Acclaim for the Work
of DONALD E. WESTLAKE!

"Dark and delicious."
—*New York Times*

"Westlake is a national literary treasure."
—*Booklist*

"Westlake knows precisely how to grab a reader, draw him
or her into the story, and then slowly tighten his grip until
escape is impossible."
—*Washington Post Book World*

"Brilliant."
—*GQ*

"A wonderful read."
—*Playboy*

"Marvelous."
—*Entertainment Weekly*

"Tantalizing."
—*Wall Street Journal*

"A brilliant invention."
—*New York Review of Books*

"A tremendously skillful, smart writer."
—*Time Out New York*

"Westlake is one of the best."
—*Los Angeles Times*

Double
FEATURE

by **Donald E. Westlake**

A HARD CASE CRIME NOVEL

A HARD CASE CRIME BOOK
(HCC-143)
First Hard Case Crime edition: February 2020

Published by

Titan Books
A division of Titan Publishing Group Ltd
144 Southwark Street
London SE1 0UP

in collaboration with Winterfall LLC

Print edition ISBN 978-1-78565-720-7
E-book ISBN 978-1-78565-721-4

Design direction by Max Phillips
www.maxphillips.net

Typeset by Swordsmith Productions

The name "Hard Case Crime" and the Hard Case Crime logo are trademarks of Winterfall LLC. Hard Case Crime books are selected and edited by Charles Ardai.

Printed in the United States of America

Visit us on the web at www.HardCaseCrime.com

For Aram Avakian, fondly, this two-reeler.

Editor's Note

Donald Westlake originally published this book under the somewhat cryptic title *Enough*, and opened it with a quote from *The Devil's Dictionary* by Ambrose Bierce: *"Enough: too much."* This did not make the title less cryptic. If you picked the book up when it was new, it's possible you might have known that just two years earlier Westlake had published another book punningly titled *Two Much*. But did that explain this new title? It did not.

This book, which contains two original novellas (two of Westlake's very best), is a favorite of mine, and when we launched on our project of bringing the best of Don's undeservedly forgotten work back into print ("The difference between in print and out of print," Don once emailed me, "is precisely the difference between life and death"), I was determined to include this book.

But what to do about that title? Oh, we could have left it alone. But detached from its moment in time and its proximity to *Two Much*, it really didn't make any sense. So I huddled with Abby Westlake and we brainstormed several dozen possible new titles, focusing on the fact that the two novellas in this book both are intertwined with the world of film. Finally, I stumbled upon the title that stuck. "Of course, *Double Feature*," Abby wrote. "It even sounds like a Don Westlake title."

I hope it does. And I hope Don wouldn't object to this modest tinkering. I take some comfort from his having tolerated such things with good grace and good humor while he was alive. Remind me to tell you the story of the turnip someday.

Charles Ardai
New York City, 2020

A TRAVESTY

If once a man indulges himself in murder, very soon he comes to think little of robbing; and from robbing he comes next to drinking and sabbath-breaking, and from that to incivility and procrastination.

THOMAS DE QUINCEY
"MURDER CONSIDERED AS ONE OF THE FINE ARTS"

ONE
The Adventure of the Missing R

Well, she was dead, and there was no use crying over spilt milk. I released her wrist—no pulse—and looked around the room, while fragments of imaginary conversations unreeled in my mind:

"And you say you hit her?"

"Well, not that hard. She slipped on the floor, that's all, and smacked her head on the coffee table."

"As a result of you hitting her."

"As a result of her polishing the goddam floor all the goddam time."

Laura's clean jagged style had, as a matter of fact, killed her more than anything else. What kind of bachelor girl apartment was this, with its hulking glass coffee table and chrome lamps and white vinyl chairs and bare black floor? Where were the pillows, the furs, the drapes and hangings, the softnesses? Sterile cold hardness everywhere; it might as well be an art gallery.

"But you did hit her, is that right?"

"But it was an accident!"

If it were an accident, it might just as well have happened when I was somewhere else. I wasn't here at all, officer, I was, uhh…Screening a film. Yes, at home by myself. Yes, I do that all the time, it's part of my job.

I got to my feet, studying the room. If I weren't here, what would be different?

Well, that glass, for one. It wouldn't be standing on the murderous coffee table with Jack Daniels in it and my fingerprints all over it.

Fingerprints. Well, there'd be fingerprints everywhere in this highly polished apartment, wouldn't there?

"Yes, officer?"

"Do you know a Miss Laura Penney?"

"Yes, I do, casually." Casually: *"Is something wrong?"*

"Have you been to her apartment?"

"A few times, I suppose, picking her up for a screening."

Fine. I took the glass to the small kitchen, washed it, put it away, and headed for the bathroom to study the medicine chest. Razor, shaving cream, toothbrush; nothing that would lead anybody to—

Wait a minute. That little medicine bottle with the drugstore label, isn't that—?

It is. My Valium, with my name typed on the prescription label: "Carey Thorpe, 1 as required for stress." So I took one—if *this* wasn't a situation of stress there is no such thing—and pocketed the bottle.

Nothing else in here, so onward quickly to the bedroom. Clothing, yes. A couple of shirts, a tie, my Emperor Nero cufflinks, some shorts, my other blue sweater—

Socks? Black, one size fits all, they could belong on anybody's feet, so leave them. This is becoming a pretty hefty package as it is.

Anything else? Bed-table drawers, with their anonymous drugstore items. Nothing under the bed, not even dust. *Fin.*

Back to the living room, with my armload of dry cleaning, and Laura spread lifelike on the glossy floor, a scene from almost any John Carroll–Vera Hruba Ralston flick. This side of her looked perfectly fine.

Into my coat. Into my topcoat, distributing shirts and shorts and ties into various pockets, wrapping the sweater around my waist under all the coats. Thank God it was February, and perfectly normal to look lumpy and bulky.

Gloves on, and one final look around. Oh, God, the letter from Warner Brothers, announcing the re-release of some hoary chestnut. My name was on it, and a date making it clear the thing couldn't have arrived earlier than today. I snatched it up and headed for the apartment door.

And what was the movie again, the one they were reissuing? I gave the letter a quick scan: *A Slight Case of Murder.*

Oh, really. Stopping, I gazed heavenward; or at least ceiling-ward. "Come on, God," I said. "That's beneath you." And I got out of there.

Until the night Laura Penney did herself in most of the violence I'd known had been secondhand. Carey Thorpe is the name, and if that rings no bells you aren't a truly serious student of the cinema. I'll admit it's easy to miss my general film reviewing, in publications such as *Third World Cinema* and *The Kips Bay Voice*, but my first book, *Author and Auteur: Dynamism And Domination In Film*, was an alternate selection of Book Find Club in the summer of 1972, and last year my second book, *The Mob at the Movies: Down from Rico to Puzo*, got universal raves.

Born in Boston in 1942, I came to consciousness concur-rently with television. Being a spindly youth, I spent most of my childhood in front of the box, watching whatever the pro-gram directors thought fit to show me. Old movies were the mainstay of local programming then, so by 1960 when I went off to college (Penn State; anything to get away from home and family) I knew more about movies than Sam Goldwyn and less than him about anything else.

College, of course, was full of other spindly youths just like me. Perhaps our predecessors in the dorms had discussed sex and beer and goldfish-swallowing, but we discussed Hitchcock and Fuller and Greta Garbo (why *did* she agree to make *Two-Faced Woman*?). In my sophomore year my film reviews were appearing in the college paper, in my junior year my first general piece—"Billy Wilder: The Smile In The Skull"—was accepted by *Montage Quarterly* (twenty-five dollars and two contributors' copies, both ripped by the mailman), and when I got my degree in American Lit I moved directly to New York City, typewriter in hand, where I've been ever since.

Fortunately, my maternal grandmother passed away just before I passed out of college, leaving me a trust fund with an income of about fifteen thousand a year. Unfortunately, the old bitch mistrusted me as much as she liked me, and tied up the fund so thoroughly with banks and lawyers that I can't *ever* get at the principal. (Believe me, I've tried.) Nevertheless, the fifteen G a year has been a reasonably comfortable base, and over the last several years my writing has brought in about as much again, so I've lived moderately well.

On the other hand, I'd prefer to live very well, and I'd been hoping to make a killing (excuse that) with *From Italy With Love*. It had seemed to me America was ready for a big glossy photo-filled coffee-table book on Italian Neo-Realism of the postwar era, but so far I haven't been able to get together with a publisher. I'll admit seven hundred stills from *Shoe Shine*, *Bicycle Thief*, *Open City* and *Paisan* might get a little depressing, but what about all those sexy women in their tattered dresses? Sometimes I don't understand the publishing industry.

I met my wife-to-be, nee Shirley Francesconi, about a year after I moved to New York, at a press screening. She was two years older than I and living with a drugs-politics-8mm freak, so we knew each other only socially for a year or so, and if I'd had any sense I'd have left it that way. But then her freak got busted on possession and went away for an extended rest, so we dated a while and then we lived together and then we got married and then we found out we hated each other.

The only reason we stuck it seven years instead of seven days is because my family thought Shirley was terrific. In fact, when the split finally did come last year it wasn't to her own folks over in Queens that Shirley went home, it was to mine up in Boston. She's been there ever since, moving slowly in the direction of divorce and annoying me about money.

The money problem is unfortunately complicated by the fact that she left while I was still high on *From Italy With Love*. I'd raved a lot about the vast sums that book would bring in, and Shirley wants some of it. My family is well off—my father's an insurance company executive, he's had his five square meals every day of his life—and they're encouraging her to squeeze me. How's that for a super family?

Then there's the kids. It's perfectly true I'm no good as a father, but I never *claimed* I'd be any good. If Shirley'd just gone ahead and taken the goddam pill like she was supposed to there wouldn't *be* any kids, but oh, no, the pill gave her migraine. Migraine! The pill maybe gave her migraine, but the diaphragm gave her a daughter named Rita and the foam gave her a son called John, and whose fault is that? Let my parents go on supporting them if they want, who I want to support is me.

So that's where we stand; or where we stood until Laura took that header. I'm no monk, I like female companionship, but for all I know Shirley has private detectives on me—she'll do anything to strengthen her position for that inevitable day in court—so I impressed on both my girls the necessity for maintaining tight security. We didn't live together, we didn't obviously date a lot, and of course I'd explained to each of them that I'd occasionally have to take other women to screenings or press parties. (The two girls also didn't know about one another. Laura and Kit were nodding acquaintances, with no reason ever to confide in each other, so I was about as safe as anybody ever is in this vale of tears. It was even possible to take one of my girls to a premiere attended by the other, with no suspicions raised.)

Well, all that had now come to an end. Laura, who'd at first come on as the most rabidly independent of Women's Lib types, had been complaining more and more about our secret life, comparing herself to *Back Street* and other absurdities, wanting to know why I didn't just get the divorce over and done with (why hurry a finish that could only be costly and difficult for me?) and even threatening once or twice to blow the whistle herself with Shirley. Of course she didn't really mean it, but it was upsetting to hear her talk that way, and in fact it was a repetition of the same threat that had caused me to lose my temper tonight and pop her one, etc.

"You say Miss Penney threatened to tell your wife about this affair?"

Mm. I was right to get clear of this, as quickly and quietly as I could. So out of the apartment I went, smearing the doorknobs with my gloved hand, checking the street before leaving the building, and walking all the way over to Sheridan Square before hailing a cab to take me home.

Where I found several messages waiting on my telephone answering machine. After divesting myself of my coats and excess wardrobe I made a drink and sat at the desk to listen.

The first was a nice female voice with a British accent: "Mr. Gautier's office calling Mr. Thorpe, in re screening on the twentieth. Could you possibly make it at four instead of two?"

I'd rather. And since I was unexpectedly dateless for that screening, perhaps the owner of the nice British accent would like to join me. Reaching for pencil and paper, I made a note to call back, while listening to the second message, from Sogeza "Tim" Kinywa, editor of *Third World Cinema*: "Sogeza here, Carey. Have you got a title yet on the Eisenstein piece?"

No, I didn't. I was about to make another note when the third message started: "Oh, you've left already. I wanted to remind you to bring the Molly Haskell book, but never mind."

Well. A strange sensation that, hearing a voice from beyond the grave. I erased the tape, finished my drink, and went to bed.

My street door intercom doesn't work. I've talked to the super about it, but he only speaks some fungoid variant of Spanish understood exclusively on a six-mile stretch of the southern coast of Puerto Rico. I've also talked to the landlord, an old man with a nose like a tumor, and his response was the same as to anything his tenants say to him; a twenty-five minute diatribe on economics, expounding a theory so arcane, so foolish, so contradictory and so absurd that I'm surprised the government has never tried it. Or maybe they have.

In any event, when the bell rang at nine-thirty the morning after Laura's accident I couldn't find out who it was before letting them in, but who could it be other than the police? Wouldn't they automatically question all of Laura's friends, everybody in her address book? Bracing myself, I left my half-eaten omelet and buzzed them in.

Him in. When I opened the apartment door and listened, only one set of footsteps was trudging up the stairs. But didn't cops always travel in pairs?

Apparently not. When he rounded the turn at the landing I saw a stranger, a chunky middle-aged man in brown topcoat and black hat, looking something like Martin Balsam in *Psycho*. And coming up the stairs toward me; so I should quick put on my Granny drag and run shrieking out to stab him.

In fact I should have, but of course I didn't. Instead, I stood in my doorway looking open and honest and innocent and friendly, and when he reached the top of the stairs I said, in a we're-here-to-help-you manner, "Yes?"

"Morning," he said, and smiled. He was puffing a bit from the climb, and seemed in no hurry to get his words out. "Mr. Thorpe, isn't it?"

"That's right. Can I help you?"

"Well, sir," he said, "I think it's the other way around. I think *I* can help *you*."

Not a cop? What was he, some sort of salesman? I said, "What's this about?"

"This," he said. Taking a white envelope from inside his coat, he extended it toward me.

Frowning, I said, "What's that supposed to be?"

"You left it behind." He was still smiling, in a casual self-contained way. "Last night," he added.

"Last night?" Unwillingly I took the thing from him and turned it over to see what was written on the other side. Return address: *Warner Brothers, 666 Fifth Ave*. Neatly centered, neatly typed, my own name and address.

The envelope! I'd remembered the damn letter, but not the envelope. Where had it been?

He answered my unasked question: "Under her."

"Um," I said.

"Why don't we talk inside?" he suggested, still smiling, and walked into the apartment. I had to move aside or we would have bumped. Then I closed the door and followed him into the living room, where he stood nodding and smiling, looking at the movie posters, the one wall of exposed brick, the mirrored alcove that gives the apartment its illusion of space, the projector and screen set up at opposite ends of the room, the unfinished breakfast on the small table by the kitchenette. "Nice place," he said. "Very nice."

I moved reluctantly closer to him. He didn't look like cops in the movies, but what else could he be? "Are you from the police?"

He gave me a quick amused glance. "Not exactly," he said, and sat down on the sofa. "The fact of the matter is, I'm a private investigator."

"A private detective?" Several thousand private eye films swirled through my head, most of them starring Dick Powell.

"I was on surveillance last night," he told me, "outside that apartment."

I didn't feel like standing any more. Sinking into my leather director's chair I said, "So she did put a tail on me."

His smile grew puzzled. "What say?"

"My wife."

"Oh, well," he said, "I wouldn't want to make trouble for an innocent party. No, sir, it didn't have anything to do with *you*. It was Mrs. Penney's husband put the agency on the job."

"Husband?" I'd known Laura had at one time been married, but *everybody* has a marriage or two somewhere in their past and I'd always assumed hers was long since over and done with. "You mean, she was still married?"

"That's my understanding," he said. "Legally separated, I believe."

And she'd been nagging *me* to break the old ties. Now I saw the whole plot; she'd hold on to husband number one until I was lined up to take his place. Devious devious women, they're all alike. Josef Von Sternberg knew what he was talking about.

The detective spoke through my interior monologue. "The point is, I was there. I watched the two of you go into the building, and then quite some time later I watched you come out alone, and I must say, Mr. Thorpe, rarely have I seen a man act as guilty as you did. I didn't know what it was all about, of course, but I thought probably I ought to keep an eye on you."

"You followed me."

"That's just what I did," he agreed. "And I noticed another

peculiar thing. You must have let half a dozen empty cabs go by, but then when you got to Sheridan Square you were suddenly in a real frantic rush to hail a cab and jump in and holler out your address."

He paused, with a bright alert smiling look, as though offering me a chance to compliment him on his powers of observation. I refrained.

He went on. "Well, it seemed to me you didn't want anybody tracing you from Mrs. Penney's apartment, and I thought *that* a little peculiar. So I followed you uptown here, and waited to see which lights went on, and got your name from the doorbell. You really ought to ask who's there before you let anybody in, you know, just as a by-the-by."

"The intercom's broken."

"Then you ought to get it fixed. Believe me, it's my business and I know, you can't have too much security."

"I've talked to the super and the landlord both. Wait a minute! What are we talking about?"

"You're right," he said, "I got myself off the subject. I'm a bug on safety, I take all kinds of precautions for myself and I'm all the time pushing safety on everybody else. Let me see, now. After I got your name from the doorbell I went back downtown and let myself into Mrs. Penney's apartment."

That surprised me. "You had a key?"

"Well," he said, with another of his little smiles, "I have a whole lot of keys. Generally there's one for the job."

"You broke in, in other words."

"Well, sir, Mr. Thorpe," he said, "I don't think you ought to start using harsh words, you know. There's two of us could do that."

"All right, all right. Get to the point."

"Well, you know what I found in the apartment."

"This envelope," I said, waggling the fist in which I had it imprisoned.

"Yes," he said, "and a body on top of it. From the marks on the coffee table and the floor, it looked to me as though there'd been some sort of fracas. You struck her—there's a bit of gray spot on the side of the jaw, she was dead before it could swell up any—and she hit her head on the coffee table going down."

"It was an accident," I said.

He did a judicious pose, pursing out his lips and stroking the line of his jaw; Sidney Greenstreet. "That's a possibility," he said. "On the other hand, you did run away, and you did try to cover your presence in the apartment, and if you'll look at this picture here you'll see you *do* just look guilty as all hell."

From inside his coat he had taken a photograph, which he now leaned forward to extend toward me. I took it, with the hand not crushing the envelope, and looked at a grainy but recognizable black-and-white picture of myself emerging from Laura's apartment building. By God, I *did* look guilty as all hell, with my mouth open and eyes staring and head half-twisted to look over my shoulder. I also looked very bulky, as though I'd just stolen all the silver. Mostly I reminded me of Peter Lorre in *M*. "I see," I said.

"Infrared," he told me. He seemed very pleased with himself. "The negative's in my desk at the office."

I looked up from my own staring eyes into his calmly humorous ones. "What now? What are you going to do?"

"Well, sir," he said, "I think of that as being up to you."

And suddenly we were in a situation I recognized from the movies. "Blackmail," I said.

He looked a bit offended. "Well, now," he said, "there you go with the harsh words again. I just thought you might be interested in buying the negative, that's all."

"And your silence?"

"I wouldn't want to get a man in trouble, if I could avoid it." He shifted his bulk on the sofa. "Now, I'm supposed to turn in my report by twelve noon, and it seems to me I could handle it one of two ways. Either I could say a gentleman—that would be you—brought Mrs. Penney home but left her at the street door and went away, or I could report that you went in with her and came out without her and please see photo attached."

I said, "How much?"

"Well," he said, "that's a very rare photograph."

"And I'm a very poor man."

He chuckled at me, disbelievingly. "Oh, come along now. You've got a nice place in a rich part of town, you've—"

"This isn't a rich part of town. A couple blocks west of here is rich, but not here."

"This is the Upper East Side," he informed me, as though I didn't know where I lived.

"Look," I said. "You just walked up the stairs yourself, do you think they have walk-ups in a rich part of town?"

"On the Upper East Side of Manhattan they do. Besides, you're a writer."

"I'm a movie reviewer. There isn't any money in that."

"You've had books out."

"Film criticism. Did you ever see a book of film criticism on the best-seller list?"

"I don't believe I've ever seen the best-seller list," he said, "but I do know from my years with the agency that successful writers tend to have nice pieces of money about themselves."

"I don't," I said. "For God's sake, man, you're a detective, surely you could check into that, find out if I'm a liar or not. I'll show you my checkbook, I'll show you letters from my wife screaming for money, I'll show you my old income tax returns."

"Well, sir," he said, "if you're *too* poor, I think I'd be better off going for the glory of making the arrest."

A cold breeze touched me. "Wait a minute," I said. "I didn't say I don't have *any* money. Obviously, if I can afford to pay I'd rather do that than go to jail. It just depends how much you want."

He frowned at me. He studied me and thought it over and glanced around the living room—and to think I'd been pleased at how expensive I'd made the place look—and at last he came to a decision: "Ten thousand dollars."

"Ten thousand dollars! I don't have it."

"I won't bargain with you, Mr. Thorpe." He sounded rueful but determined. "I couldn't falsify my report for a penny less."

"I don't have the money, it's as simple as that."

He heaved himself to his feet. "I'm truly sorry, Mr. Thorpe."

"I'll tell them, you know. That you tried to blackmail me."

He gave me a mildly curious frown. "So?"

"They'll know it's the truth." I jammed the photograph into my trouser pocket. "I'll have this picture for evidence."

He shrugged and smiled and shook his head. "Oh, they'd probably believe you," he said, "but they wouldn't care. Funny thing about police, they'd rather catch a murderer than a black-mailer any day in the week."

"They'll have both. I may go to jail, but you'll go right along with me."

"Oh, I don't think so." He could not have been more calm. "I'd be their whole case, you know," he said. "Their star witness. I don't think they'd want to cast any aspersions on their own star witness, do you? I think you'd generally be called a liar. I think generally people would say you were doing it out of spite."

I thought. He watched me thinking, with his curly little smile, and finally I said, "Two thousand. I could raise that somewhere, I'm sure I could."

"I'm sorry, Mr. Thorpe, I told you I won't bargain. It's ten thousand or nothing."

"But I don't *have* it! That's the Lord's own truth!"

"Oh, come on, Mr. Thorpe, surely you've got something set aside for a rainy day."

"But I don't. I've never had the knack, it's one of the things my father's always hated about me. He's the squirrel, I'm the grasshopper."

He frowned, deeply. "What was that?"

"I don't save up my nuts," I explained, "or whatever grasshoppers save up. You know, you know, the children's story. I'm the one that doesn't save."

"Well, Mr. Thorpe," he said, "it seems to me you should have listened to your father." And turning away, he crossed the room toward the front door.

I should have killed him, that would have been the most sensible thing to do. Picked up something heavy—that can containing *North By Northwest*, for instance—and brained him with it. Unfortunately, I wasn't sufficiently used to being a killer, so what I did was grit my teeth and get to my feet and say, "Wait."

He waited, turning to look at me again, the same patient smile on his face, letting me know I could have all the time I needed. But that's all I could have.

I said, "I'm not sure I can do it. I'll have to borrow, I'll have to— I don't know what I'll have to do."

"Well, sir," he said, coming back to me, "I don't want to make things difficult for you if I can possibly avoid it. Here's my card."

His card. I took it.

He said, "You call me at that number before eleven-thirty if you decide to pay."

"You mean, if I *can* pay."

"Any way you want," he said. "I'd mostly like a cashier's check, made out to bearer."

"Yes, I suppose you would." I looked at the card he'd given me. Blue lettering read *Tobin–Global Investigations Service— Matrimonial Specialists*. In the lower left was a phone number, and in the lower right a name: John Edgarson.

"If you do call," John Edgarson told me, "ask for Ed."

"I'll do that."

"And Mr. Thorpe," he said, "do try to look on the bright side."

I stared at him. "The bright side?"

"You've had an early warning," he told me. "If you decide not to pay, you've got almost three hours' head start."

It's amazing what you can do in an hour when your life depends on it. By eleven o'clock I'd converted into cash the following:

Savings account	$2,763.80
Checking account	275.14
To pawnshops: (Projector 120.; Leica camera 100.;	
8mm camera 70.; portable tape unit 160.;	
8mm projector 50.; stereo system 180.;	
typewriter 50.; watch 40.; wedding ring &	
jewelry 90.)	860.00
Films, posters, stills, etc.	450.00
Loan from publisher against future earnings	1,500.00
$100. bad checks to liquor store, florist, grocer,	
dry cleaner, barber & hardware store	600.00
GRAND TOTAL	6,448.94
Needed	10,000.00
Shortage	3,551.06

Eleven o'clock. Five after eleven. I was back in my apartment, my pockets full of cash. But where was I going to get three thousand five hundred fifty-one dollars and six cents?

My grandmother's trust fund? Not a chance. I'd cried wolf with the people at the bank two or three times already, and they'd made it perfectly clear *my* well-being didn't matter to them one one-hundredth as much as the fund's well-being.

My father? Another blank. He had the money, all right, and plenty to spare, but even if he was willing to help—which he wouldn't be—the cash would never get here from Boston in the next twenty-four minutes. Besides, if I did ask him the first thing he'd say—even before *no*—would be *why*.

Would Edgarson take less? Six thousand dollars in the hand was surely better than ten thousand dollars in the bush. I dialed the number on the card he'd given me, and when a harsh female voice answered with the company's name I asked for Ed. "Minute," she said, and clicked away.

It was a long minute, but it finally ended with a too-familiar voice: "Hello?"

"Edgarson?"

"Is that Mr. Thorpe? You're a few minutes early."

"All I can raise is, uh, six thousand, uh, dollars. And four hundred. Six thousand four hundred dollars."

"Well, that's fine," he said. "And you've still got twenty minutes to get the rest."

"I can't. I've done everything I could."

"Mr. Thorpe," he said, "I thought we had an understanding, you and I."

"But I can't *raise* any more!"

"Then if I were you, Mr. Thorpe, I'd take that six thousand four hundred dollars and buy a ticket to some place a long way from here."

South America. *The Lavender Hill Mob.* But I liked the life I had here in New York, my career, my girlfriends, my name on books and magazines. I didn't want to run away to some absurd place and learn how to be somebody else.

"Well, goodbye, Mr. Thorpe," the rotten bastard was saying, "and good luck to you."

"Wait!"

The line buzzed at me; Edgarson, politely waiting.

"Somehow," I told him. "Somehow I'll do it."

"Well, that's fine," he said. "I'm really relieved to hear that."

"But it might take a little longer. You can give me that much."

He sighed; the sound of a just and merciful man who knows he's being taken advantage of but who is just too darn good-hearted to refuse. "I'll tell you what I'll do, Mr. Thorpe," he said. "Do you know a place in your neighborhood called P. J. Malone's?"

"Yes, of course. It's three or four blocks from here."

"Well, that's where I'll have my lunch. And I'll leave there at twenty after twelve to go turn in my report. Now, that's the best I can do for you."

An extra twenty minutes; the man was all heart. "All right," I said. "I'll be there." And I broke the connection.

And now what? I went to the john to pop another Valium—my second this morning—and then I sat at my desk in the living room, forearms resting where my typewriter used to sit, and waited for inspiration. And nothing happened. I blinked around at my pencils and reference books and souvenirs and trivia, all the remaining bits and pieces of the life I was on the verge of losing, and I tried to think how and where to get the rest of that damned money.

From my brother Gordon? No. My sister Fern? No. Not Shirley, not Kit, none of my friends here in New York.

It was too much money, just too much.

What story could I tell my father? "Hello, Dad, I want you to wire me four thousand dollars in the next ten minutes because—" Finish that sentence in twenty-five words or less and win...a free trip...a free chance to stay home.

There was a pistol on my desk; not a real one, a mock-up that had been used in a movie called *Heller In Harlem*. I'd watched some of the filming uptown, for a piece in *Third World Cinema*, and the producer had given me this pistol as a kind of thank-you. His name and the name of the movie and my name and a date were all inscribed on the handle.

I picked up this pistol, hefted it, turned it until I was looking into the barrel. Realistic little devil. If it actually were real I could kill Edgarson with it.

But it wasn't real. So there was only one thing to do.

"This is a stick-up," I said.

The teller, a skinny young black girl with her hair in rows of tight knots like a fresh-plowed field, looked at me in amused disbelief. "You're putting me on, man."

"I have a gun," I said, drawing it out from beneath my top-coat lapel and then sliding it back out of sight. "You'd better read that note."

It was a note I'd worked on for nearly fifteen minutes. I'd wanted the strongest possible message in the fewest possible words, and what I had eventually come up with—derived from any number of robbery movies—was printed in clear legible block letters on that piece of paper in the teller's hand, and what it said was:

> *MY BABY WILL DIE WITHOUT THE*
> *OPERATION. PUT ALL THE MONEY*
> *IN THE SACK, OR I'LL KILL US BOTH.*

I realize there was a certain ambiguity in that word "us," that I might have been threatening either to kill the teller and myself or my baby and myself, but I was relying on the context to make the message clear. My baby wasn't present, but the teller was.

The only sack I'd had available, unfortunately, had originally come with a bottle of champagne in it, and in white lettering on its green side it clearly stated *Gold Seal Charles Fournier Blanc de Blancs New York State Champagne.* I'd been using it to hold the tiles in my Scrabble set. I knew it wasn't quite the right image for somebody trying to establish himself as driven to crime by the financial crisis of his baby's operation, but I was hoping the note and the gun and my own desperate self would carry the day.

I also had the impression, from some newspaper article or somewhere, that banks were advising their employees—telling their tellers—not to resist robbers or raise any immediate alarm. They preferred to rely on their electronic surveillance—the photographs being taken of me at this very instant, for instance—and not risk shoot-outs in banks if they could possibly avoid it.

Well, this time I was ready to have my picture taken. The clear-glass hornrim spectacles on my face were another movie souvenir, the black cloth cap pulled low over my forehead had just been purchased half a block from here, and the pieces of tissue stuffed in on both sides of my face between cheek and lower gum altered my appearance just as much as they'd altered Marlon Brando's in *The Godfather.* So click away, electronic surveillance, this is one picture I won't have to buy back.

In the meantime, the teller was reading. Her eyes had widened when I'd flashed the pistol, but they narrowed again when she studied the note. She frowned at it, turned it over to look at the blank back, picked up the champagne sack and hefted it—an R fell out, dammit—and said to me, "You *sure* you on the level?"

"Hurry up," I hissed at her, "before I get nervous and start shooting." And I flashed the gun again.

"You're nervous, all right," she told me. "You got sweat all over your face."

"Hurry up!" I was repeating myself, and running out of threats. Once a toy gun has been brandished, there's nothing left to do with it; brandishing is its entire repertoire.

Fortunately, nothing else was needed. With an elaborately unruffled shrug—I envied her calm under pressure—the teller said, "Well, it's not my money" (my point exactly), and began to transfer handfuls of cash from her drawer to the sack.

At last. But everything was taking too long. The big clock on the wall read five minutes past twelve and I was a long long way from P. J. Malone's. (I'd thought it better to do my bank robbing outside my own immediate neighborhood.) I wanted to again urge speed on the girl, but I was afraid to emphasize even more the contrast between her calm and my frenzy so I remained silent, jittering from foot to foot as wads of twenties and tens and fives disappeared into my nice green sack.

She filled it, till it looked like Long John Silver's Christmas stocking, and then she pulled the little white drawstrings at the top and pushed the sack across the counter to me. "Have a nice day," she said, with an irony I found out of keeping under the circumstances. *She* might not be taking this seriously, but I was.

I was three minutes late but Edgarson was still there, lunching at his leisure in a high-sided booth at the back. I slid in across from him and he gave me his encouraging smile, saying, "There you are. I was beginning to worry about you."

"Save your worry." In his presence I realized how much I hated him. I'm not used to being helpless, at the mercy of another person, and if I ever had the chance to even the score with this bastard I'd leap for it.

He must have seen something of that in my face, because he became immediately more businesslike, saying, "You have the money?"

"You have the negative?"

"I sure do." He withdrew from inside his coat a small envelope, opened it, held up an orange-black negative, and then put it back inside the envelope.

"I'll want to inspect that," I said. (Scenario: He hands me the negative, I pop it into my mouth and swallow it. Then what does he do?)

But he was smiling at me and shaking his head. Revised scenario: He keeps the negative, mistrusting me. "First you give me the money," he said. "Then you can inspect this picture all you want."

"Oh, all right." Reaching into my pockets, I said, "I didn't have time to get a cashier's check. You won't mind cash, will you?" Fistfuls of the stuff began to pile up on my paper place mat. Even Edgarson lost his bucolic cool at that. Staring at the money, he said, "Well, I'll be damned. No, I don't mind cash, not at all."

The waiter arrived then, gave the money an astonished look, and said, "Did you intend to order anything, sir?"

"Jack Daniels," I said. "On the rocks."

"Just one glass?"

"Ha ha," I said. Gesturing at the money, I explained, "I robbed a bank."

"Ha ha," the waiter said, and went away.

I looked at Edgarson. "I *did* rob a bank, you know. You've put me through a lot today."

He'd had time to recover. Smiling in bemusement, shaking his head, he said, "You sure are an interesting fella to watch. I'll say that for you."

"Don't bore me with your shoptalk." I tossed over a small envelope from my publisher's bank, where I'd cashed his advance check. "There's fifteen hundred. You can count it, if you want."

"I might as well," he said, and proceeded to do so.

I kept dragging out my other money, most of it in twenties and tens with a few fifties sprinkled here and there. The eight-sixty from various pawnshops, the six hundred from the bad checks, the four-fifty from the nostalgia shops, the two seventy-five from the checking account. And another envelope; tossing it to him, I said, "My former savings account. Two thousand seven hundred sixty-three dollars and eighty cents."

"It's an amazing thing," he said, placidly counting, "but most everybody's worth more than they realize."

"Fascinating," I said, and pushed across the pyramid of loose bills. "Here's another twenty-one eighty-five."

The waiter, returning, placed my drink where my money had been and said, "How does a person get to be your friend?"

I picked up the drink. "Put this on *his* bill," I said.

"I should think so," the waiter said, and left.

I sipped and Edgarson counted. Then I sipped some more and Edgarson counted some more. Then I sipped some more and Edgarson said, "I make that six thousand four hundred and forty-eight dollars so far." The bills, upon being counted, had disappeared into his clothing, and now he shoved my eight cents back across the table to me, saying, "We don't mess with change. But we would like to see some more greenbacks."

"Out of my green sack," I said, delving down inside my shirt and bringing out the swag. Propping the sack like a dildo in my lap, I loosened the drawstrings and started pulling out more cash.

This time I also did some counting, since I hadn't had a chance yet to find out how much I'd made from my first excursion into major crime. Sorry, second excursion; I was forgetting Laura. "Two hundred," I said, and flipped a stack of twenties across the table. "One eighty," and a stack of tens. And so on and so on and so on.

And yet the bottom of the sack was reached too soon. I'd needed thirty-six hundred dollars, but my total profit from the bank job was only two thousand, seven hundred eighty.

Edgarson noticed it, too. "Nine thousand, two hundred and twenty-eight dollars," he said at last. "I make you seven hundred and seventy-two dollars short."

"I can't rob another bank," I said. "You're just going to have to bend your principles in this case, or by God I'll kill us both." I clutched at the toy gun beneath my coat, letting Edgarson see as much of it as the bank teller had seen. "I've gone through enough today. I can't go through any more." My voice was rising, and it was by no means entirely fake.

Edgarson made calming patting motions in the air. "Take it easy," he told me. "Take it easy, Mr. Thorpe, there's no reason to get upset. Why, if I can't make allowances here and there, what sort of fella would I be?"

I could tell him what sort of fella he was, but I didn't. I merely sat there and glared at him and clutched the inscribed handle of my pistol.

"Now," he said, and it seemed to me that through his professional calm I detected just the slightest hint of uneasiness. "Now, I think you're being honest with me," he said, "and you really can't raise any more money than this, and I think it just wouldn't be fair of me not to accept this nine thousand dollars and call it square."

I relaxed somewhat, but my hand remained on my gun. "All right," I said.

He took out that envelope again and extended it to me. "Here you are, my friend."

I finally released the gun, and used that hand to take the envelope. Having peered at the negative and seen vaguely that it was the right one, I said, "And this is the only copy, right? I shudder to think what would happen if you suddenly came back with another one."

"Mr. Thorpe," he said, "you wrong me. There aren't any more negatives, and there aren't any more prints. And once I put in a false report, I couldn't very well go back and call myself a liar, now, could I?"

That made sense. "All right," I said.

"Speaking of which," he said, withdrawing two larger envelopes from an inner pocket, "here's the report I won't be turning in. You might want to keep it yourself. This other one's the report I *will* turn in, if you'd like to take a look at it."

I would, but I glanced through the truthful one first. "Agitated manner…hurrying in a guilty fashion…seeming nervous and upset…" This Edgarson wasn't a subtle writer, but he got his message across.

The false report made for pleasanter reading. Making sure which was which, I gave him back the false one and put the truthful copy in one of my moneyless pockets.

Edgarson signalled for the check, then said to me, "There's something else I wanted to talk to you about."

My hand strayed toward my pistol. "What was that?"

He did his air-patting gesture again. "Nothing to get upset about," he assured me. "You just happened to mention you were in some sort of marital difficulty with your wife, so I'd like to suggest you have a talk with one of the staff people at my agency. It's surprising sometimes just how—"

"*What?*" I couldn't believe it. "You're sitting there and hawking your goddam *detective agency* at me?"

Very earnestly he said, "You can't do better than Tobin–Global, Mr. Thorpe. Seventy-four years of reli—"

"Stop talking," I told him. "Do us both a favor, Edgarson, and stop talking."

The waiter provided a welcome interruption by showing up with the check. While Edgarson gathered pieces of my money with which to pay it, the waiter gave me a look and said, "I get off at three."

"Tell *him*," I said.

Edgarson paid, and the waiter went away, and I said, "I want to come along with you when you turn in the report."

He frowned. "That might not be wise, having the two of us seen together."

"I'll wait outside. But I want to know for sure you've gone straight to your agency and turned in *that* report."

Shrugging, he said, "If it will ease your mind, Mr. Thorpe, come right ahead."

Tobin–Global Investigations was in the Graybar Building, back of Grand Central. I rode up in the elevator with Edgarson and paced the corridor while he went inside. He was gone about three minutes, and then he came back, smiling, flashing his jacket pocket where the envelope no longer protruded, saying, "All done, Mr. Thorpe. It's turned in and your worries are over."

"I have to be sure," I said. "I want to be able to sleep nights."

"Mr. Thorpe," he said, "I'm not any kind of trouble for you at all. Now, a man in my job has to turn in his reports, and I just turned in mine, and I wouldn't dare tell a different story later. Not where there's a murder mixed in."

"So I'm safe from you."

"Absolutely."

"Good," I said. "Now I wonder if I could ask you a favor."

He seemed doubtful. "Yes, sir?"

"Sooner or later the police will come ask me about last night, and I'd like to try on you what I plan to tell them and see what you think of it. From a professional point of view, I mean."

Relieved, expansive, he said, "Well, I'd be happy to, Mr. Thorpe. That's a very good idea."

So, standing there in the corridor with him, I told him the story: "I took Laura to a press preview late yesterday afternoon, and then to dinner, and then home. At dinner, she told me she was worried because she believed her husband had hired somebody to murder her."

He frowned at that. "Oh, now, Mr. Thorpe," he said, "I don't think you ought to start making things up, you'll just create suspicion. It's better to tell a simple straightforward story."

"Well, wait a minute," I said. "Listen to the way this one works out, and see what you think."

Shrugging, he said, "If you insist, Mr. Thorpe, I'll listen."

"Fine. Anyway, at dinner Laura told me there'd been somebody hanging around and she was afraid it was the hired killer. Well, of course I didn't believe her, I told her she was imagining things. Then, when I took her home, she pointed out a man loitering on the other side of the street and said that was the one she'd meant." I gave Edgarson a long slow look up and down. "I think I could give a pretty clear description of that man," I said.

His brows were coming down in an angry straight line over his eyes. "Just what the hell is all this?"

"To get on with the story," I said, "I volunteered to go upstairs with Laura to her apartment and stay with her a while, but she said no, she'd rather be alone because she was going to try phoning her husband and maybe settling their differences once and for all. So I said good night and went home."

"I don't know what you think you can gain with a story like that," Edgarson told me, "but if you tell it to anybody you'll just make trouble for yourself, not for anybody else."

"You told me you entered that apartment last night," I reminded him. "I know you moved the body, because you found that envelope under it. Are you absolutely sure you didn't leave any fingerprints, any traces of yourself at *all*? If you're certain, then you're probably safe, it'll just be your word against mine."

"Mr. Thorpe," he said, "you're a grade A son of a bitch, do you know that?"

"Of course," I said, "I *could* tell a simpler story."

If it weren't for the pistol he knew to be in my pocket, I think he would have tried taking a poke at me. "You'd goddam better," he said.

I smiled at him. "And *you'd* goddam better give me back my nine thousand dollars."

It was good to be home again, my possessions once more about me. And it was *very* good to have been able to do Edgarson in the eye. If I hadn't been able to even the score with him somehow it would surely have rankled in my mind a good long time, but as it was the expression on his face as he'd handed back fistful after fistful of green paper was a memory I would treasure always.

After a leisurely shower and shave, and a nice lunch of chicken breasts in grape sauce (left over from Kit's last visit), I sat at my desk to tot up the results of the day's activities and to learn that Edgarson had stiffed me for two hundred thirty dollars. I chuckled indulgently; let him save face if he wanted. Even with that petty larceny, and the incredible interest the pawnbrokers had charged me for the two-hour use of their money, my bank robbery had left me nearly twenty-four hundred dollars richer than when I'd gotten up this morning. My checking account was healthy, Edgarson was no longer a threat, and surely it wouldn't be impossible to replace that R left behind at the bank. Life, all in all, was not unpleasant.

And what did the evening hold in store? A screening, a dinner for two? Checking my calendar, I saw that today's notation read, "Dinner, Laura, 7:3o."

Well. Well, it looked as though I had an unexpected free evening. Wonder what Kit's doing tonight?

I had nearly finished dialing Kit's number when it suddenly struck me that I had better keep that original date with Laura. It was noted on *my* calendar, why wouldn't it also appear on hers? At seven-thirty tonight I'd better be in the lobby of Laura's apartment building, ready for our date, ringing her doorbell.

TWO
The Affair of the Hidden Lover

Somebody buzzed to let me in.

Laura? *Laura,* I thought, and I wasn't sure myself whether I was thinking of Laura Penney or of the 1944 Otto Preminger movie. Either way it was the dead girl come back to life, and a nasty shock. Gene Tierney moved in the shadowy recesses of my mind, and I felt uncomfortably like Dana Andrews as I pushed open the door and crossed the pocket lobby to the pocket elevator.

When I emerged on the fourth floor a man wearing an open black overcoat and a dark gray suit was standing in Laura's open doorway. A cop, obviously. He looked like Dana Andrews, so what did that make me? Clifton Webb?

I know nothing, I reminded myself. *I am here to pick up my dinner date, and I have no idea who this man is.*

I stopped, just into the vestibule, frowning and looking around as though thinking I might have gotten off at the wrong floor. In fact, I held the elevator, in case I should want to reboard.

The policeman, a black-haired fortyish Dana Andrews with cold eyes and blue chin and dandruffy shoulders, said, "Can I help you?"

My outer self remained bewildered. "I'm looking for Laura Penney."

"Would you be Mr. Thorpe?"

So she had made a note. "Yes, I am," I said, and released the elevator door, which grumbled shut behind me. "Is something wrong?" My hands hid themselves in my topcoat pockets.

"Come in."

I crossed the threshold as he stood to one side, watching me. I tried not to look at the spot where I'd last seen her, but my eyes insisted, and it was with great relief that I saw nobody there. To cover my eyes' indiscretion, I turned my head left and right, looking at everything in the room, continuing to fail to understand the situation. "Where *is* Laura?" I turned to the policeman, who was closing the door. "And who are you?"

"Detective Sergeant Bray," he said. "I'm a police officer. There's been an accident."

"An accident? Laura?"

"Did you know Mrs. Penney well?"

"*Did* I know her? For God's sake, man, what's happened?"

"I'm sorry to break it to you this way, Mr. Thorpe," he said, "but I'm afraid she's dead."

"Dead!"

"Come along," he said, taking my elbow. "Come sit down."

I permitted myself to be moved, as though too stunned to act from my own volition, and when he'd seated us, me on the sofa and himself to my right in the chrome-and-leather chair, I said, "An accident? What kind of accident?"

"Frankly, Mr. Thorpe," he said, "there's some question about that. When was the last time you saw Mrs. Penney?"

"Yesterday. We had dinner together."

"You brought her home?"

"Yes, of course."

"At about what time?"

"Possibly nine, nine-thirty, I don't know exactly."

"And when did you leave?"

"Oh, I didn't stay," I said. "In fact, I didn't come up, I simply saw her to the door."

"You didn't come up?" He sounded mildly surprised. "Wasn't that unusual?"

"Not at all. I wouldn't want to give the wrong impression about our relationship, we weren't…lovers, or anything like that. I have a steady girlfriend, named Kit Markowitz."

"You and Mrs. Penney were just good friends," he suggested.

Was there irony in that remark? His manner seemed bland, unsuspicious; I took him at face value and said, "That's right. But are you suggesting—" I paused, as though struck by a sudden disquieting thought. "Did somebody *do* something to her?"

He frowned. "Such as what, Mr. Thorpe?"

"I don't know, I was just—I just remembered what she was saying last night."

"And what was that?"

"It was all very vague," I said. "She had the idea there was a man hanging around, following her. She pointed him out last night, standing on the sidewalk across the street."

"You saw this man?"

"He was just a man," I said. "He didn't seem interested in Laura or me in particular. She had the idea her ex-husband had hired somebody to make trouble for her."

"Do you know Mr. Penney?"

"No. I believe he's in Chicago or somewhere."

He nodded. "Could you describe the man you saw last night?"

"I only saw him for a minute. Across the street."

"As best you can."

"Well, I'd say he was in his mid-forties. Wearing a brown topcoat. He seemed heavyset, and I got the impression of a large nose. Sort of a W.C. Fields nose." Bray nodded throughout my description, but wrote nothing down. "And you say Mrs. Penney seemed afraid of this man?"

"Well, not *afraid*, exactly. Upset, I suppose. I offered to come upstairs with her if she was worried, but she said she wanted to phone her husband. I had the idea she wanted privacy for that."

"Mm-hm."

"Sergeant Bray, uh— Is it Sergeant Bray?"

"That's right."

"Well— Could you tell me what happened?"

"We're not entirely sure as yet," he told me. "Mrs. Penney fell in this room and struck her head. She might have been alone here, she might have slipped. On the other hand, it seems likely there was someone with her."

"Why?" I asked, and movement to my left made me turn my head.

It was another one, in black pea jacket and brown slacks, coming into the room from deeper in the apartment and carrying what I recognized immediately as my socks. As I caught sight of him he said, "Al, I found these and— Oh, sorry."

"Come on in, Fred. This is Carey Thorpe."

Fred grinned in recognition. "Right. Dinner, seven-thirty."

"Mr. Thorpe," Bray said, "my partner, Detective Sergeant Staples."

I got to my feet, unsure whether or not we were supposed to shake hands. "How do you do?"

"Fair to middling." This one was a bit younger than Bray and looked more easygoing. He said, "Would you be the movie reviewer?"

"As a matter of fact, yes."

"I read you all the time," Staples told me. "In *The Kips Bay Voice*. My wife and I both, we think you're terrific, we swear by you."

"Well, thank you very much."

"If you say a movie's good, we go. If you say it stinks, we stay away from it."

"I hardly know what to say," I admitted, and it was the truth. Such extravagant praise had *never* come my way before.

"Pauline Kael, Vincent Canby, we just don't care."

Even praise can reach a surfeit, and I was happy to be rescued by Bray, who interrupted his partner by saying, "What have you got there, Fred?"

"Oh, yeah." He held them up like a dead rabbit. "Socks."

Bray seemed to find that significant. "Ah hah," he said. "I thought so."

I said, "Excuse me, is that a clue?"

Staples probably would have answered, but Bray asked me a question first: "Was Mrs. Penney involved with any man in particular, that you know of?"

"A lover?" I shook my head, frowning with thought. "I don't think so. She was usually available for an evening out, and I never heard her talk about any steady boyfriend."

"Well, there was one," Staples said. "And he looks like our man, doesn't he, Al?"

"Could be."

I found myself watching these two as though they were characters in a movie I'd be writing up, noticing with approval the complementary types they offered. Bray was the slower and more methodical, while Staples was intuitive and emotional. Bray, in character, now said, "On the other hand, he could have come in afterward, found the body, and figured he ought to keep himself out of it."

"I still think it's the boyfriend," Staples said.

"Except for the glass," Bray told him. "If he lived here, wouldn't he have known about that?"

Something trembled in my stomach. Trying to sound no more than ordinarily curious, I said, "Glass?"

This time Staples got to answer the question. "There was one glass in the living room here," he said, "with a partly consumed drink in it. But in the kitchen cabinet was another glass that had been washed and put away. So the killer had a drink with her, and then after she was dead he washed his glass."

"Fantastic," I said. "How did you know all that? If he washed the glass, how did you find out?"

"He put it in the cabinet right side up. Mrs. Penney stored her glasses upside down, so that one glass was put away by somebody else."

"By God," I said, "real-life detectives *are* just like the movies."

Staples grinned like an Irish setter. "We get lucky sometimes."

"No, I can see it's a special kind of talent," I insisted, giving him a return overdose of praise while at the same time cursing myself for that stupidity about the glass. Of *course* she kept her damn glasses upside down, I *knew* that, but I must have been more rattled than I'd thought. The shelf is high, and the damn glasses look the same right side up or upside down.

Bray said to his partner, "If the guy was living here, he'd know which way the glasses went."

"Not if he got rattled," Staples said. "Besides, I don't think he actually lived here, I think he just stayed overnight sometimes."

I said, "That's the significance of the socks?"

Staples grinned again; by golly, this was another chance to dazzle me with his sleuthing. "They're more significant than that," he said, and when he went on he addressed himself equally to his partner and to me. "These socks were the only male clothing in the bedroom. Now, the razor and stuff in the bathroom don't mean much, they could even belong to the victim herself. But these socks mean a man, and one that stayed here often enough to keep some extra clothing around. And you see what else they mean?"

I had to admit I didn't, but Bray already knew. "He cleaned his stuff out," he said.

Staples pointed an approving finger at him. "Right! He left the socks because there's no way to trace anybody from socks like these. But he took everything else because maybe they *could* be traced. Laundry marks, initials, whatever." Turning his beaming face toward me, he said, "Now, you see what that means. That means guilty knowledge."

"Ah," I said.

Bray, the cautious one, said, "I agree with you, Fred, up to a point. There is a boyfriend and he did clear his stuff out after the victim was killed. But I still think there's a good chance he came in *after* she was dead, realized he could be in a lot of trouble, and tried to cover his tracks."

"Maybe so," Staples said. "Maybe there's two guys out there in front of us, but I still think there's only one."

"And there's something else," Bray told him. He then had me repeat my story about the mysterious man across the street, after which he said, "So he could be the killer, too."

I said, "Excuse me, I'm not trying to play detective with you, but she didn't know who that man was, so she wouldn't sit down and have a drink with him, would she?"

Staples now did his finger-pointing in my direction, saying, "Very good, Mr. Thorpe, very good. Of course it's *possible*, the guy could have come up and said he had a message from her husband or whatever, she asks him in for a drink and he kills her. That's possible, but it isn't very likely."

I said, "Or maybe the killer did the thing with the glass to throw you off, make you think it was somebody Laura knew socially."

This time Staples' smile was condescending. "Mr. Thorpe," he said, "I hate to say this, but you've been seeing too many movies. In real life killers don't get that cute. Visualize it for yourself; the guy gets in the apartment, kills Mrs. Penney, then he comes into the kitchen and turns over one glass so we'll think he knows her socially. People just don't act that way."

"I suppose not," I said.

Bray said, "I guess that's about all we'll need you for at the moment, Mr. Thorpe. If we want to talk to you again, I suppose you'll be around."

"Of course." Smiling at them both I said, "I wasn't planning on going out of town."

Staples smiled back, but Bray didn't.

Home again, I swallowed a Valium with bourbon and sat down to listen to the messages on my answering machine. The first was from Shirley, in her harsh ex-wife's voice with its recently acquired Boston accent: "There are some papers for you to sign, whether you like it or not. I'm sending them today, special delivery, and if we *don't* get them back by Tuesday your father says I should hire a New York attorney. At your expense."

Lovely. Next came the voice of Tim Kinywa of *Third World Cinema*, also sounding petulant: "Sogeza here, Carey. Could you *possibly* give us a title on the Eisenstein piece? I need it before noon tomorrow if at *all* possible." Damn; I'd forgotten about that. Here before me was the note I'd made, along with the note about the changed time for the screening. I underlined both, while listening to my next message. A secretary-type voice: "Mr. Thorpe, Mr. Brant will be in New York for a week, arriving Friday. If you'd care to arrange an appointment, would you phone the Sherry–Netherland sometime Saturday morning?"

I would. For six months I'd been trying to set up an interview with Big John Brant, famous old-time director of such classics as *Fury At Sundown*, *Tank Command*, *Fatal Lady* and *Smart Alex*, and finally it was going to happen. Good.

The last message was from Kit: "Hello, machine. Just wondered what your master was doing tonight. I'll be in if he feels like calling."

Did I feel like calling? I considered the question while I dialed Tim's number and listened to his recorded announcement: "Hello, caller, this is the number of Sogeza Kinywa and *Third World Cinema.* We aren't answering the phone just now, but if you'll leave your name and phone number on this tape we'll get back to you very soon. Kwaheri, and peace."

Nobody talks to anybody any more. We just talk to each other's machines. "Hello, Tim," I said to the machine. "This is Carey, and the title is 'The Influence of Eisenstein: Stairway To The Stars.' I have an early screening tomorrow, but if there's any problem you can reach me at home after one."

And now Kit. After the day I'd had I wasn't sure I could handle the warm-human-being role tonight, but I ought to call her back anyway and see if anything developed. So I dialed, and damn if I didn't get *her* machine: "Kit Markowitz here, on tape. I'm really sorry not to answer in person, but if you'll leave a message right after the little beep, I'll call you back just as soon as I can. Wait for it now, wait for it. Here it comes."

She'd changed her announcement; the previous one had been more standard. After the little beep I said, "Too cute, Kit. This is Carey, and I'm home for the evening."

After that, I settled down for a little work. A new *New York*-type magazine called *The Loop* had started in Chicago, and I'd promised them a piece called "Bogdanovich: The Kid Brother As Leader Of The Pack." Linking Bogdanovich and Ryan O'Neal through the seminal figure of Lee Tracy was turning out to be more complicated than I'd anticipated.

Kit phoned half an hour later to say, "*I* don't think it's too cute."

"It's the 'wait for it' that gets me."

"But that's the whole idea."

"I know."

"You're too linear," she said; one of her au courant but mean-ingless insults, the result of reading too many trade paperbacks. "You doing anything tonight?"

I'd decided by now how to handle my news. "The fact is," I said, "I'm mostly getting over a shock. You remember Laura Penney?"

"The girl with the mouse-brown hair? The one you've been seeing so much of lately?"

Ah. Maybe I hadn't been covering my tracks quite so well as I'd thought. "Well, I won't see much of her any more," I said. "She's dead."

"Good God!"

"Killed, in fact."

"Oh, Jesus. One of those rape things?"

"I don't think so. It happened in her apartment. I was sup-posed to take her to dinner tonight, I went over th—"

"You *found* her! Oh, my *God!*"

"Not quite that bad. The police were there."

"Oh, baby, what an experience. Do they suspect *you?*"

I was shocked—truly shocked—at the suggestion. "Why would they do that?"

"I thought the police were supposed to suspect everybody."

"Oh. Then maybe they do suspect me, I don't know. They didn't act that way."

"You sound *very* jittery. Want me to come over?"

Did I? The half-finished page in the typewriter grayed before my eyes. "I'd love it," I said.

"I love your pubic hair," I said.

She came over to the bed, carrying the two drinks. "What kind of compliment is *that?*"

"A sincere one." I took my drink and made room for her

beside me in the bed. Looking at the feature in question, I said, "It's furry, but not too much. It has a friendly quality."

"I bet you say that to all your girls."

I did, as a matter of fact, so I remained silent while she arranged the covers over herself. On the TV facing the bed the fifty all-time greatest hits of some obsolescent teenage castrati were being peddled in an extremely hard sell. "As somebody once said about Marion Davies," I said, nodding at the screen, " 'Forgotten, but not gone.' " It was nearly midnight, and if that Kallikak on the tube would ever stop yowling we would go on watching *The Thin Man*, a film I was enjoying this evening in a very new and different way. The day was ending far better than it had begun. Kit had come over around nine-thirty, we'd gone at once to bed, and then I'd been subjected to an hour's conversation on the general subject What Happened To Laura Penney And Why? Kit, like Detective Staples, believed that Laura had a secret boyfriend and that he was the killer. I couldn't tell her she was absolutely right, of course, but on the other hand I didn't want to be suspiciously negative, so I maintained a thoughtful neutrality on the subject and let Kit do most of the talking.

A good girl, Kit, all in all, about the best of my recent women. An acquisitions editor for a reprint publisher, she was attractive, divorced, childless, bright, funny, and self-supporting; what more could a liberated male want?

William Powell returned, with Asta. They put Myrna Loy in a cab headed for Grant's Tomb and went off hunting the murderer by themselves. Kit said, "Could it be Jay English?"

I looked at her. "Could *what* be Jay English?"

"The secret lover."

"He's a fag," I pointed out.

"Well, maybe he's trying to go straight." She squinted at the

TV, but it was Laura's murder she was trying to solve, not Julia Wolf's. "That's why they kept it secret, because they weren't sure it would work out."

"In the first place," I said, "Jay English doesn't *want* to go straight. And in the second place, he's still living with that fellow whatsisname."

"Dave Something."

"That's the one."

"Ah!" Sitting up straighter in the bed, she said, "*He's* the killer!"

"Who?"

"Dave. Because he found out about Jay and Laura!"

"You're a madwoman," I told her.

"Then who do you think it is?"

"I haven't the faintest idea."

She studied me, as though trying to guess my weight. "*You* were hanging around her a lot lately," she said. "Maybe you're the one."

"If I am," I said, "you're in a lot of trouble right now."

There was no way to tell from her expression whether she was serious or joking. "You took her to that press screening yesterday."

"Only because you couldn't go."

"What did you do after?"

"We went to dinner, I took her home, I came back here."

"You weren't here at ten o'clock."

"Of course I was."

"I called at ten and got your machine."

I put my drink on the bedside table and half-turned to face her. "Are you serious?"

"I called at ten," she repeated, "and I got your machine." Yet she didn't look or act as though she thought of herself as being in bed with a murderer.

I said, "I was running a film, for a piece I'm doing, *Top Hat*. You know I turn the machine on when I do that."

"I bet the police suspect you," she said.

"Do you?"

"What?" She stared at me, startled, and said, "Hey! You're really upset."

"Of course I am."

"I don't *really* think it's you, silly," she said, thumping me on the belly. "I think it's Jay's boyfriend Dave."

"So do I," I said. "But the big question is, who do you think killed Julia Wolfe?"

"Who?"

I nodded at the TV screen, where Asta was finding another body. "In the movie we're allegedly watching."

"Oh." She shrugged, not very interested. "I've seen it before," she said. "It's the lawyer."

THREE
The Wicker Case

In the morning Kit called her office with some lie, and then we went to the screening together; some French *ancien vague* item called *L'Abbé de Lancaster*, full of reaction shots and shrugged shoulders. "They smoke a lot in the provinces, don't they?" Kit said after a while.

Following a quick lunch together, Kit went on to work and I returned to the apartment to put together my review of *L'Abbé de Lancaster* for *The Kips Bay Voice*. But before that I had telephone messages to run.

Three of them. The first, from Tim Kinywa, thanked me for the title and told me there were no problems, while the third was from a "friend" of mine, a fellow film critic, saying, "Nothing important, I'll call again." I knew what that was; he had a collection of his magazine pieces coming out, and he wanted a plug.

But it was the second call that disturbed me. "That recording sounds exactly like you, Mr. Thorpe," said the cheery voice of Detective Sergeant Fred Staples. "When you get home, would you give Detective Staples a call? The number is seven seven five, five four nine nine. Thanks a lot."

Now what? Kit's casual unsuspicious questioning last night had shaken my confidence, and I was no longer sure I could keep ahead of the team of dour-methodical-Bray and cheerful-intuitive-Staples. Why would he be calling me? What had I forgotten?

So I swallowed a Valium and returned the call. He was in, and he said, "Hi, Mr. Thorpe. You free for a while this afternoon?"

"I, well, yes, I suppose so. Why?"

"I'd like to ask your help," he said.

The recurring police line from British mystery movies came into my head: *"We'd like you to help us with our inquiries."* That line was never spoken to anybody but the murderer. I said, "I'll be happy to help, if I can. I'll be in all afternoon."

"I'll come over in about, oh, half an hour. Okay?"

"Fine," I said.

I spent the half hour doing the film review, and I'm afraid I gave the poor Abbé of Lancaster a heavier drubbing than he deserved. I was still pounding away when the bell rang. Taking it for granted this was Staples, I buzzed to let him in and popped another Valium while he came upstairs.

It was Staples; cheerful and bouncy as ever, but puffing a bit from the climb. He shook my hand and greeted me merrily enough, but was there a hint of suspicion deep within his eyes? Remembering the movie lore that policemen don't drink with people they intend to arrest—wasn't that from *Beat The Devil*?— I said, "Care for a drink? A beer? Some wine?"

"No, thanks," he said, still smiling. "Too early in the day for me."

Hell and damnation. Hoping only that he would turn out to be another blackmailer, I closed the door and offered him a chair. Taking it, he said, "First off, I might as well tell you you're off the hook. Not that you were ever on it, at least not very much."

I looked at him, not sure I understood. "Off the hook?"

"Your innocence has been established," he said.

I sat down in the director's chair. "Well," I said. "Thank you very much."

"The funny thing is," he told me, "it was through that fella that Laura Penney told you about. The one she said was following her."

"It was?"

"We got in touch with the husband last night. Mr. Penney. And darn if he didn't have private detectives watching his wife. He'd just put them on the case a few days ago."

"They don't seem to have helped much."

"They were supposed to collect evidence for a divorce or something." Shaking his head, he said, "I can't understand anybody like that, can you? Sneaking around, putting detectives to watch their wife. Maybe it's because my own marriage is so good, but I just can't comprehend a man who'd do a thing like that."

Nodding, I said, "I know, it doesn't seem right. But if you look in the Yellow Pages, there's a lot of agencies specializing in that sort of thing. They must get their customers somewhere."

"I suppose so." This insight into a darker corner of human nature had robbed Staples almost entirely of his sunny smile, but now he rallied, saying, "But in this case it did us some good."

"You found the killer?"

"Not yet, but we've narrowed things down. We got in touch with the detective agency this morning, and they gave us their dossier. We have photographs of just about everybody Mrs. Penney saw in the last few days. We even have a picture of you. Want to see it?"

Peter Lorre in *M*. "I'd be fascinated."

He took from his jacket pocket a white envelope with a red rubber band around it. First he transferred the rubber band to his wrist, then he opened the envelope and took out a little bunch of photographs; small ones, about two-and-a-half by four-and-a-half. He selected one of these, chuckled at it, and handed it over.

Not Peter Lorre in *M*. Rock Hudson and Doris Day in *Pillow Talk*. That was me there, seeing Laura chastely to her door, and this photograph did not suggest that I would next go upstairs with her and commit murder. "Nice picture," Staples suggested.

I sighed. "The last time Laura was alive. May I keep this?"

"Well, sure," he said. "We don't need it, because you aren't the killer."

"This picture tells you that?"

"No, the fellow who took the picture told us. He was on watch outside the apartment building until one in the morning, and he's willing to swear you never went back into the place during that time."

Why wouldn't he swear to it? Never went *back* in; that was the simple truth. (And how it must have galled Edgarson that he couldn't put my head in the noose.)

Could I still make a little trouble for him? I said, "Then the private detective must have seen the killer."

"If he did," Staples said, "he didn't recognize him. Or it's possible the killer was already in the apartment, waiting for Mrs. Penney, and he used another way out of the building. Say through the side exit from the basement. Which would suggest premeditation."

"From Sergeant Bray's description," I said, "it didn't sound like premeditation. It sounded more like a fight, an angry flare-up or something."

Staples nodded. "Everything points to a sudden argument with a friend. That's why I'd like you to take a look at the rest of these pictures—" extending them across to me "—and see how many of the men you can identify."

"Ah. You think it might be one of these." Half a dozen photos; I riffled through them and saw a succession of blurred but familiar faces.

"We're not limiting ourselves to those," Staples told me. "At this point, it could be anybody."

"Except me," I said, and the phone rang.

Chuckling and nodding, Staples said, "That's right, except you."

I got to my feet, crossing toward the desk, saying over my shoulder, "I'll turn on my answering machine, so we won't be interrupted."

But, through the phone's second ring, Staples said, "I'd rather you did answer it, if you don't mind. I left this number at the office, so it might be for me."

"Oh. Fine."

And damned if it wasn't. When I picked up the receiver and said hello, a gruff male voice that might have been Sergeant Bray said, "Staples there?"

"Coming up." I turned and extended the receiver, saying, "You were right."

He came smiling over to take the phone and announced himself cheerily into it. To be polite I pretended absorption in the photographs—cold faces, bulky overcoated bodies, Laura in several unimportant public moods, *cinema verité* at its absolute lowest—while I listened to Staples' share of the conversation.

It turned out to be the wrong share; the meat was with the other participant. Staples limited himself mostly to *yeah* and *nope* and *got it*, while making quick pencil notes in a small pad. Finishing with, "Be right there," he hung up and put his pad away.

He was leaving? Good; exonerated or not, I still felt nervous in his presence.

But even though he'd promised to be right there, he showed no hurry about moving on. Turning to me, he said, "Would you know a movie director named Jim Wicker?"

"Two features," I said. "Neither very good. I don't know him personally, he's a West Coast type. Young, up from television commercials, hasn't shown much promise yet."

"Well, he won't show any at all from now on," Staples told me. "Somebody just shot him."

"*Shot* him?"

"About four blocks from here, while he was watching his new movie." Chuckling in his bubbly way he said, "I guess that's *real* criticism, huh?"

"New movie?" I tried to remember what I'd read in the trades recently about Jim Wicker. "Oh, that would be *A Sound of Distant Drums*, for Lanisch–Sanssky."

"Lanisch–Sanssky? Do you know these people?"

"I know who they are, they're in my field."

"Would that be Hugo Lanisch?"

"Yes, of course. He ran Twentieth Century Fox for six weeks three or four years ago. Why?"

"Because it was in his house that Wicker got killed," Staples said. Then, apparently struck by a sudden thought, he said, "Listen, Mr. Thorpe, how would you like to come along?"

"Come along? In what way?"

"You could see the way a police investigation works in real life," he said. "And you could fill us in on who these people are. I wouldn't introduce you or anything, you'd just be that sort of quiet cop in the corner. What do you say?"

I laughed; I couldn't help it. I had become the detective's sidekick. "I say, lead on!" I told him.

Edgarson was in a car across the street. He was bundled up in there, but I recognized him right away, with his glinting little eyes glaring out from around the sides of his nose.

I turned my back, and Staples and I, barrel-shaped in our overcoats, stuffed ourselves into his battered green Ford with the police ID on the sun visor, and then we waited quite a while for Staples to get the engine going. He kept flooding it, but remained cheerful, with continuing comments about the cold weather. "I'd like to go down to Puerto Rico right after New Year's," he said, "and not come back till St. Patrick's Day."

"Amen," I said.

"If only I could afford it."

"Amen again."

He looked surprised. "Really? Not prying or anything, Mr. Thorpe, but I had the idea you were sort of well off."

"I suppose I give that impression," I said. (And didn't I know it.) "But I pretty much live up to the hilt of my income. And then, I don't have a family to support. Or a car," I added, as the Ford's engine at last turned over.

"That makes a difference," Staples agreed. He gunned the motor a lot, and finally we got underway, with Staples saying, "There's no point turning on the heater. Takes it ten minutes to warm up, and we'll be there by then."

I'd brought the Laura photos with me, and now I said, "Did you want to talk about these pictures first, or the Jim Wicker business?"

"Fill me in on Wicker," he said. "And this fellow Hugo Whatsit."

"Lanisch," I said, and went on to tell him what I knew of Lanisch–Sanssky Productions and Jim Wicker. Hugo Lanisch and Gregor Sanssky, both old-line movie executives who'd been with the studios thirty or thirty-five years ago when the studios really meant something, had gone into independent production about fifteen years back, turning out whatever was popular at the moment. They'd made some science-fiction movies in England at one time, and more recently they'd done a few period murder mysteries. They'd done well enough, but they'd never had a major success.

Nor had Jim Wicker, a young man of about thirty, a Californian who had served his apprenticeship grinding out television commercials, graduated to a season of television adventure shows, and then made two unremarkable theatrical feature films, the first for American International and the second for some independent producer down in Florida. Wicker was a technician, a man who did unexciting work but who always brought his projects in on time and within budget. He was a perfect choice for Lanisch–Sanssky; dependable and inexpensive.

All the time I was telling Staples this unoriginal set of film lives I was also feeling the peevish stare of Edgarson on the back of my neck. Was he following us? I didn't dare turn around to look, and the doubt made it hard to keep track of what I was saying.

Staples asked a few questions about Wicker and Lanisch, but once he moved from the business level to the personal I was no longer any help to him. I didn't know if Wicker was married or even heterosexual. I didn't know if Lanisch was in debt.

"Well, here we are," Staples said, and pulled in at a handy hydrant on 67th Street between Madison and Park. "It's that town house there. You just keep silent and leave everything to me."

"Right."

We got out of the car and I chanced a quick look back. I didn't see Edgarson anywhere, but I could still feel him.

Bray didn't like my presence, and he made no bones about it. Staples and I met him just inside the front door, where he'd been chatting with a uniformed policeman, and he gave me one quick disapproving glance before saying to his partner, "What's this?"

"Mr. Thorpe can be very helpful, Al," Staples said. "He knows a lot about these people."

Bray studied me. "You know Lanisch?"

"I don't know any of them personally," I said. "But I do know who they are."

Staples said, "He filled me in on the way over. Don't worry, Al, he'll stand in the corner and he won't say a word."

"He's your guest," Bray said, as though saying *he's your responsibility*. Turning away, he said, "They're all upstairs."

Staples gave me an encouraging smile, which I hesitantly returned. Leaving the uniformed cop to his guard duty at the front, we followed Bray through a stark high-ceilinged living room to a small elevator with a porthole window in the door.

The movie business had apparently been very good indeed to Hugo Lanisch, if it had bought him this town house. It was quite some place, five stories high, done in a kind of Bauhaus-modern style, full of white walls and chrome balls and sharp diagonals. There was also this elevator, which the three of us crowded into and which rose at a slow enough pace for Bray to give us the full story en route. "There's a special room upstairs where they show movies," he said. "Six people were in there, including Wicker, and when the movie was over Wicker was dead in his chair. He'd been shot in the back of the head and the gun was on the floor behind him. No prints."

Staples said, "Could anybody else get in during the movie?"

"No. There's only one door, and anybody coming in has to walk right in front of the screen."

"So the killer's definitely one of the five others watching the movie."

Bray looked sour. "One of them," he agreed, and the elevator stopped. He pushed open the door and we followed him into a square high-ceilinged room with black carpeting and puffy white low chairs and another uniformed cop. "This way," Bray said, and the three of us trooped across the room and through an open doorway on the far side.

The scene of the crime. Oh, my God, and the victim himself, lying sprawled in a white leather chair and looking perfectly ghastly. His eyes were open and staring ceilingward, but the eyeballs were sunk too deep in the sockets, as though everything inside there had shriveled. A great sticky-looking stain the color of beaujolais smeared the white leather back of the chair. *My* victim had been much more discreet.

With difficulty, I forced myself to look at the rest of the place, which was a very plush little screening room. Ten of the white leather chairs, on chrome rollers, were scattered about the gray carpet, intermixed with small white formica Parsons tables. The entire wall to the left of the entrance formed the screen, flanked by drapes which would probably close when no movie was being shown. Framed movie posters were mounted on the side walls, and a small but generous bar was built in at the back.

Staples said, "I thought you said there was only one door." He nodded toward a second door, next to the bar.

"Projection booth," Bray told him. "It's like a little closet in there, and no other way out."

"Ah." Staples walked around the body in the chair, studying it from different angles. "Deader'n hell, isn't he?"

Bray said to me, "If you're going to throw up, there's a john past the elevator."

"I'm not going to throw up." In fact, I wasn't at all queasy, though I preferred not to look at the dead man. Bray had simply been letting me know again that he didn't like my being here.

Staples, having studied the corpse long enough to memorize it, now said, "Fine. Where's our suspects?"

"Back this way."

We went out through the other room again, past the elevator, down a short white hall, and into a bookcase-enclosed room done in shades of orange and brown. Tall narrow windows at the far end of the room showed the February nakedness of tree branches and the rear of some building on 68th Street. The low chrome-armed chairs in here were covered with brown corduroy and on them were sitting half a dozen distressed-looking people. I saw no one I knew, but two or three of the faces were familiar, probably from press parties. All of the faces were troubled and nervous, as though we were tax men here for an audit. Another uniformed policeman stood stolidly in a corner, pretending to be a guard in a bank.

Bray addressed the group: "I'm sorry for the delay, ladies and gentlemen, we'll try not to take much longer. I'm Detective Sergeant Bray, and this is Detective Sergeant Staples. We'd like to find out what happened. Does anybody have any suggestions?"

The troubled faces turned toward one another, this way and that, but the only one who spoke was a tall slender ash-blonde woman in black slacks and a pearl gray sweater, who asked, as though hoping against hope, "I suppose it must have been one of us?"

"It does seem that way," Bray told her. "I'm sorry. Unless someone has another theory?"

But no one did. The faces remained troubled, and attentive.

Bray said, "All right. Then we might as well begin." The interrogation that followed was informal in style but very thorough, starting with the names and functions of everyone present. The oldest man here, sixtyish, almost completely bald, stocky, with a vaguely Mittel-European accent, was our host, Hugo Lanisch, co-producer of the film they'd been watching. The slender blonde in the black slacks was his most recent wife, Jennifer; in her early thirties, cool and beautiful and well-bred, she looked as though she'd come with the town house, and probably she had.

There was one black among the white faces, a bearded plump fortyish man named Gideon Fergus, who'd been hired to write the music for the film. I remembered his work from several black exploitation movies; mostly bongos and electric guitars.

Then there were two people from United Films, the company that had financed the movie and would be its distributor. The stout black-haired woman with the serious hornrim glasses and the overly loud way of speaking was Ruth Carr, the East Coast story editor and presumably the one who had interested United Films in the project in the first place. And the 35-year-old slender fag in the leather pullover and big yellow glasses and long blond hair was Barry McGivern, the company's assistant advertising director.

Finally there was the projectionist, a neatly dressed young man of about 25 named Jack March. An executive in embryo, March had an earnest expression, short blond hair, metal-rim glasses and a modest California tan. He had apparently decided his role at a murder was to look very alert, in case anybody should want coffee.

Having established names and pedigrees, Bray turned the floor over to Staples, who cheerfully but insistently worked out where everybody had been seated during the screening. With only six in the audience, they had not clustered together but had been fairly widely distributed through the room. Staples eventually had to produce paper and pencil and do a sketch plan of everybody's position, but when he was finished the layout was clear. Wicker had been the farthest from the screen, so that any of the others could have left his or her seat, traveled on hands and knees, and approached him from behind without being seen by anyone else.

Except the projectionist. Young March had been watching the film through a small window next to the projector, but it turned out he'd seen the movie before—he was the messenger who'd brought it here from the cutting room on the west coast—and he hadn't been completely attentive. He explained there were always things to be done in the projection booth, but that was undoubtedly a polite falsehood; the second time through, *A Sound Of Distant Drums* was probably more than a bit boring. Besides, if the killer had stayed on his knees behind Wicker the projectionist would have been unlikely to see him in any case.

So now the characters and the setting had been established. A rich old movie producer, his rich young wife, a third-rate black composer, two studio functionaries and a reliable small-time director had gathered in a room to watch for the first time a film in which they were all interested. What they were seeing was a rough cut, still several minutes too long and with no musical score. In the course of this screening, one of the others had shot the director, for reasons yet to be established.

But before getting to motive, Bray was interested in one more physical aspect of the crime: the sound of it. Taking over from Staples, he said, "Mr. Wicker was killed with a .25 caliber revolver. Now, that wouldn't make as much noise as a .45 automatic, but it wouldn't exactly be quiet either. Just how loud is this movie you were watching?"

It was Gideon Fergus, the black composer, who answered: "Not very loud at all. It's much more of a mood piece than Jim's other films, probably because it's the first time he was doing his own original script. And there wasn't any music yet, of course."

Barry McGivern, the advertising man from United Films, said, "Well, there was that one shot in the movie. Remember? Just after they get off the train."

Ruth Carr, the stout story editor with the loud voice, loudly said, "Do I remember? *I'll* say I remember, it scared me half to death."

Bray, the patient bulldog, said, "There was a gunshot in the movie?"

There was general agreement; yes, there had been one gunshot in the movie. Barry McGivern drove home the obvious point: "The killer could have fired *his* gun at the same precise moment."

"Very tricky to get it that close," Bray said. "But possible, I suppose. Did anybody hear Wicker make any kind of sound just after the shot?"

Ruth Carr said, "I'm afraid nobody heard *anything*, just after the shot, because I gave out a yell."

Barry McGivern told her indulgently, "I must say, Ruth, *you* startled me more than the gunshot did."

Bray said, "You screamed?"

"I'm sorry," Ruth Carr said, but her smile was more proud than sheepish. "I've always been that way, I'm a real sucker for movies. They catch me every time."

"All right." Bray's disinterest in Ruth Carr's little personality traits was so total that even she noticed it, and looked offended. He ignored that, too, saying to the group at large, "Were there any other loud noises in the course of the film? Anything else that might have covered the sound of a shot?"

Gideon Fergus said, "There were two or three door slams, but I don't know that they were *that* loud."

Ruth Carr said, "And the jet taking off. That one hurt my eardrums."

A little discussion ensued among Gideon Fergus, Ruth Carr and Barry McGivern as to whether or not the wail of a jet taking off was the kind of sound that would cover the noise of a gun being fired. Hugo and Jennifer Lanisch, I noticed, took no part in this discussion, nor in any of the talk that had preceded it. They sat fairly close together, but not touching and not looking

at one another, and though God knows they were far from twins
—he with his gleaming round bald head and deeply lined face,
she with her oval face framed by heavy ash-blonde hair—their
expressions were nearly identical. Both were defensive, blank,
rigidly controlled, tightly held in check. Looking at them, the
thought came to me: *Was Jennifer playing around with young
Jim Wicker?*

This same thought had apparently occurred to both Bray
and Staples, and once the sound-effects discussion ran itself
out the two detectives began poking delicately into the general
question of motive. How long had each of our suspects known
Jim Wicker, what was the state of each relationship, how had
the relationship been formed? The questions were general,
and ostensibly aimed at all the suspects equally, but it was plain
that the questions were focusing more and more frequently on
Jennifer Lanisch.

Were Bray and Staples doing this out of perversity? Or was it
possible they didn't know who the murderer was? Finally it
seemed to me the only thing to do was break my promise of
silence, which I did by saying, "Well, of course Jack March is
the killer, but that still leaves the question of why. I suppose
once we find out his real name the motive will become more
clear." Everybody stared at me, even the uniformed cop in the
corner. Bray looked as though he might burst a blood vessel,
but Staples was merely bewildered, and when he said, "What
are you talking about?" I heard in his voice the forlorn prayer
that I would actually know what I was talking about.

I did. "I suggest his real name isn't Jack March," I said,
"because he's so obviously in disguise. You'll notice the tan on
the lower half of his face is lighter than on the upper half,
meaning he's just recently shaved off a full beard. Also, his
clothing is all brand spanking new, suggesting he's been used to
a different sort of garb. That short haircut also looks very

recent, and those spectacles are fakes, with clear glass. I have a pair myself, they were a prop in a movie, and they reflect light differently."

By now, everybody was staring at young March instead of at me, and March didn't like it at all. "That's silly," he said. "Yes, I shaved off my beard when I got this job, but that doesn't mean I killed anybody."

"You were the only one behind Wicker while the film was being screened," I pointed out.

Staples, looking at me with hope and terror and warning all mixed in his expression, said, "Any of the others could have crawled around behind Wicker, we already established that."

"Taking a chance on being seen by the projectionist? Besides, I haven't yet mentioned the real proof."

"Then I wish you would," Staples said, and I could see Bray silently agreeing.

"The gun was fired," I said, "in conjunction with a loud sound in the film, probably a gunshot. But the gunshot in the film was so unexpected that Miss Carr screamed when it happened. Only someone who had seen the picture before would know about that gunshot and be able to anticipate it and use it. And only March, who carried the print here from Los Angeles, had seen the picture before. Only March *knew* the film."

"I knew it, all right," March said, and by the sudden harshness in his voice I knew we'd be hearing the truth now. "I knew it because I wrote it! And that son of a bitch stole it from me! I trusted him, I—I— This was my only chance to get even with him, while he's watching it himself, sitting there watching the script he, he—" And March dropped to his knees and buried his face in his hands.

I turned smiling to Staples. "Elementary, my dear Watson," I said.

FOUR
The Problem of the Copywriter's Island

Staples went whee-whee-whee all the way home. "Did you see Al Bray's *face?* he demanded, and answered his own question by laughing out loud and slapping his gloved palm against the steering wheel.

I had in fact seen Al Bray's face, and he'd looked as though a movie marquee had fallen on him. He didn't say anything to me, but he kept looking in my direction like a Flat Earther faced with an astronaut. I, on the other hand, had sense enough to remain modest and to fade into the background after I'd done my little turn. There was no point preening; any man who intends to rub a cop's nose in it had better be on safer ground than I was.

Anyway, March's breakdown and confession had essentially finished that job, so Staples soon took me away, leaving Bray to care for the details. Morgue and technical people were just arriving as we reached the sidewalk, and while Staples had a word or two with them I scanned the block for Edgarson. He was nowhere to be seen; had the presence of the police scared him off?

Now Staples was driving me home, crowing all the way, and not sobering till he'd parked again next to the fire hydrant near my building. Then he said, "If you could do the same thing on the Laura Penney killing, it would be a great help."

I *could* do the same thing, as a matter of fact, but I wasn't going to. Young Jack March had been a great lesson to me, had I been in need of a great lesson: he'd demonstrated the folly of quitting. I had made a very nice circumstantial case against him, and no doubt in time the police would have established his true identity and his motive for killing Jim Wicker, but without the confession would it ever have been proved? If the gun couldn't be traced directly to March—and my guess was that it couldn't—some small doubt would have to remain, and with a halfway decent defense attorney that small doubt could surely be turned into an acquittal. March, the premeditated murderer, had planned everything up to the crime itself, but then had lost his moorings, his sense of purpose and his nerve. I, the unpremeditated murderer, hadn't planned anything until after the event, but because I'd retained my nerve and my sense of purpose I was now the only human being on Earth who had been fully cleared in that killing.

But what Staples wanted was an expression of cooperation and sincerity of purpose. I obliged, telling him, "By God, I wish I *could* just point a finger and say, 'That's the killer.' I was very fond of Laura, you know, I've realized that more and more since her death."

Sympathetic understanding gleamed in Staples' eyes. "I know what you mean. But we do have those photographs. We could go over them now, and maybe something'll click for you."

"Fine." Then, because hospitality seemed necessary under the circumstances, and also because it was damn cold in Staples' unheated car, I said, "Want to come up? We can have coffee and be comfortable."

"Good idea."

So the two of us climbed the stairs to my apartment and spent a while uncoating ourselves. Then I went to the kitchenette to make coffee, while Staples wandered around the living room, looking at my memorabilia. Seeing him near the desk, I called, "Would you mind switching on the phone machine? I want to hear my messages."

"Sure." He hovered over it, willing but unschooled. "What do I do?"

"Turn the switch to playback and press the rewind button."

He did both, and I went on with my coffeemaking while the machine gibberished itself backward at high speed and then began to unreel my latest messages: "Hi, Carey, it's, um, Jack Freelander. Um. It looks as though, um, *Esquire*, um, might want that piece, um, um, I told you about, um, about the pornographic movie biz. Um. Would you be, um, free some time soon? I'd like to, um, pick your brains. Also, um. Do you happen to know, um, where Laura Penney is? Um. She doesn't answer her phone. Um. See you later. Um. Um."

I called, through the final stutters of Jack Freelander's message, "How do you like your coffee?"

"Regular." Staples came to the kitchenette doorway, saying, "I feel like I'm eavesdropping, listening to all that."

"Don't be silly," I said. "I've got nothing to hide." Meantime, the second message had started. "Hi, sweetie, it's Kit. I'll be tied up this evening, but give me a call tomorrow. And I still say Jay English did it."

"Christ," I muttered. I gave Staples his coffee, and the two of us went back to the living room and message number three:

"Hello, Mr. Thorpe. How does it feel to be a murderer?"

After I put the mop away and made myself another cup of coffee, Staples insisted we listen to that last message another half dozen times, in hopes I'd eventually recognize the voice:

"Hello, Mr. Thorpe. How does it feel to be a murderer? Hello, Mr. Thorpe. How does it Hello, Mr. Thorpe feel to be a how does it Hello, Mr. how does it feel how does it, Mr. Thorpe, feel to be a murderer? a murderer? a murderer?"

"I just don't know," I said. "The voice sounds familiar, but I can't quite place it."

Finally Staples gave up, saying, "He called you 'Mr. Thorpe', so I guess whoever he is he doesn't know you all that well."

"I guess he doesn't. Excuse me a minute." And off I went to the john, to pop a Valium. What did humanity do before these wonderful pills?

Back in the living room Staples was reading my movie posters, but his mind was still on the message, because he said, "Would you run it just once more? I'm sorry, I know it upsets you, but I want to record it."

Turned out he had a cassette recorder in his overcoat pocket. Damn it to hell. I considered accidentally erasing the message but I was afraid I'd trigger Staples' suspicions, so we played the thing one last time while his little machine turned a beady ear on my little machine, and then at last I could erase the bastard and sit down with my coffee, waiting for the Valium to take hold.

Staples tried to reassure me: "We run into a lot of nuts like that, Mr. Thorpe. They get an idea in their heads, and they don't want to be distracted by facts."

I said, "What if you hadn't already cleared me, what would you be thinking now?"

He chuckled. "I'd be a lot more interested in talking with that particular nut, to tell the truth." Then he said, "Forget about it, Mr. Thorpe, it's a closed incident. Let's look at those photos."

So we did. Six pictures of Laura, with as many men, all of whom I knew to one extent or another. Going through them one at a time, I gave Staples a name and capsule biography for each, and resisted the temptation to plant suspicion in his mind about any specific one of these prime suspects.

That was a question I hadn't as yet resolved in my own mind. If *I* hadn't killed Laura—and the official line was that I had not—then someone else must have done it. Would it be better to provide that someone else, or could we content ourselves with a simple unsolved murder? There are hundreds of unsolved murders every year, why shouldn't Laura Penney's be among them? For the moment, at least, that seemed the better way, so I made none of the leading remarks that occurred to me concerning each of these escorts, but simply provided Staples with basic uncolored information: name, occupation, relationship with the deceased.

And one of them turned out to be that same Jay English whose name Staples had heard Kit mention on my answering machine, in the sentence, "I still say Jay English did it." He remembered that comment, of course, and asked several questions, with me assuring him the whole thing had been a joke, if not in very good taste, considering the unequivocal homosexuality of its subject. Joke or not, Staples made sure to get the roommate's name spelled right: David Poumon.

One of the other photos was of Laura with her father, a straight-backed well-preserved old gent I'd met once several months ago, when he was in town from upstate. If Staples was so interested in unusual sexual relationships, how about intimating something incestuous there to keep his busy mind occupied? No; once again I restrained myself and moved on to the next, which happened to be the same stammering Jack Freelander who'd just left, um, a message on my machine.

After I'd done all the pictures once, with Staples making notes in his small pad and giving each subject his own page, he led me back through all six again, asking leading questions, poking here and there in search of motive, and damn if he didn't suggest father–daughter incest himself. He led up to it gradually, with questions about whether Laura saw her father seldom or often, what she had to say about him, and so on, and finally he asked the question straight out: "Do you think there was anything going on there?"

"Going on?"

"Well, you say he's a widower, and she's separated from her husband."

I was astounded, not at the concept but that Staples should voice it. Apparently he specialized in thinking the unthinkable. I said, "He's her father! You don't think— I mean, what *do* you think?"

He shrugged, his expression as open and cheerful as ever. "I think people have love lives," he told me. "One way or the other, they make that connection. Now, here's a woman, she's thirty-two years old, she's been married, she's separated from her husband, all she has is these casual non-sexual dates with a number of different men. She doesn't seem to have *anybody* that's really important to her."

"That's possible," I said. "There are people who prefer to be alone."

"Not many. And not Laura Penney. It doesn't feel right, Mr. Thorpe. She had a lover, I'm sure of it." Gesturing at the photos on the table next to me, he said, "In among all those men in her life was the *man* in her life. But he was kept hidden. Why?"

"I see what you mean," I said. "A lover wouldn't be kept hidden unless there was a reason for it."

"Right." He checked off the possibilities on his fingers. "He's married. He's homosexual and doesn't want to make a complete break with the homosexual world. He's her father."

"I don't believe it."

"Neither do I," Staples assured me. "But at this stage of the game, I keep an open mind."

I was beginning to feel a bit wary of that open mind of Staples'. If he was so eager to think the unthinkable, why wouldn't it occur to him to play with the thought that my guaranteed innocence might in itself be an indication of guilt? I was, after all, the Least Likely Suspect. And as with all Least Likely Suspects, I was in reality the Murderer.

Staples and I talked for half an hour more, with him drawing another three or four names from me of men who knew Laura but whose pictures had not been snapped by the private detectives. Finally he seemed satisfied that he'd squeezed me dry, and he made ready to leave, saying, "I do appreciate your cooperation, Mr. Thorpe. And the coup you pulled in the Wicker killing this afternoon was really beautiful. You made my day."

"It'd be interesting to find out the rest of that story."

"Oh, I'm sure Al Bray's got the whole thing by now." Then, seeming to be struck by a sudden thought, he said, "Say. That girlfriend of yours is tied up tonight, isn't she?"

Meaning Kit, who had said so on the machine. "Yes, I guess she is."

"Why not have dinner with us? Patricia and me. She'd love to meet you, she's as big a fan as I am. And I'll have the story from Al by then, I can tell it to you at dinner."

"Oh, I don't think I should—"

"Listen, you're not imposing." He was very eager, very determined. "And Patricia's a wonderful cook. I tell you what, I'll call her from here, you'll see there's no problem. Okay?"

I was ambivalent. On the one hand, I wanted to be near Staples as much as possible, I wanted to know what he was thinking so I could steer him away from dangerous shallows. On the other hand, his presence made me nervous. As to the grubby details of Jack March and his fatal grudge against Jim Wicker, they interested me not at all.

But Staples was waiting for an answer, all eagerness and bounce. "All right," I said. "If it's all right with your wife."

"Patricia's gonna flip," he assured me. "Okay if I use your phone?"

"Go right ahead."

He did, and though he kept his voice too low for me to hear the exact words—I had politely removed myself to the far end of the room—the syrupy note in everything he said suggested he couldn't have been a husband more than fifteen minutes. True love birds, icky-wickies together. But it was too late now to back out.

Cradling the phone at last, Staples turned his beaming smile toward me and said, "It's all set, Mr. Thorpe. I'll pick you up around seven-thirty, okay?"

"Fine," I said. "But if I'm going to eat at your table, I think you'd better call me Carey."

"Terrific." He stuck out his hand, saying, "And I'm Fred."

The hunter and the quarry shook hands.

It was like being stuck in one of the sweeter Disney cartoons, one of the early ones where the sentimentality really cloys. Great pink clouds of love floated everywhere, and tiny blue-birds seemed to flutter just beyond my peripheral vision.

Patricia Staples wasn't at all difficult to look at, but God have mercy if she wasn't a penance to listen to. Of medium height and weight, with silky blonde hair and clear innocent blue eyes, pert lips and straight nose, she looked like something on a corn flakes box or on the cover of a 1943 issue of *Liberty* magazine, and in the course of dinner alone she called her husband "sweet-ness" and "honey" and "sugar" often enough to produce terminal diabetes. (Even though he did send nearly half of them back.)

Staples had told me that he and his Patricia had been mar-ried almost three years, yet they looked and sounded and acted like the most simpering of honeymooners. Staples later claimed this aspect was the result of their decision not to have children, apparently allowing them to be infantile without competition, but I prefer to believe that Staples was attracted to her lavish wholesomeness because of its contrast with the seamier side of his own work.

The gilded cage enclosing this contented canary was a seventh-floor co-op apartment in a grim red-brick building in Corona,

Queens, not far enough from the Long Island Expressway. One saw it out there, churning away in the blighted darkness beyond the living room windows like a diorama of life on the planet Jupiter. The apartment itself was warm and yellow and bright, with furniture that must have looked just as flimsy and just as tacky in the various Long Island showrooms from which it had been purchased. A great rectangular green-and-yellow painting of a meadow glade in spring, the grandmother of all jigsaw puzzles, dangled over the sofa like an eavesdropper, while Staples and I sat daringly beneath it, drinking Corona Hills Scotch with club soda and chatting about great murder mysteries of fact and fancy.

Patricia, meantime, bustled about. Queen of her domain, a housewife so utterly satisfied with her lot as to make all the efforts of Women's Lib seem like an exercise in counting grains of sand, Patricia Staples spent that entire evening, it seemed to me, with a white apron over her pale blue dress, carrying a casserole to the table between two heat-mittened hands. This, by God, was what the boys of *Guadalcanal Diary* had been fighting for.

Well of course it wasn't *quite* that bad. It doesn't take that long to carry a casserole, nor to cook one, but even when Patricia Staples was sitting in the uneasy chair on her husband's left hand her mind and heart appeared to be still in the kitchen.

As to her being a fan of mine, I saw early on that she was a fan of no one and nothing but her husband. She gave eager agreement to everything he said, whether sensible or foolish, and he gave her the blind compliment of assuming that all her parrot responses were the product of an independent but wonderfully sympatico mind.

Staples apparently preferred not to talk shop in his wife's presence, so when we all sat down to dinner—chicken, rice, tomatoes, celery and much much more, all in the same Corning ovenproof bowl—the talk turned to movies, and I'm afraid I found it impossible not to become a pompous bore. But they did keep demanding it; Patricia invariably agreed with Fred, who invariably agreed with me, who had no one to agree with but myself. It would take a far more Calvinist personality than mine to resist such an opportunity for pontification. I spoke in long compound sentences, like an early draft of one of my own articles, and in fact I quoted from my previous works several times. Patricia didn't mind, since she wasn't particularly aware of my existence anyway, but Fred for all his eagerness did begin to glaze after a while.

Dinner, like all good things, came to an end, and while Patricia retired again to her kitchen to "tidy up" (a phrase they both used, *both* of them) Staples and I seated ourselves once more beneath the leaning painting, this time with Corona Hill VSOP Olde Brandy, and after the few obligatory propaganda remarks from Staples about how good it must be for a bachelor to eat a real meal for a change we went back to shoptalk, the subject being murder. This time, though, it was murder closer to home: "You haven't asked," Staples pointed out, "about the Wicker case."

"That's right," I agreed. "I haven't."

He took that to mean I wanted to know, so he told me. It was one of those convoluted stories of betrayal, disguise, coincidence and overly complicated scheming that mystery stories *always* end with, and though I nodded a lot while Staples reeled it off I didn't retain a word of it, except the fact that Jack March's real name turned out to be Andrew Thomas Cauldenfield. (Ever since Lee Harvey Oswald, murderers have had prominent middle names, just as tall farm youths used to have prominent adam's apples.)

Patricia joined us soon after that, and the talk switched back to movies, and that was when *Gaslight* came up. Staples announced it to be one of his all-time favorite pictures, "but Patricia's never seen it."

"I have a print," I said. And I found myself extending an invitation: "Would you like to come see it?"

Staples stared at me. "A *print?* You mean you own that movie, you have it right there in your apartment?"

"I have copies of more than twenty films," I told him, "and access to almost anything else I'd like to see. The studios loan prints to people in the field."

Staples viewed me with something like awe, and even Patricia seemed impressed. Staples said, "By golly, if I had that I don't think I'd *ever* leave the house."

"It's like anything else," I told him. "You get used to it after a while."

We then discussed the best time for them to come see *Gaslight* and decided on Sunday afternoon at three. Staples would be working earlier that day, but Patricia could take the subway to Manhattan, meet her husband for lunch, and then the two would come over to my place for the screening.

Soon after that it was time to leave. Staples suggested he drive me back to Manhattan, and though I insisted I'd be perfectly content in the subway he wouldn't take no for an answer. So I thanked Patricia for a delicious dinner, shook her cool hand, and her husband and I rode the elevator down to the basement garage where he kept his car.

The ride back was full of conversation, by which I mean that Staples kept up a cheerful flow of talk to which I added occasional appropriate punctuation. It was becoming clear that in Staples' eyes I was a celebrity, and he was delighted to have collected me. My own feelings were too complicated for me to think about, so I simply floated on the surface of my mind, letting it all happen. At my door, Staples pulled to a stop and shook my hand, saying, "It was really nice to have you out, Carey. Really nice."

"I appreciated it, Fred. And that's a wonderful girl you have there."

"Don't I know it," he said, with a big grin.

"See you Sunday, Fred," I said, and opened the car door.

"Right you are. Goodnight, Carey."

"Goodnight, Fred."

I stepped out onto the street, closed the door after me, and the Ford growled away, its exhaust thick and white in the cold air. I crossed the sidewalk, went up the stoop reaching for my keys, and a dark figure came out of a corner of the vestibule to hit me very hard in the stomach. I doubled over in pain and shock, trying not to lose my balance and fall backwards down the steps, and he hit me again, this time in the side, just above the waist.

It was brief, but horrible, and I suspect very professional. Grabbing a handful of my coat, he pulled and tugged and crowded me into the darkness of the vestibule and then punched and kicked and kneed me half a dozen times in quick succession, as I sagged down the wall. All of the blows were to my body, and all seemed placed with some kind of anatomical precision, and all were very painful.

Then it was over and he was gone, without my ever seeing his face or hearing his voice; though of course I knew at once who it was. I sat on the floor of the vestibule, having trouble breathing, and a while later I found the keys I'd dropped and let myself into the building and up several thousand stairs to the apartment, where Edgarson's voice on my answering machine said, "We're calling about your debt, Mr. Thorpe. We look forward to early payment."

Two hours in a hot tub helped somewhat, and so did both

Valium and bourbon, but when I dragged myself out of bed Friday morning I was as stiff and sore as though Edgarson had just finished kicking me that very second.

I was supposed to go to a noon screening at MGM, but I found myself reluctant to leave the apartment. Also to answer the phone; so I turned on the answering machine with the monitor button pushed, enabling me to hear my callers as they were leaving their messages. That way, I could speak to anyone I chose, and avoid the rest. Meaning Edgarson.

Even such painful clouds as this one have silver linings. After another long soak in the tub, followed by more pills, I decided to table the problem of Edgarson for a while, and actually managed to get some work done on my next projected piece for *Third World Cinema*, with the tentative title, "John Cassavetes: The Apotheosis Of The Inarticulate." Though Edgarson didn't call, several other people did, but I wasn't in the mood for any of them and I ignored their messages and went on with my work.

Then, just as I had written, "On-set improvisation sounds so good in theory that it's a shame it sounds so bad in practice," the phone rang again, and after my recorded announcement ("Hi. Carey Thorpe's answering machine here. Please leave your name and a phone number where I can reach you, and I'll be back to you first chance I get.") Staples' voice said, "Fred here, Carey. I was hoping to catch you at home. We've got another—"

A policeman; exactly what I needed. Not waiting to listen to any more, I picked up the phone, switched off the machine, and said, "Here I am. I'm here."

Staples, headed off in mid-message, floundered briefly before saying, "Hello? Carey?"

"I was working," I told him, "so I left the machine on."

"Oh, I won't bother you, then, I just—"

"No, no, that's fine, I'm ready to take a break. What's happening?"

"Well, we've got another one," he said. "Feel brilliant today?"

"Another murder?"

"Another tricky murder. Regular murders we get all the time. Want to come along?"

With Staples I would be safe from Edgarson. "Absolutely," I said.

This time, happily, the body had been removed. In fact, Staples and I had the small apartment on West 76th Street entirely to ourselves.

The victim was a thirty-three-year-old bachelor, an advertising copywriter named Bart Ailburg. His one-bedroom apartment on the third floor of a brownstone half a block from Central Park featured a pleasant large living room with windows overlooking back gardens featuring plane trees.

Much could be gathered about Ailburg from his home. The excessive masculinity of his imitation lion-skin bed throw and all those hoofs and horns scattered about as paperweights, ashtrays, lamps and general decoration, combined with the sloppy pile of male physique magazines under the bed, suggested rather strongly a homosexual tendency. The travel posters on the walls, the two shelves of travel reference books handy to his desk, and the small souvenirs grouped on the mantle over the nonfunctional fireplace indicated that his job was connected with travel advertising. And the three locks on his front door, taken with the fact that he had medicine chests in the bathroom, both crammed with prescription bottles and all kinds of patent medicines, suggested a timid hypochondriac, a cautious unassertive sort of man.

Staples reconstructed the crime for me. This living room was rectangular, with sofa, TV and so on at the end near the kitchen and with the desk and bookcase at the end by the windows. The desk was centered in front of the windows, and Ailburg had been sitting at it, facing the room, working. Doing a travel ad, in fact, writing out a draft in pencil on a lined yellow legal pad; his writing was spidery, neat, rather small. The killer had picked up a bone-handled letter opener from the desk and had stabbed Ailburg six times in the neck and back. Ailburg, bleeding a terrific amount, had fallen forward onto the desk and had shortly afterward died, leaving most of the desk drenched in blood except for the legal pad, which had been under him.

Judging from stains on the bathroom floor, the killer had become smeared with blood and had next taken a bath. Since it had been necessary for him to take a bath rather than merely wash at the sink, it was a reasonable presumption that he had been naked when he'd done the killing.

The apartment had not been ransacked, nothing appeared to have been stolen.

The ad Ailburg had been working on had been due this morning, for a deadline later today. When Ailburg, invariably a prompt and reliable worker, had failed to show up and also failed to answer his phone, one of the partners in the ad agency sent a messenger, who persuaded the building's superintendent to enter the apartment. They discovered first that only the door's regular lock was fastened, leaving both the chainlock and the police lock undone, and then they discovered Ailburg himself.

The report had reached Staples and Bray shortly after ten this morning. All of the normal things had been done, neighbors questioned, movements checked, and nothing interesting had turned up. Ailburg, a man of regular habits, had apparently come home directly from the office yesterday, had spent a quiet evening at home, and had then been murdered sometime between midnight and three in the morning.

"Al Bray," Staples finished, "is ready to put it down to one of your fag murders. Rough trade. You know, where a fellow goes cruising in Central Park and comes back with some tough young stud who bumps him off."

"No," I said. "Not this time."

Staples grinned at me. "That's what I say, too."

"In the first place," I said, "Ailburg might have gone cruising, but he wouldn't come back with anybody tough. That wasn't his style."

"Well, you can't say that for sure," Staples said. "When you get into people's sex lives, it's hard to make predictions."

"Ailburg had a deadline this morning," I said. "If he was such a conscientious type, he might go out looking for a friend *after* he got the work done, but not before."

"There I agree with you," Staples said. "That was my point exactly with Al."

"Also," I said, "a cautious man wouldn't let a stranger behind him with a sharp letter opener."

"No, he wouldn't. But the killer was probably naked, don't forget that."

"A lover," I said. "But someone Ailburg knew, not some pickup. You don't go get yourself a brand new sex partner and then sit down calmly to do some work while this new body prances around naked."

Staples said, "That's right. The feeling I had in this room was that it was somebody Ailburg was comfortable with, somebody he didn't have to play host to."

I said, "I don't see the problem. It was one of Ailburg's boyfriends. How many did he have?"

Staples held up a well-thumbed black address book. "There

are over sixty men's names in here," he said. "Homosexuals still tend to be pretty secretive about who their lovers are. We've got no fingerprints, no witnesses, no clues, nothing. It would be a long, hard, dull job to check out every one of these guys, and we could *still* never come up with the right one."

"Ah," I said. "That's why Bray's content to think it's a pick-up killing."

"Sure," Staples said. "If the job's tough, we have to do it, but if it's impossible we can forget it."

Walking around the room, I said, "I suppose you've looked for letters, anything that could give you specific names of boy-friends."

"Nothing," Staples said.

I'd been avoiding the desk, which was still smeared with caked brown blood. The rough outline of Ailburg's torso and arms was clear in the center, with the pencil and the legal pad. Going over at last to that part of the room, I saw that both windows were securely locked, that there was no fire escape here, and that we were too high for anyone to have climbed in from the back. Finally I turned my reluctant attention to the desk.

Other than the bloodstains, it was neat, the work space of a methodical man. A small Olympia portable typewriter was pushed to one side, near the beige telephone. And on the legal pad was written:

> "ST. MARTIN!
> *Carefree days, exotic nights!*
> *The peace of the beaches, the thrill of the casinos!*
> *And only a mile and a half away, the charming*
> *capital city of Antigua."*

"A very rough draft, apparently," I said. "There weren't any other worksheets around?"

Staples shook his head. "From the looks of things, he'd just started to work when he was killed."

I said, "Which was sometime between midnight and three in the morning. That wasn't in character for the man, not to start work until so late at night on something that was supposed to be turned in the next morning."

"That bothered me, too," Staples said. "But I'm not sure what it means."

"An argument," I suggested. "The killer came here probably in the early evening, and they had one of those droning dragged-out arguments that lovers get into."

"*Most* lovers," Staples said, with a big smile, suggesting that he and his Patricia should be exempted.

"Certainly," I said. "Anyway, Ailburg had this work to do, so finally he just told his boyfriend, 'I'm going to work,' and he sat down here and started writing. And not doing very well, either, probably because he was still troubled about the fight. I mean, 'The peace of the beaches,' that's a terrible line."

"It does sound funny," Staples said.

"Now, the boyfriend," I went on, "got *really* mad when Ailburg started to ignore him. The fight wasn't settled, and there Ailburg was at his desk, writing away just as though nothing had happened. So the boyfriend came over, in a rage, and let him have it."

"Fine." Staples waved the address book again. "Which one?"

"I don't know," I said.

We spent another five minutes looking at the place, but there was nothing left to see. Staples, who'd been expecting me to come up with another of my little magic turns, watched me with fading hope, but I knew I wasn't going to repeat my success. Finally I said, "I guess the Wicker case was just beginner's luck."

"I knew this was a tough one," Staples said, with a game smile, "that's why I called you."

"Sorry I couldn't—" Then I stopped, and frowned over at the desk.

Staples was saying, "Oh, come on, Carey, if *I* can't do my job there's no reason you should— What's up?"

"There's something wrong," I said. "Just a minute."

I went back to the desk, Staples following me, and frowned again at that bit of copywriting. "That isn't right," I said.

"What isn't right?"

"I've been to the Caribbean, and Antigua isn't that close to St. Martin. Not at all. Wait, hold on."

Sitting at Ailburg's desk, forgetting for the moment any squeamishness I might have felt, I looked through his reference books for an atlas. Finding one, I turned to a map of the Caribbean and said, "See? Here's St. Martin, and here's Antigua way down here."

Staples touched the map with a blunt finger. "What's that little island there? The one by St. Martin."

When he removed his finger, I bent to read the lettering: "Anguilla."

"Anguilla, Antigua." Staples shrugged, saying, "He was upset from the argument, that's all, he just got mixed up."

"Does that make sense?" I studied Ailburg's writing again, shaking my head. "No, it doesn't. This was his job, he knew what island was where. And look how he broke that sentence, starting a new line after the word 'charming.' It looks awkward."

Staples said, "I don't see what you're driving at."

I was sitting now where Ailburg had been, and I rested my forearms on a blood-free part of the desk. "Ailburg is sitting here," I said. "The boyfriend comes around behind him, Ailburg sees him pick up the letter opener. He isn't sure what's happening, but he's afraid. And he quick starts a new line of copy, telling us who the boyfriend is."

Staples leaned over my shoulder to read aloud. " 'Capital city of Antigua.' You mean that's supposed to be a message?"

"Let's see." Back to the atlas I went. "The capital city of Antigua is St. John. Is there anybody named St. John in that address book?"

Staples, obviously unsure whether I was a genius or a lunatic, leafed through the address book, ran his finger down a column, and gave me a slow smile. "How about Jack St. Pierre?"

"That's your man," I said. "It's up to you to prove it, but he's the guy to concentrate on."

FIVE
The Footprints in the Snow

Staples drove me home, and on the way we discussed the murder that had first brought us together. All of Laura's male friends and acquaintances had been interviewed by now, several had been eliminated via unassailable alibis, and the active list had been reduced to five; not including, I was happy to see, Laura's father.

But farther reduction from five was proving difficult, if not impossible. No one of the suspects was more or less likely to be the elusive secret boyfriend, none would admit to any but the most casual relationship with Laura, and unfortunately this victim had not left behind a clue to the boyfriend's identity. (Using Ailburg as an example, Laura might have been found, for instance, clutching a publicity still of Cary Grant. Or Harry Carey. Or perhaps a tattered paperback copy of *Herself Surprised*.)

In any event, the investigation was currently at a standstill. "But that doesn't mean we've given up," Staples assured me. "Whenever you've got a good-looking career girl murdered, there's always a lot of media pressure to keep the case alive. Channel Five won't even mention Bart Ailburg, but they still talk about Laura Penney on the news every night."

"From my point of view, of course," I said, "I'm glad to hear that. That's one killer I really want found."

"Well, I told you our five suspects," he said, and reeled off the names again. (There's no point my giving the list; the killer's name wasn't on it.) "If you could come up with another of your brilliant deductions," Staples told me, "we could really use it."

"I'll do my best."

Shortly thereafter he dropped me at my apartment, and went on to pick up Al Bray and go question Jack St. Pierre. It was still daylight, though rapidly growing dark with heavy clouds and the threat of impending snow, and no one was lurking for me in the vestibule. I let myself into the building, climbed the stairs, unlocked my apartment door, and entered to find Edgarson sitting in my leather director's chair, reading this afternoon's *Post*. "Well, there you are," he said, folded his paper, and got to his feet.

I went down the steps three at a time, out the front door, and directly into a passing cab.

I spent the night at Kit's place on East 19th Street. We awoke late—it was Saturday, so Kit didn't have to work—and found that the promised snowstorm had indeed arrived, creating a cold slushy world of difficulty and discomfort. Fat white flakes were still drifting endlessly downward from a dirty gray sky, the radio weather forecast spoke of "gradual clearing"—by April, probably—and Kit had decided she had the flu.

Which created an additional complication. Like most independent people, minor illness made Kit bad-tempered, and I soon realized she wanted me the hell out of there so she could snuffle in peace.

But where would I go? Was Edgarson still in my apartment? I dialed my number, but only heard my own confident voice on the machine. I left me no message.

Then I remembered Big John Brant, the movie director. He was in town, and I was supposed to phone him this morning about our interview. So I called the Sherry-Netherland, and soon had Brant on the line sounding gruff but friendly. I identified myself, and reminded him of the interview, and he said, "Well, what about right now?"

"That's fine," I said. "I'm downtown."

"Then come uptown," he said, and chuckled, and broke the connection.

I pocketed half a dozen of Kit's Valiums, my own supply being in captured territory. "Get well soon," I told Kit, and kissed her irritable cold cheek, and went out into the disgusting world.

Q: "In your film, *Don't Eat The Yellow Snow*, what is the symbolism of the repeated appearance of the small black dog in the background of so many of the shots?"

A: "Oh, yeah, that damn dog. Well, I'll tell you, that's a funny story. That was Sassi's dog, you know. Wha'd she call that damn thing? Rudolph, that was it. Anyway, that was her third— no, second—her second feature with American Artists. She was shacked up with Kleinberg then, you know, so he'd give her anything she wanted. She wasn't even supposed to be in that picture, only Kate said she wouldn't work for Kleinberg for any amount of money, and Kleinberg left the script around in the bathroom or some damn place, and Sassi read it and said, I wanna do that picture. So we were stuck with her. And she had this shitty little dog, Rudolph, and that dog wasn't trained at *all*. Run around, you couldn't control it, and finally I just said shit, I said, let the damn little thing stay in there, *I* don't give a rat's ass. Just so it doesn't get in the airplane sequence, that's all, and you know, it damn near did. Just about the end of the picture, the shitty little thing got itself run over by an Oregon state trooper. Sassi tried to get the fellow fired, but Kleinberg didn't run Oregon, so that was that."

The interview was not going at all well. I suppose it was mostly my fault, since I was distracted by the problem of Edgarson, but Big John Brant wasn't helping very much. No matter what I asked him, from the broadest possible questions about thematic undercurrents to the narrowest points of technique, all I got back were these rambling reminiscences about nothing in particular. Scatology and gossip seemed to be his only subjects.

And I'd spent sixty dollars on a cassette recorder to preserve this tripe. It wasn't until after I'd left Kit's place that I'd realized I was carrying none of my normal interviewing tools, so when I'd reached midtown I'd bought a pen and a pad and this cheap little recorder, and all I was recording so far was sex and shit.

Nevertheless, it's my own conviction that a bad interview is never really the interviewee's fault. There are two participants in an interview, but only one of them is supposed to be professional. I've interviewed actors with an IQ of seven and managed to make them sound at least competent, if not brilliant. It was the Edgarson business that was clouding my mind, with the result that I was permitting Brant to maunder along with virtually no guidance at all.

The setting also encouraged this feckless informality. Brant had a high-floor suite here at the Sherry–Netherland, with windows overlooking Central Park and the Plaza, where the still-falling snow made the world look like a Currier & Ives Christmas card that had inadvertently gone through the washing machine. A tall and slender and mind-crunchingly beautiful girl came into the room from time to time to add another couple of logs to the fire. Brant and I both sipped bourbon over ice as we sat before the crackling flames, and the contrast between this warm beautiful room and the cold snowy aspect of Central Park almost demanded a discursive droning conversational style, in which nothing could get accomplished.

Brant, too, was a problem. An old man now, with liver spots

on hands and forehead, with great knobby knuckles and wrists, with that old man's style of sitting as though he were a sack of rusty machine parts, his best work was behind him and he no longer kept his brain tuned to the sharp clarity that had given the world such films as *Meet The Gobs*, *All These Forgotten* and *Caper*. He was garrulous and relaxed and perfectly content to bend a young stranger's ear for an hour or so while the snow fell outside and the beautiful girl performed her function of keeping his old body warm.

But something had to be done, if any useful material at all were to come out of this meeting, so finally, after the memoir of the dog Rudolph, I decided my only choice, since Edgarson persisted in distracting me from my job, was bring him into the interview. Maybe he would help us get moving in a more useful direction.

Q: "I'd like to ask you now a more or less specific question of technique, based on a film other than one of yours."

A: "Somebody else's picture?"

Q: "Yes. This is a work in progress being done by a young filmmaker here in New York. I've seen the completed portion, and I'd like to ask you how *you* would handle the problem this young filmmaker has set for himself."

A: "Well, I'm not sure I get the idea what you want here, but let's give it a try and see what happens."

Q: "Fine. Now, the hero of this film is being blackmailed in the early part of the picture. But then he gets rid of the evidence against himself, but the blackmailer keeps coming around anyway. He's bigger than the hero, he threatens to beat him up and so on, he even moves into the hero's apartment, he still wants his blackmail money even though the evidence is gone. The hero doesn't want to go to the police, because he's afraid they'll get too interested in *him* and start looking around and maybe find some other evidence. So that's the situation, as far as this young filmmaker has taken it. The blackmailer is in the hero's apartment, the hero is trying to decide what to do next. Now, if this was one of your pictures, how would you handle it from there?"

A: "Well, that depends on your story."

Q: "Well, I think he wants the hero to win in the end."

A: "Okay. Fine."

Q: "The question is, where would you yourself take it from there?"

A: "Well, what's the script say?"

Q: "That doesn't matter. That's still open."

A: "Open? You have to know what happens next."

Q: "Well, that's up to you. What would *you* have happen next?"

A: "I'd follow the script."

Q: "Well, they're doing this as they go along."

A: "They're crazy. You can't do anything without a script."

Q: "Well…They're working this from an *auteur* assumption, that it's up to the director to color and shape the material and so on."

A: "Yeah, that's fine, but you got to have the material to start with. You got to have the story. You got to have the script."

Q: "Well…I thought the director was the dominant influence in film."

A: "Well, shit, sure the director's the dominant influence in film. But you still gotta have a script."

Well, that wasn't any help. What was I supposed to do, go ask three or four screenwriters for suggestions? Is the director the *auteur* or what the hell is he?

I did keep trying along in this vein for a few more questions, but they didn't get me anywhere. So far as I could see, Big John

Brant's career had come down to this; he was the fellow who told the cameraman to point the camera at the people who were talking. And to think how high in the pantheon I'd always placed this man.

The script. Only a *hack* cares about the goddam script. What I needed was to talk to a *real* director; Hitchcock, or John Ford, or John Huston, or Howard Hawks. *What happens next?* that was my question. Sam Fuller would have an answer to that. Roger Corman, even.

Well, it was all hopeless. The interview with Brant meandered along, being of no use personally and damn little professionally, until Miss Fireperson came in a little after twelve with a pointed reminder: "Don't forget your luncheon appointment, J.T." So I also wouldn't be getting lunch. I gathered up my paraphernalia, shook hands, smiled, said some lies, listened to just one more scatological anecdote, and took my departure.

As far as the hotel bar, where I swallowed another of Kit's Valiums with bourbon and water, ate a handful of peanuts for lunch, and gradually came to a decision. I could no longer spend my life wandering through a snowstorm from one reluctant haven to the next. I had to reclaim my own home. I had to get Edgarson *out*, and me *in*, and I had to do it *now*.

I had one more bourbon to confirm this decision and to warm me for the trek uptown, and then I left the hotel and turned toward home. Since I lived less than ten blocks from here—up four and over five, approximately—and since traffic was utterly snarled by the snow, there was no point trying to find a cab, so I walked. I was dressed warmly enough, except for my shoes, and I simply kept stumping through the slush, irritable but determined.

There's something both lazy and inexorable about a major

snowstorm. No wind, no real storm at all, just billions and billions of wet white smudges floating down like Chinese armies, and after a while there doesn't seem to be any reason why it should *ever* stop. Maybe that low gray-black sky contains unlimited quantities of these wet white smudges, maybe they'll just keep drifting down like this forever. Maybe human life developed on the wrong planet.

Along the way, I bought a chainlock at a hardware store on Third Avenue. I couldn't help remembering Bart Ailburg, whose door had been armed with a lock like this but who had been murdered anyway. However, no true parallel applied. Ailburg had been murdered by a loved one, which in my case was not the issue.

At the house, I spent ten minutes searching out Romeo, the super, and finally found him drinking wine in the tenants' storeroom in the basement. He wasn't drunk, I was happy to see, but he was surly. "I doan wuk Sahdy," he told me, trying to hide the brown paper bag with its cargo of Hombre or Ripple.

"You don't work ever," I informed him. "But you'll come upstairs with me now or I'll call Goldbender and tell him I found you drunk in the basement and lighting matches."

Surliness turned to a kind of clogged outrage. "I ayn drunk!" Then he comprehended the rest of my sentence and was, for just an instant, completely baffled. Innocence bewildered him, he didn't know at first what to do with it. But he soon enough recovered, crying out, "Motches? I doan got no motches! I doan *hob* no stinkin' motches!"

"And," I went on, wanting to be certain he understood the threat I was making, "I'll tell Goldbender that I intend to call the *police* about a super being drunk and lighting matches in the basement."

Maddened by this maligning of his virtue, Romeo waved his

arms in the air, slopping wine on himself and on the stored possessions of the tenants as he cried, "*I doan hob no motches!*"

"Goldbender is going to think about his insurance," I pointed
out, "and—"

"*I doan hob no motches!*"

"And," I insisted, "he is going to fire you. Particularly," I
added, "when he smells you."

Romeo became aware of the spillage and began fretfully to
pat himself with his free hand. "You makin me nervis," he said,
and he sounded as though soon he might cry.

"Come along, Romeo," I said. "Put your lunch down over
there and come along."

"This ay muh lunch." He frowned from the bag to me, and
returned to an earlier worry. "An I doan hob no motches."

"Come, Romeo." I turned away, not looking back till I reached
the stairs, when I saw that Romeo, however much he might be
bewildered and mistreated, was also sensible. He was coming
along.

As we plodded up the several flights of stairs together, me
squoshing in my cold wet shoes, Romeo said, "Wha jew wan,
anyway?"

"Just come along," I told him.

What I wanted from Romeo was his presence. We would
enter, Edgarson would approach me, Edgarson would see the
witness, Edgarson would depart. The details would work themselves out, but at the finish Edgarson would definitely depart.

Except that he wasn't there. Gingerly I let myself into the
apartment, Romeo snuffling in my wake, and nothing moved in
the semi-darkness of the living room. I switched on lights,
I looked quickly in bedroom and kitchen and bath, and the
apartment was empty. Edgarson had vacated on his own.

Romeo had remained by the door, shoulders hunched against

injustice, and when I emerged from the kitchen he said, "O.K. Here I am. Wha jew wan?"

"That's fine, Romeo," I told him. "Thank you very much, I won't be needing you any more."

Then, of course, he didn't want to leave. At first he'd been bewildered and surly when I'd brought him up here, and now he was bewildered and surly when I released him. There's no pleasing some people.

But he did finally go, and I immediately brought out my hammer and screwdriver from the storage cabinet under the bathroom sink and proceeded to mount the chainlock. It was in two parts; a metal plate from which dangled a six-inch chain with a metal ball on the end of it, and a longer metal plate with a long slot. The plate-with-chain I screwed into place on the doorframe at about chest height, then stretched the length of chain out horizontally and marked on the door how far the ball would reach. Next I fixed the longer plate onto the door in the right position, slipped the ball in the wide space in the slot, and experimentally opened the door. When I did so the chain tightened, because the ball was stuck in the narrower part of the slot, and the door wouldn't open more than four inches.

There. Let Edgarson play with his keys now, it would take more than a key to come through that door. He could open it wide enough to reach his arm in, but that was all.

Safe at last, I turned my attention back to the apartment. Surely Edgarson would have done something to commemorate his visit. Excrement on the floor? Mousetraps in the bed? Something destructive, or nasty, or both?

But I'd misjudged him. The man had beaten me up Thursday night, and yet when he'd had a full day and night to himself in my apartment he'd done nothing to it at all. He seemed to have no pattern, no consistency in his behavior, and if that was deliberately planned to increase my nervousness it was very successful. If I'd found all my dishes broken or all the furniture knocked over in the living room I would have been more angry but less tense, because I would have known what I was up against and what he was likely to do next. This way, it was impossible to guess where or when Edgarson would once more pop up, or what his manner would be when he did make his next appearance.

This time, he had contented himself with going through my personal papers and with leaving me a short but complete note, typewritten and sitting on my answering machine:

You have until noon Monday.

The phone woke me at nine-thirty Sunday morning and it was Staples, sounding slightly irritated through his normal cheeriness. "Do you feel brilliant this morning, Carey?"

"What? What?"

"Oh, I'm sorry, did I wake you?"

"No, but you might. What time is it?"

"Nine twenty-seven. Up late last night?"

Yes, as a matter of fact. I'd stayed up till nearly three, distracting myself from thoughts of Edgarson by trying to make a sensible interview out of Brant's twaddle. But I was awake now, so I sat straighter in the bed and said, "That's okay, I ought to get up anyway. What's happening?"

"Another little problem."

"Problem? You mean a murder?"

"Well, that's the question. *I* say it's a clear-cut case of suicide, but Al Bray keeps saying it *feels* funny. He doesn't have a bit of evidence, it just *feels* funny."

So that was why Staples was annoyed. It wasn't so much

that Bray disagreed with him, which surely must have happened more than once in the course of their partnership, as that Bray was disagreeing on Staples' grounds. It was Staples who was supposed to have feelings and be intuitive, while Bray was assigned the role of the methodical plodder. To have the plodder suddenly intuit all over the place could be unsettling.

I said, "You mean you think it's suicide and he thinks it's murder?"

"He doesn't know what he thinks," Staples said. "It just doesn't *feel* right. So he asked me to call you."

"He asked? Al Bray?"

"We made a deal. If you agree with me it was suicide, Al won't make any more fuss and we'll put in our report and that's the end of it."

"What if I think it's murder?"

He chuckled; a bit challengingly, I thought. "Then you'll have to prove it," he said.

They sent a car for me, with a uniformed policeman as chauffeur. I hadn't been happy about leaving the apartment untended, since the chainlock only works when there's someone inside to attach it, but then I remembered a stunt from several hundred spy movies. I took a paper match, bent it double, and wedged it between door and frame just below the bottom hinge. It protruded just enough to be seen, if you knew where to look, and if anyone opened my apartment door the match would fall. It wouldn't keep Edgarson out, but it would warn me in time if he'd returned. If the match was on the floor when I came back I'd know Edgarson was once again in residence, and off I'd go for Romeo.

Outside, the policeman was standing beside his unmarked black Plymouth, his breath steaming in the cold air. The snow had stopped but the sky was still gray and heavy with low clouds, and the temperature was dropping.

Our destination was Central Park West near 89th Street, and on the way the cop filled me in on the situation. At eight-twenty this morning, a tenant of the building in question had come out to walk his dog, and found the crushed body of a woman lying face up on the sidewalk. The tenant returned immediately to the building and informed the doorman, who called the police. The doorman also obtained a blanket and went out to cover the body, at which point he realized the victim was someone he knew, a tenant who had occupied one of the penthouse duplexes atop the building. Apparently she had fallen or jumped or been pushed from the terrace up there.

A patrol car responded to the first call, but no one went up to the dead woman's apartment until the precinct detectives arrived, and then it took considerable banging and doorbell-ringing to rouse the woman's husband, who had been asleep and had not been aware of his wife's absence from the apart-ment. According to the husband, his wife had been despondent and depressed recently and had spoken of suicide.

The couple's name was Templeton, George and Margo, and they were both in their early fifties. He was a millionaire in the real estate business in the city, with ownership of office build-ings and Broadway theaters among his holdings, and she was a one-time actress who had given up her career twenty-five years ago to marry him. They had two sons, both now grown and living away from New York. They had been to a party last night where both had become very drunk and where George Templeton freely admitted they had quarreled publicly over whether or not he had ruined her life twenty-five years ago by marrying her. They had returned home, continuing the argument in their chauffeur-driven limousine and in their bedroom, until Templeton had either gone to sleep or passed out from drink. And he had known nothing more until the pounding of the police at his door had awakened him.

The Templetons kept a staff of three servants, but only one of these—the maid—lived in the apartment, and she invariably spent her Saturday nights and Sundays with her family in New Hyde Park.

As to the time of death, the Weather Bureau said the snow had stopped at just about eight o'clock this morning. The body had been found at eight-twenty, and both the tenant who'd found it and the doorman who'd covered it swore there was no snow on top of the body. After eight o'clock, then, and before eight-twenty.

I was primed with all of this by the time we reached the building, and I was happy to see the body was no longer on the sidewalk. Clean and neat, that's the way I like my murders.

My chauffeur-cop accompanied me into the building and up in the elevator. Going up I reviewed what he'd told me, and decided Al Bray was probably right. It not only sounded like murder, it sounded like *my* murder, plus a terrace. I mean the murder I'd committed. Argumentative women don't commit suicide, they don't want to give the opposition the satisfaction. What most likely happened was that George Templeton, tired and drunk and getting older by the second, had finally popped Margo a good one to shut her up and she'd done herself a fatal injury in hitting the floor. Not wanting the scandal or the trouble of a manslaughter trial, George had chucked her over the terrace, pretended to be asleep, and then told the police his wife had been suicidal lately.

I felt ambivalent about exposing old George; in a way, we were members of the same fraternity.

*

It was a two-story apartment, with a spiral staircase.

The elevator let me off directly into the living room, on the apartment's lower floor, where Staples and Bray were sitting together on green velvet sofas, having a stiff-necked discussion. It ended when they saw me, and they both got up and came over. Staples looking a bit cocky and defiant, Bray awkward but determined.

It was Bray who did the talking, after we'd exchanged ritual hellos. "I feel a little funny about this situation, Mr. Thorpe," he said. "It goes against the grain with me. But there's something wrong here, I know there is, and I just can't put my finger on it. You've come up with a couple of off-the-wall solutions the last week, so maybe you can do something this time."

Staples added, "Even if it's just to put those *feelings* of Al's to rest."

"I don't know what to say," I admitted. "You people are trained, I'm not. I've just had beginner's luck."

"Maybe you've still got it," Bray said. "Come along."

We went up the spiral staircase in single file, Bray and then me and then Staples, who said, "Templeton isn't here right now. His doctor's in this building and he's down there, under sedation. If you need to talk with him, we can work something out."

At the head of the stairs was the master bedroom, large and ornately furnished, with French doors leading to the terrace. Windows flanking the French doors featured hanging plants, with frost-blackened leaves.

Staples now took over, saying, "No one's gone out on the terrace yet. It's exactly the way we found it. Come take a look."

I went with him. He opened the French doors and I stood in the doorway as he pointed out the obvious, saying, "You'll notice there's footprints in the fresh snow. But there's only one set of them, and they lead straight out to the railing, and they don't come back."

I nodded. "So I see."

"We took the shoes off the body," he went on, "and compared them with the nearest prints, and those prints were definitely made by those shoes."

"Ah."

I stood frowning at the terrace. The recent windless snow, the current bitter cold, had combined to create an almost perfect tableau for us, as though it were a model made out of papier maché. Two lawn chairs were folded away to one side of the terrace, which was otherwise unfurnished. The layer of snow on the floor was two to three inches thick, and in it the footprints showed clearly. There was no other disturbance of the snow of any kind out there. Beyond the snow-topped wrought iron railing was Central Park, far below, shrouded in grayish white.

Cold air was seeping in, despite the lack of wind. I stepped back from the doorway, shivering a little and looking again at the frostbitten hanging plants. I said, "Have you been keeping this door open very much?"

"Not much at all," Bray said. "Why? Does it matter?"

"I don't know if anything matters," I told him. "I'm just trying to get a picture of the situation."

Staples said, "Shall I close it now?"

"Might as well."

Staples closed the French doors and then he and Bray watched me as I wandered around the bedroom, studying things at random and trying to come to a decision. Finally I turned to Bray and said, "I'm sorry, Sergeant Bray. I'm not saying you're wrong, but this time inspiration just refuses to hit."

He frowned at me, and I could feel his confusion and his

mistrust. He believed I was lying, but he didn't know why. He said, "You don't see any indication of murder, eh?"

"Indication? I don't see any *proof*. There's plenty of indication, but you already know that. The argument at the party, the amount of alcohol they'd drunk, all the rest of it."

"But no proof." Now it was Bray's turn to wander the room, glowering at this and that. "There's something here," he said. "I know it, but I just can't get hold of it."

"I'm sorry I can't help," I told him. "I hate to spoil a perfect batting average."

"You're not spoiling it," Staples assured me. Now that he was being vindicated his manner was bluff and hearty. "If there's nothing here, and you find nothing, then you're still batting a thousand."

"Oh, no," I said. "I'm not saying Sergeant Bray is wrong. I do know what he means, that there's a certain something about all this that doesn't feel just right. But I don't know what it is any more than he does."

That mollified Bray, without spoiling Staples' pleasure, and soon afterwards they sent me off again to be driven home. Staples' farewell to me was, "See you at three."

"What? Oh, *Gaslight*." That had entirely slipped my mind. "You and your wife at three. Absolutely."

Bray being present for this exchange, it became necessary to widen the invitation to include him, and he thanked me and said he'd try to make it. But his mind was still on the death of Margo Templeton, and his vague conviction that something was wrong.

Well, he would find it or he wouldn't. I'd done what I could for my fraternity brother.

Good luck, George.

SIX
The Chainlock Mystery

I was rewriting my questions to match Big John Brant's answers when Staples called again. "It looks like I'm going to be late," he said. "We've had a new development."

Poor George. "In the Templeton case?"

Not poor George. "No, as a matter of fact, it's in the Laura Penney case."

Why did my heart flutter? I was the one in the clear. "A new development? That's wonderful."

"We're not sure yet," Staples told me. "It's an anonymous letter with a tip in it."

Edgarson! That son of a bitch, that rotten filthy bastard! Clutching the phone so tightly that my fingers hurt, I said, "A tip? What kind of tip?"

"It's all very vague and roundabout. But it isn't just some crank who read about it in the papers, because it's got details in it that only an insider would know." Then he dropped the other shoe: "Do you know any friend of Mrs. Penney's with connections in Boston?"

"Boston? You mean, besides me?"

Staples said, "You? I thought you were a native New Yorker."

"No, I'm a Boston boy."

"Well, it can't be you. Can you think of anybody else?"

"I'll put my mind to it," I promised.

"Fine. Anyway, the reason I called, I might be a little late for the movie. Patricia's coming direct to your place and I'll meet her there. If that's okay with you."

"Of course. No problem."

"Fine. See you then."

✤

I was in the kitchenette, putting together a quick lunch prior to the screening, when it seemed to me I heard some scratching sounds at the front door. Stepping out to the living room, a piece of baloney in my hand, I saw the door partway open and a hand reaching through to poke at the chainlock.

"Hah!" I cried. "Hah, you son of a bitch, you won't get in now!"

The hand withdrew and the door closed. He'd given up, the bastard.

Wait a minute. Was there something on the chainlock? Squinting, trying to see, I moved toward the door as the man on the other side gave it a sudden loud thump. The door shook, and the chainlock ball fell out of its slot. The chain swung free, and the door opened wide, and Edgarson came walking into my apartment.

"Yak!" I ran back to the kitchenette, exchanged the slice of baloney for my longest and sharpest knife—which was neither particularly long nor particularly sharp—and then I crouched in the doorway, snarling and at bay. "Don't come any closer!"

Edgarson gave me a pitying smile. "Do you want to see how I'd take that knife away from you?"

"I'm serious about this," I said.

So he came over and took the knife away and tossed it into the sink and released my arm. "Now we can talk," he said.

I headed toward the door, but he didn't follow. Instead, he stood in the kitchenette doorway and called after me, "It's mighty cold out there."

And I in my shirtsleeves. Hand on the doorknob, I looked back at him and saw he wasn't behaving in a threatening manner. He was simply standing there by the kitchenette, watching me, waiting for me to settle down. Also, he hadn't been more physical than necessary in disarming me of the knife. Hesitant, not sure what I should do next, I said, "What do you want, Edgarson?"

"You know what I want."

"I have friends coming here pretty soon," I told him. "Including two policemen."

"I've noticed that about you, Mr. Thorpe," he said, and crossed the room casually to sit on my sofa. "You've gotten real chummy with those two officers."

"They told me about that anonymous letter you wrote."

That produced a happy smile. "Oh, you know about that already, do you? I was going to mention it."

Releasing the doorknob, I moved back into the living room, saying, "This isn't fair, you know. It really isn't fair."

He spread his hands. "What isn't fair, Mr. Thorpe? You owe me ten thousand dollars. You'll pay me before twelve o'clock noon tomorrow."

"I *don't* owe you! The evidence is destroyed, you don't have anything on me any more."

"Oh, that little razzle-dazzle you pulled, about what story you'd tell." He shook his head, his smile turning down at the corners. "Well, that's in the past now, isn't it, Mr. Thorpe? You've already told your story, haven't you? And you can't change your story any more than I can change mine."

"So it's a stalemate," I said.

"Not quite." His smile became happier again. "There's still one difference between us," he said. "I *didn't* kill Mrs. Laura Penney, but you did. And I know you did."

"But you can't do anything about it. You just admitted as much, you can't change your story."

"That's right, Mr. Thorpe. About the only way I can be a good citizen now is anonymously."

"You can't prove anything."

"Well, sir, Mr. Thorpe, what proof do I have to have to write an anonymous letter? All I need do is attract their attention, wouldn't you say so? And leave the rest to them?"

"You already did that."

"Oh, that one." Modestly he smiled and shook his head. "I could do a *lot* better than that, Mr. Thorpe."

"Is that right? What could you say? How is an anonymous letter going to—"

The phone rang. I glanced over at it, annoyed, and then finished my sentence as I crossed the room to answer it. "—be more persuasive than *I* am? I know them now, they're my friends. Hello?"

Staples: "Fred again, Carey. Listen, this is taking a while, I'm definitely going to be late."

Glowering at Edgarson, I said, "I'm sorry to hear that, Fred."

"Patricia's on her way, though. And I'll get there just as soon as I can."

"We won't start without you," I promised.

"You know," he said, "it's amazing how many people don't really come from New York."

"Is that right?"

"Tell you all about it when I see you."

"Right. So long."

I hung up, and Edgarson said, "Let's see, now, would that be Fred Staples? Detective Sergeant, Homicide South?"

"Excuse me a minute," I said, and went into the bathroom, where I swallowed a Valium with Alka Seltzer. Then I stood for a long minute looking at my reflection in the mirror.

I knew what I had to do. What choice was there?

I got the hammer from the storage cabinet under the sink, and then I eased open the door just far enough to see him out there. He was on his feet, strolling comfortably around, at home and at ease. He stopped at the bookcases, he browsed, he selected an issue of *Third World Cinema* and leafed through it. Would he stop at the two-page spread of stills from the porno movie?

He would. Clutching the hammer, I slipped out of the bathroom and across the carpeted living room floor. Remembering how readily he had taken that knife from me, wincingly aware of what he might do if he saw me coming at him with a hammer in my hand, I found myself torn between the needs of speed and silence, and I did a sort of frantic tiptoe plunge across the room, lifting the hammer high over my head.

I was zipping Edgarson into the Valpack when the doorbell rang.

I looked up. The digital clock on my desk read 3:02; Staples, or possibly his wife.

I finished zipping, then ran into the bathroom, turned off the water, dried the hammer, put it away. As I was coming out of the bathroom the doorbell rang again. To stall any longer would be suspicious, so I buzzed my visitor in and then dragged the Valpack into the bedroom, where with great difficulty I managed to hang it in the closet.

Trotting back to the living room, I scooped into a desk drawer the former contents of Edgarson's pockets, and then just had time to double-check that the bloodstain on the floor was completely cleaned up. Then there came the knock at the hall door, and I opened it to admit Patricia Staples, bundled up like Anna Karenina. "Mrs. Staples. Come in."

She came in, and we transferred a series of hats, coats, scarves and gloves from her person to the hall closet, during which I told her of her husband's most recent phone call and she agreed that yes, Fred had told her he might be late, but she was used to that. It was hard to keep to a schedule if you were a policeman's wife.

While agreeing with all that, I took a few seconds to frown at my breached chainlock. It looked no different from before, it appeared not to have been damaged in any way, and yet Edgarson had come through it as though it were made of grass. How had he done it?

"What a nice place you have here," Mrs. Staples was saying, moving on into the living room.

So we had a few minutes of chitchat of the normal type, ending with her deciding to have a bourbon and water if that's what I was having. It was.

I went off to the kitchenette to mix the drinks, and she made me very nervous by roaming around the living room, looking at this and that. Was there anything left to be noticed?

I brought the drinks out as quickly as possible, and she smiled at me and said, "You know, bachelors aren't supposed to be good housekeepers, but you keep this place just spick and span."

"Well," I said, "I just shove everything out of sight."

I induced her to sit on the sofa, and sat down beside her. She raised her glass. "Cheers."

I agreed, and we drank, and I said, "Of course, I'm not really a bachelor."

She raised mildly interested eyebrows. "You're married?"

"Separated. My wife is in Boston, getting a divorce."

"How sad." She leaned toward me slightly. "Do you have children?"

"Two. A boy and a girl."

"Do you get to see them?"

What a thought. "Sometimes," I said. "Not as much as I'd like, of course."

"Of course." She sipped at her drink, ruminating. "Divorce is such a terrible thing."

I could do this conversation from across the street: "And yet, sometimes it's the only answer."

She sighed, and sipped, and sighed again, and said, "Did you read that article in last month's *Reader's Digest?*"

" 'New Hope For Dead People'?"

Big blue eyes blinked slowly. "What?"

"Sorry," I said. "Which article did you mean?"

"The one by the Monsignor about divorce."

"No, I missed that one."

"He felt it was a very serious step."

"I feel that way, too."

"Particularly for the children."

Enough about the damn children. I said, "Well, the grown-ups feel it too, of course."

"Oh, of course." She paused, thinking her goldfish thoughts, sipping away at her bourbon, looking as beautiful and as intelligent as a sunset. Gazing away across the room, she said, "Fred can't have children."

"Ah," I said.

"Not on a sergeant's salary."

"Oh," I said.

Another sigh, another sip. "It's difficult to bring a child into the world these days."

"Sometimes it's difficult not to."

Those eyes beamed at me again. "Beg pardon?"

"Nothing. I was just agreeing with you," I explained, and the sound of the telephone saved me.

It was Fred: "Listen, Carey, I'm terribly sorry, but I'm just not going to get there at all. Al Bray and I are up to our asses in this thing, it looks as though it might be the break we were looking for."

My back was to Patricia. I closed my eyes and said, "The anonymous letter?"

"It just might do it. Wish us luck."

"Oh, I do."

"The problem is, we aren't going to be able to get away, not for hours."

I looked at Patricia Staples, sitting on my couch. I would have to go on talking with her, and there would be no search parties to rescue me. "That's a shame," I said.

"Well anyway, Patricia's there, isn't she?"

"Right here," I said brightly.

"And the whole point was for her to see the picture. Would you mind? I mean, as long as she's there."

"You're sure you wouldn't like me to wait?"

"We'll be hours, Carey. Thanks for the thought, but you and Patricia go ahead, okay?"

"If you say so."

"Could I talk to her?"

"Of course."

I turned the phone over to Patricia, and noted that both glasses seemed to be empty. While husband and wife spoke together, I carried the glasses into the kitchen, built new drinks, and fretted over Edgarson's anonymous damn letter. Was he coming from beyond the grave—or the Valpack—to even the score? Had he revealed more than he'd realized in that first anonymous letter?

And yet, it seemed unlikely Fred Staples would have talked to me the way he had if the trail were leading in my direction. Or that he would cheerfully leave me alone with his wife.

Encouraged by those thoughts, I carried the drinks back to the living room to discover that Patricia was off the phone now and looking at my movie posters. She accepted the new drink with thanks, downed some of it, and said, "Well, I guess we're supposed to go ahead and see the movie."

"Right," I said, and while I got out the print and threaded

the first reel into the projector I said, "I want you to know I feel proud that Fred trusts me alone with you."

"Oh, it's me he trusts," she said carelessly. "He thinks if you made a pass at me I'd push you away."

Was there something ambivalent in that remark? I frowned at her, but her expression was as blank as ever. I went back to threading the film. (I would have had everything set up ahead of time, except for Edgarson dropping in.) With the film ready, I placed the projector, turned the sofa at right angles to the wall, and switched on my telephone machine so we wouldn't be disturbed. "There we are," I said. "All set. If you'll just sit where you were…"

She did. I switched off the lights and on the projector, waited to be sure the focus and frame were right, and then sat down next to her. *Gaslight* began.

The first time Ingrid Bergman became frightened, Patricia clutched my hand. She held it tight, while all the time gazing at the screen, and the second time Ingrid Bergman became frightened Patricia drew my hand into her lap and held it there with both of hers.

What a warm lap. The backs of my knuckles were being pressed downward into the cleft, and heat radiated up like rose petals from that crotch. On-screen, Joseph Cotten suspected something was wrong, but smooth Charles Boyer had command of the situation. And the third time Ingrid Bergman became frightened Patricia did some complex rubbing movement involving hands and body and knuckles, and at that point enough was enough. So I reached across with my free hand, and drew her face to mine, and drank deeply the nectar of her lips.

She did not struggle. Nor, on the other hand, did she particularly enter into the proceedings, though both her hands did continue to press my hand deeply into her lap. Generally I would say that she took this kiss the way she had taken the conversation that had preceded it; with mild polite interest.

All kisses must end, and at the finish of this one Patricia drew back her face just far enough so we could see one another's eyes in the flickering reflected light from the screen. Solemnly we looked at one another. Solemnly she said, "We shouldn't."

Okay, kid, I know all about that line. "Right," I said, and rolled her off onto the floor.

"I love your pubic hair," I said.

She gazed down at herself. "It is nice, isn't it? All furry and soft. But boy, in the summertime I just have to shave and shave and shave. Because of the bathing suits."

"You must look fantastic in a bikini."

She smiled at me. I was learning that she loved compliments above all other things. "You'll have to see me sometime."

"I intend to."

We were in the bedroom now. The first reel of *Gaslight* had been running itself out as we'd finished our first encounter, so I'd quickly shut down the projector and hustled this incredible woman in here onto the bed, where we could vary our approaches without danger of skinning our elbows or knees.

It was the first time I'd ever made love to a woman in a bedroom with a murder victim hanging in the closet, particularly a victim of my own, and I must say it made absolutely no difference at all. I was neither turned off nor were my responses heightened. Possibly I'm abnormal.

My reaction, however, was completely normal when Patricia got off the bed and crossed the room to open the closet door. "Ummm," I said. "Ummm, unnn, ungg."

"Do you have a robe? Oh, here it is. Terrycloth, I love terrycloth, it feels so nice against my skin."

Beyond her the pole sagged from the weight of the Valpack. She closed the door, slipped into my robe, gave me a smile and a bye-bye finger waggle, and went off to the bathroom.

Christ. Since the Valium supply was temporarily cut off, I padded barefoot out to the living room, switched on the smallest dimmest light, found my glass, and made myself a fresh bourbon on the rocks. When I carried it back to the bedroom Patricia was there, getting dressed. "It's terribly late," she told me.

"Don't worry about it. Want a drink?"

"No, I'd better go on home. Fred worries."

Fred was entitled, though I didn't say so. "Listen," I said. "You just saw *Gaslight*, remember?"

"Of course," she said, and gave me a surprisingly lewd smile.

"I mean you have to be able to talk about the movie," I pointed out, and while she dressed and did her face and fussed with her hair and generally cared for herself like a conscientious gardener I gave her the plot and principal incidents of *Gaslight*. By then she was ready to leave, so still naked I walked her to the door. "Now, remember," I said, helping her to bundle into her coats and hats and gloves and scarves, "Charles Boyer was doing it, and the jewels were the decoration in the dress."

She nodded. "The jewels were in the dress."

"See you soon," I said.

"Oh, yes," she said, sparkly-eyed, and kissed my nose, and left. I watched her down the first flight of stairs, then shut the door, turned, and stepped smack on a thumbtack.

"Ow!" I said, naturally, and hopped around on one foot till I got the thumbtack out. Then I limped around on one and a half feet, cursing, until it occurred to me to wonder where that damn thumbtack had come from. Surely not from my desk, way over at the other end of the room.

I turned on more lights, bewildered, and at first I found nothing at all. Then, also on the floor, I came across a smallish rubber band. Where had these things come from?

Edgarson. The chainlock.

Yes. When I closely studied the chainlock, there was a tiny puncture in the wood of the door just past the metal plate with the slot. Now I saw what Edgarson had done. He had looped the rubber band around the chain, then with the thumbtack had fastened both ends of the rubber band to the door. With the door open, the rubber band was stretched out across the metal plate with the slot in it. When Edgarson closed the door, the rubber band naturally contracted, pulling the chain with it, sliding the ball through the slot to the wide opening. When he thumped the door, the ball fell out.

Another illusion shattered.

SEVEN
The Riddle of the Other Woman

The phone had rung three times while Patricia was here, so I listened to my messages while going through the drawerful of Edgarson's possessions, the things formerly in his pockets.

Only two messages; one caller had hung up without saying anything. The first of the verbal callers was Jack Freelander, umming and stuttering his way through another request to pick my brains for his damn porno article that *Esquire* would never publish anyway, and the other was Kit: "Hi, baby. I'm feeling a lot better all at once. I was mean yesterday, wasn't I? Drove you out into the storm. Come on back, and I'll make it up to you."

Any other time, honey, but just at the moment I am (a) rather drained of my vital fluids, and (b) occupied with an unexpected guest who just keeps hanging around.

Edgarson's effects: One wallet, containing thirty-seven dollars, four credit cards, a Tobin–Global laminated ID card with his photograph on it, a New York driver's license, about twenty assorted business cards, a few crumpled old newspaper clippings that made no sense to me, and several pieces of paper scribbled over with notes to himself; phone numbers and the like. Three key rings, loaded with keys. A claim check for a parking garage over on First Avenue. A Boy Scout knife, with enough doohickeys and thingamabobs to dismantle a tank. A plastic pouch with a little pocket screwdriver set. A circuit tester. Various envelopes containing official-looking documents concerning bail-bond jumpers and repossessable automobiles. A small address book—I wasn't in it. A half-used checkbook, with all the stubs blank. A little metal box containing thumb-tacks, paper clips, rubber bands, washers and so on. A small roll of black electric tape. A tattered paperback copy of *One Of Our Agents Is Missing* by E. Howard Hunt. A dollar and thirty-seven cents in change.

I pocketed the wallet and claim check and change, stuffed the key rings and knife and screwdriver set and circuit tester and little metal box and roll of electric tape back into the drawer, and shredded the envelopes, checkbook and address book into the wastebasket, on top of the paperback. Then I bundled into my overcoat and left the apartment.

It was now shortly after eight in the evening, and the neighborhood was full of cars from Queens, which is the normal weekend cross we have to bear in this part of the city. The air was very cold, the sky was still leaden and low, and while the main avenues had been cleared of snow the side streets were still rather clogged.

I found the parking garage on First Avenue, and Edgarson's claim check got me the same dirty blue Plymouth Fury he'd been following me around in. I paid the tab out of Edgarson's wallet, tipped the boy an Edgarson quarter, and drove on back to my place, where I parked next to Staples' favorite fire hydrant.

Lugging that Valpack down the stairs was the hardest and least appetizing part of the whole job. Thump, thump, thump all the way down. I couldn't lift the thing, so I also had to drag it through the snow on the sidewalk and then heave and push and cram it up over the rear bumper and into the trunk. Finally it arranged itself in there, and I slammed the lid and drove out to Kennedy Airport, where a TWA skycap said, "You can't park here, sir."

"I just want to leave my luggage. It's too heavy for me to carry."

He gave me a superior smile, but when I opened the trunk and he tried to lift the Valpack by the handle his expression suggested he'd just found a hernia. "My my," he said. "That *is* heavy."

Should I do a joke about there being a body in it? No, I should not.

The skycap struggled the Valpack onto his cart and said, "Do you have your ticket, sir?"

"Not yet."

"And where will you be going?"

Feeling a cool climate was best under the circumstances, I said, "Seattle."

"Fine, sir. You'll find your bag at the ticket counter." I thanked him, gave him one of Edgarson's dollars, and he wheeled Edgarson away.

Driving out to the long-term parking lot, I considered leaving it at that, but time and confusion were my allies here, so I took the inter-airport bus back to TWA, and used one of Edgarson's credit cards to buy him a nonstop round-trip ticket to Seattle, first class. My Valpack was tagged, two clerks wrestled it onto the conveyor belt, and Edgarson rolled away on the start of his journey westward. My clerk compared the quickly scrawled signature I'd just perpetrated with Edgarson's quickly scrawled signature on the credit card, was satisfied, gave me the card and the ticket, and wished me a pleasant journey. "Thank you very much," I said. "I love Seattle this time of year."

For only fifteen more of Edgarson's dollars, a taxi took me to my general neighborhood in Manhattan. I had emptied his wallet en route, keeping the money and stuffing the cards and papers into my overcoat pockets, and in the course of a six-block stroll I distributed the wallet and its former contents into twenty-five or thirty trash receptacles. Then I returned home, to find that more people had been in conversation with my answering machine.

Two of them; the Staples family. Patricia's message was first, and was both brief and evocative. What an astonishing way for that woman to talk. When Fred's voice came on immediately after I felt a certain brief discomfort, which was not at all eased by what he had to say:

"More developments in the Laura Penney case, Carey. I think maybe you could be a big help after all. Call me at the office." And he gave his number.

I phoned Patricia first, and we said warm things back and forth, about how much we *had* enjoyed and how much we *would* enjoy and so on, and then she said she'd be in Manhattan tomorrow afternoon and would I be home between two and three? Oddly enough, I would.

Next, I said, "Sweetheart, I hate to mention this, but Fred does come here sometimes. I'd hate to have him accidentally recognize any voices on my answering machine, if you follow me."

"You mean you don't want me to tell you those things any more?"

"Don't talk to some cold machine," I explained. "Talk to my warm ear."

So she did, at some length and in some detail concerning the morrow, and when at last I managed to end the conversation I was feeling a bit humid. I went and washed my face in cold water before phoning her husband.

The guttural New York voice that answered told me Staples wasn't there, but when I identified myself he gave me a number where Fred could be reached. I jotted it down, hung up, and realized I had just written Kit's phone number.

Could that be right? Confused notions of swapping, keys-on-the-floor, *Fred And Patricia And Carey And Kit*, mingled in my mind with the more realistic thought that Staples was at work right now on Laura's murder, and this work of his had apparently brought him to an interview with *my* girl.

Which meant I had a choice. I could phone Staples to find out precisely what was going on, or I could use that ticket to Seattle. (Replacing it first, since the original was now in a dozen pieces in as many trash baskets.) So far, though, Seattle was still the alternate; I dialed Kit's number.

And Kit answered. She sounded, I thought, a little tense. I said, "It's me, honey. I got two messages to call."

"Oh, hello, Carey." Enunciated with clarity but no warmth; announcing me to Staples, of course.

Pretending I hadn't a care in the world, I said, "Feeling better, eh?"

"Yes. I guess it was one of those twenty-four hour bugs."

"When I get a twenty-four hour bug, it stays a week."

"Could I call you back, Carey? I'm a little tied up right now."

"With Fred Staples," I said. "That was my other message, he wants to talk to me."

"Oh? I didn't— Hold on."

I held on, and the next voice I heard belonged to Fred Staples. I listened hard for nuances in that voice, changes in his attitude toward me, but he was the same ebullient Fred as ever: "Hey, there, Carey, how you doing?"

"Just fine," I said.

"You never told me you had such a terrific girlfriend."

I answered in appropriate mode: "Keeping her for myself, Fred."

He chuckled, then said, "You going to be around the rest of the evening?"

"Sure." Some long-winded explanation of my absence from the apartment trembled on my lips, but I forced it down. The guilty man flees, as they say, where no man pursueth. Also, there's the fella that protests too much.

"I'd like to drop over," Staples was saying. "In half an hour or so, okay?"

"Coffee or bourbon?" (No drink with potential arrestee.)

"Mmmm…Better make it coffee "

Taking comfort from that hesitation, I said, "I'll have it waiting." But I missed the first time, when I tried to cradle the phone.

If you're going to commit a murder—and in the first place, I don't recommend it—one thing you should definitely *not* do afterward is have sex with the investigating officer's wife. It merely makes for a lot of extraneous complication.

In fact, generally speaking, it seems to me that *all* police officers' wives are better left alone. In the first place, their husbands walk around all the time with *guns*. And in the second place, there are so many other things a cop can do to you if he's annoyed; he carries as much power in his badge as in his pistol. So all in all I would suggest that policemen's wives, like nuns, should be left to Mexican bandits.

There's nothing like ignoring your own advice. But I hadn't after all intended all that with Patricia Staples; it had just, well, happened.

Whatever my intentions, though, well-armed police officer Fred Staples was about to walk into the scene of (a) Edgarson's launching, and (b) his own cuckolding. No matter how much Valium or how much bourbon I put away, I remained convinced that something, some small tiny forgotten thing, from at least one of those misadventures would attract Fred's bright eye. Though I ran the vacuum cleaner, though I made the bed, though I went over the apartment half a dozen times, I still didn't feel secure when the doorbell rang nearly an hour later. I wasn't ready, but I let him in.

Al Bray wasn't along, which I took as another hopeful sign. He came up the stairs, we smiled at one another, and said hello and shook one another's hands, and then he came on in without apparently noticing anything about anything. I poured coffee for both of us, he sat on the sofa where Patricia lately had lain, and I settled tensely into the director's chair.

"I called Patricia before I came over," he told me. "She said she had a terrific time."

"That's good," I said. "It was my pleasure."

"She asked me to tell you she really loved *Gaslight*."

In my own recent conversation with Patricia, the word 'gaslight' had become a kind of double entendre private joke. Was she deciding to play a dangerous game? Hoping she wasn't, I made some sort of conventional response and then said, "But you've got to tell me why you went to see Kit. I'm burning with curiosity."

He said, "Well, she did know Mrs. Penney, of course."

"Not all that well."

Was he being evasive? He said, "When a case doesn't break right away, you tend to reach out farther and farther, hoping to pick up one end of the string."

"Kit's only relationship with Laura was through me," I pointed out.

"That's right. And you're from Boston."

Good God; was he suspecting me? Carefully I said, "I don't think I follow."

"Here's the anonymous letter." He extended it toward me.

A sheet of ordinary white paper, with a typewritten message and no signature:

Laura Penney died in New York while her husband was in Chicago. He doesn't know anything about it. Look the other way. Think about the Boston connection. If A got too close to B, what would C do?

I cleared my throat. "That's the least intelligible letter I've ever seen in my life," I said, noticing that that bastard Edgarson had even managed to use my own first initial in the right place. "C," indeed.

Taking the letter back, putting it away inside his jacket, Staples said, "You and Kit Markowitz have been going together for five or six months, haven't you?"

"That's right."

"But you've been keeping it quiet, because you've got this divorce underway with your wife."

"Right again."

"That's why you'd go out with other women sometimes, Laura Penney and different other women."

"Sure." I shrugged, being casual if it killed me. "Kit knows all about that. The idea was, if I went out with a number of different women it would make less trouble in dealing with my ex-wife. But if I seemed to be heavily involved with just one girl, then Shirley might start to act like a woman scorned, if you know what I mean."

"Shirley. That's your wife."

"Right."

Nodding, thinking things over, Staples said, "The other day, you told me you missed Laura Penney more than you'd thought you would. She was closer to you than you realized."

"Yes?"

Staples leaned forward, his face much more serious than usual. "Women understand emotions a lot more quickly than men. I've noticed it time and again."

"You're probably right. But I don't know where you're heading."

"Kit Markowitz understood more than you did about your feelings for Laura Penney."

"She did?"

"What if," he said, and he was watching my face as though he expected to see words form on it, "what if Kit thought you were even closer with Laura Penney than you were?"

"I don't know. What if she did?"

But he had another hypothetical question to ask: "What if I told you she went through her date book for the last four months, and she'd seen you less than one-quarter of those days?"

"Well, we both work, we both have lives of our own."

"But she did that with the date book before I ever talked with her," Staples said. "She was thinking about it, you see what I mean?"

Which was an insight into Kit I could have lived without. I said, "Maybe she feels neglected."

"I think she does."

"She never let *me* know about it."

"Well, she's an independent woman, isn't she? She wouldn't, uh, what's that saying? Wear her heart on her sleeve."

"I suppose she wouldn't."

Back he went to his hypothetical questions: "But what if she looked around," he said, "to see what you were doing that three-quarters of the time you weren't with her? Wouldn't she see that you were spending a lot of time with Laura Penney?"

"Oh, not that much."

"As a matter of fact, yes. Al Bray went through Laura Penney's calendar again this afternoon, and she saw a *lot* of you, Carey. A *lot* of you. Over a four-month period, you had dates with Kit Markowitz forty-three times and with Laura Penney forty-five times. That's two *more*."

I coughed, and cleared my throat, and said, "What's all this building up to, Fred?"

He said, "Maybe we've been making a mistake all this time, Carey. We've been concentrating on men friends, but it doesn't have to be that way."

Now what in hell was he talking about? "I'm just not following you, Fred."

So he explained: "Laura Penney died when she hit her head

on the glass coffee table in her living room. It was the fall that killed her, and it didn't necessarily have to be a very strong punch that knocked her down. A little struggle, she loses her balance, it could happen just like that."

"Meaning what? Come on, Fred, for God's sake what are you driving at?"

"A woman could have done it," he said.

He suspected Kit! Kit!

I stared at him. Relief washed through me like sunrise, and I barely restrained myself from laughing in his face.

He said, "Think about it. Here's a woman thinks Laura Penney is taking *her* man away. She goes over to have it out. They argue, they fight, Laura falls and is killed. The other woman is frightened, she's going to run away, but then she looks around and finds male clothing in the bedroom. Either she thinks the clothing belongs to her boyfriend, or she decides to confuse the issue. In either case, she takes the clothing away with her. Or there's Al Bray's theory that she just leaves and *then* the boyfriend shows up, finds the body, and clears his stuff out himself. But in any case, the woman did the killing."

I said, "You mean Kit? Kit wouldn't kill anybody, that's just ridiculous."

"Not on purpose, maybe. But an accident, in the middle of a fight? She has a pretty good temper, doesn't she?"

"She isn't *violent*, for God's sake."

"Nevertheless," Staples insisted, "of all the Boston connections, that's the one that shows the most promise."

"But there isn't any Boston connection," I told him. "Kit's a New Yorker."

"The Boston connection is you." Pulling out the anonymous letter again, he said, "Listen to this, if we put your names in here instead of these letters, making Laura Penney 'A' and you 'B' and Kit Markowitz 'C.' Then it reads, 'If Laura Penney got too close to Carey Thorpe, what would Kit Markowitz do?' "

"Call me up and yell at me," I said. "That's what she'd do."

"Did she call you up and tell you about her date book?"

"No. So what?"

"So she's maybe a little more secretive than you think." Satisfied with himself, he leaned back on the sofa, putting the letter away again as he said, "Tomorrow we'll get hold of that private detective who was watching Mrs. Penney's building, and we'll run Kit Markowitz through a lineup and see if he recognizes her."

Oh, you will, eh? And good luck to you, too. Aloud I said, "I just don't believe any of it."

"We'll see." Staples nodded, and sipped at his coffee. "We were making too quick an assumption," he told me. "Assuming it had to be a man." He patted the pocket containing Edgarson's troublemaking letter. "This tip may have put us on the right track after all."

"Not if it makes you believe Kit Markowitz killed anybody," I said. "Is that really what you've been working on all day?"

"We started with half a dozen possibilities, but pretty soon they narrowed down to her. For one thing, she doesn't have an alibi."

"Why? Where does she say she was?"

"At home, alone. No witnesses."

"Didn't anybody call her? Didn't she talk to anybody on the phone?"

"She tried calling you, she says," Staples told me, "but she got your answering machine and she didn't leave any message."

"That's right," I said. "She told me that the next day. I was home, but I was screening a film."

Staples finished his coffee, then said, "I'll tell you something else, Carey. You're an absolutely brilliant natural detective, the most fantastic I've ever seen. You've got a real knack for it. But you can't get anywhere with this case, and do you know why?"

I did know, as a matter of fact, but it would be interesting to hear what he thought so I said, "No. Why?"

"You're too close to it. You're emotionally involved."

"You may be right," I said.

I phoned Kit and she said, "Is he gone?"

"Staples? Just left."

"I'll be right there," she said, and hung up, and arrived fifteen minutes later, looking angry and determined. Taking off her coat, she said, "He thinks I did it."

"Slow down," I advised her. "You want a drink?"

"I will not slow down." She hung up her coat and marched into the living room. "That damn fool thinks I killed Laura Penney. Over *you*!" And she turned to glare at me as though it were *my* fault. (Well, I suppose it was, at that.)

"Absurd on the face of it," I said.

"There's only one thing to do."

I didn't like her glower. "And what would that be?" I asked.

"We have to find the killer ourselves."

"*What?*"

"That idiot Staples is out there right now," she said, waving an arm at the window and the cold dark snowy world beyond it, which as it happened did not at this moment contain Staples, who had gone home for dinner with his Patricia, "and all he's trying to do is find evidence to convict *me*."

"Which he'll never find."

"Don't be so sure of that," she said. "I have no alibi."

"Millions could say the same."

"He could build up a case against me."

"Staples? I don't see how. You didn't do it, so where's his proof?"

"Circumstantial evidence," she said, in the manner in which people in Victorian novels used to say "madness in the family."

"*What* circumstantial evidence?"

"How do *I* know?" She was pacing around my room, waving her arms. "Remember *The Wrong Man*?"

"The Hitchcock film, with Henry Fonda?"

"*He* was convicted of murder, and he didn't do it."

"That was a mistaken identification."

"How about *Call Northside 777*? Jimmy Stewart as the reporter. And both of those movies were based on real-life cases."

"You need a drink," I decided, because I needed a drink, and headed for the kitchenette.

She followed me, still waving her arms. "And while he's spending all his time trying to railroad *me*, who's looking for the real killer? Nobody! And he'll get away."

Amen. I said, "Kit, you're making a mountain out of a molehill. This is just another one of Staples' brainstorms, he gets one a day, like rain in Mexico City. The other day he thought Laura was having an affair with her father, and the father killed her."

"Well, now he's *convinced* that I killed her. And it's up to us to prove him wrong."

I made the drinks while she raved on, and carried them back to the living room. Kit wasn't prepared to sit, but I was, and when she paused briefly to deal with her drink I said, "Life doesn't work like the movies, Kit. The innocent person getting off the hook by finding the real killer, that doesn't *happen*."

"Well, it's going to happen this time." She stood in front of me, straddle-legged with determination. "And you're going to help."

"How? There isn't even anything to do."

"Of course there is. For one thing, we'll go to the funeral."

"Funeral?"

"Laura's funeral, tomorrow morning at ten."

Laura's funeral. She'd been dead almost a week by now, and I'd taken it for granted she'd already been dispatched to her final resting place, but probably the coroner had delayed things. In any event, I certainly didn't want to go to the funeral. "What on earth do you want to go *there* for?"

"We'll see who shows up." She plopped down beside me on the sofa, eager and intent. "And you've been talking with Staples, you know what's been done in the investigation so far. Have they definitely eliminated anybody? I mean, besides you."

"Well, they were hot on the idea of the secret lover for a while," I said. "And they narrowed that down to five."

"Five? Terrific! Just a minute, let me get pen and paper." And up she jumped.

Gloomily I watched her cross the room to rummage through my desk. This was ridiculous, but what could I do about it?

Back she came, bristling with pen and paper. "I'll stay here tonight, all right?"

"Wonderful," I said, with less than my usual enthusiasm.

"Then we can go to the funeral together in the morning." She readied the pen. "Now, who are these five?"

EIGHT
The Secret of the Locked Room

Oddly enough, all five were at the funeral. And so were Kit and I, and so was Staples.

It was quite a large turnout, in fact, mostly with faces I was used to seeing at cocktail parties. Laura's father was in the front row with a heavy-faced black-haired gent I took to be the husband from Chicago. There appeared to be no other family members in attendance.

This funeral was taking place in some Croatian or Ukrainian chapel on East 9th Street. The style of the place was early *Frankenstein*, and so were the huddled old charladies intermixed with the mourners, mumbling to themselves like so many Madame Khrushchevs in a bad mood. These people had been ethnic since before the word was popular.

And Laura, it turned out, had been one of them. She had introduced her father to me once as "Frank Ward," but now I learned another seven or eight Eastern syllables had been lurking behind that Anglo brevity all the time. And what about that husband, the alleged Penney? Did those flat cheekbones look WASP? They did not.

Poor Laura. Born in upstate New York, she'd spent her life as a full-fledged American, only to depart as an immigrant. Remembering her bigotry—I don't think there were *any* groups she cared for—I knew this ceremony would only upset her. It was just as well she wasn't here to see it.

Kit kept whispering and murmuring to me throughout the service, but I paid little attention, since all she was doing was adding to the original list of five suspects. Taking a leaf from

Staples' book, she was casting a critical eye on the women in attendance and finding most of them suspicious. She'd bought a steno pad on the way down, and did a lot of cramped note-taking, as though she'd be writing up this affair for the old home town paper.

The box containing the remains was prominent in the center aisle, on a wheeled bier draped in purple and black. Gazing at it, I did regret my touch of bad temper.

After the ceremony, a dozen cars would follow the hearse out to the graveyard in Queens, but Kit's detective ardor, I'm happy to say, didn't extend that far. Nor did Staples'; seeing him move away from the line of mourners shuffling out to the cars, I went over to him and said, "Anything new?"

"Not with me. How about you?"

"Well, you got Kit mad."

He seemed amused. "I did?"

"She's decided to find the killer herself, and show you up."

"Fine. But if Edgarson says he saw her last Tuesday night, it'll be all over."

Edgarson? Was I supposed to know that name? Playing it safe, I repeated it with a question mark, and Staples explained he was the detective, etc. "Oh," I said. "Is that all set up?"

"Not yet. He's supposed to call me next time he checks in with his office."

Don't hold your breath. I said, "Let me know when you switch to a new theory, okay? Kit's about to drive me crazy."

Grinning, he said, "Why don't *you* come up with something? If you can't show that somebody else is guilty, at least prove to my satisfaction that your girl is innocent."

"I'll work on it," I promised.

"Come along with me," he suggested. "If we spend one con-centrated day on this case maybe we can crack it."

"Sorry. I've already promised Kit I'd play Mr. and Mrs. North."

I gestured to where she was standing in a corner of the chapel, arms folded as she glowered in our direction.

"Later on, then. Around two?"

At two, Patricia would be dropping by for more *Gaslight*. "I don't think so, Fred. I'll be with Kit most of the day."

"Well, I wish you luck."

"I believe I'm going to need it." I left Staples and rejoined Kit, who wanted to know everything that had been said. "Let's go back to the States first," I suggested, "and have a cup of coffee."

Which we did, in a Second Avenue health food restaurant full of heroin addicts. Kit went through her expanded list of suspects and I managed to contract it again slightly by removing three of the women who I knew happened to be a part of the alibis of various former male suspects. Another of the female suspects I eliminated by simply laughing the idea to scorn, but that still left two women and five men on the list. Six men, since she insisted on adding Jay English, the famous homosexual. Seven men; Jay's boyfriend Dave Poumon was swept ashore on the next tide.

"Nine suspects," I said. "What are you going to do with all those people?"

"Throw a party," she said. "We'll get them all drinking and relaxed, and ask some penetrating questions."

"God help us," I said. "And when will this overdone scene take place?"

"Today's Monday. Why not Friday? Everybody spends their weekends in town this time of year."

"Friday's a long way off," I pointed out. "I thought you were feeling a certain urgency about all this."

"Oh, we have lots to do before the party." She had this all thoroughly planned, I could see that much. "We'll want to know which penetrating questions to ask," she explained.

"Ah, of course."

She ruminated over her list. "I'll make some phone calls this afternoon. I can ask Betty about Claire." She made a note, then another, saying, "And Lucy Fishman used to go with Jack Henderson, so I'll find out about him from her." She frowned at her list, made another note, made a question mark, underlined something, and switched her frown to me. "You can start with Staples," she said.

"I can?"

"There was something about an anonymous letter. See if you can get a look at it."

"I'll try," I promised.

She tapped her list with the pencil point. "There's a possibility he already checked out Jay English and Dave. Could you find out?"

"Clever questioning might turn the trick," I said.

"Also Claire and Ellen. See if he has anything on them."

"Will do."

"Could you get to him this afternoon?"

An unexpected mobile of deceit suspended itself delicately in my brain. "I think maybe I could," I said.

"Then come down to my place for dinner and we'll compare notes."

"Lovely idea."

"Around seven?"

"Perfect," I said.

Between two and three, when Staples thought I was with Kit and Kit thought I was with Staples, I was with Patricia, enjoying *Gaslight*. At twenty past three, alone and refreshed and energetic from the shower, I popped a Valium and phoned Staples at his office, but he wasn't there. I left a message and worked on the Cassavetes article until four-thirty, when Staples called. "I thought you were with Miss Markowitz."

"We laid our plans," I said, "but then she went off to do some girl-talk type sleuthing of her own."

"Would you like to do some boy-type sleuthing? We've got another one."

"New York must be on the verge of depopulation."

"This one's imported. From Visaria."

"From what?"

"Visaria." He spelled it, which didn't help.

"Is that a country?"

"I don't know if they've got a country," he said, "but they've got a mission at the UN, and the head of it just got himself killed. You feel ready for a locked room mystery?"

Staples had sent a car for me again, which delivered me to a small remodeled brick town house on 46th Street between First and Second Avenues. This entire neighborhood was full of United Nations missions and foreign embassies, each nation putting on as much show as it could afford. At East Side prices, the smaller countries couldn't afford much, and this narrow four-story architectural nonentity was about par for a modest mission like that from Visaria.

If I'd hoped for some insight into the style and culture of Visaria from the interior of the mission I was doomed to disappointment. The building, probably in advanced disrepair when Visaria bought it, had apparently been purchased as a Handyman's Special and furnished out of Sears, Roebuck. The floors, which felt spongy and unreliable underfoot, had all been covered with cheap solid-color wall-to-wall carpeting. Dropped ceilings, those fiberboard rectangles in a white metal grid, screened off the no-doubt-hideous original ceilings with clean new hideousness, and the original walls were covered with paletone panelings in simulated wood grain. Light was provided by fluorescent panels in the dropped ceilings. It was like being in a real estate office in a shopping center, with furnishing to match; imitation-wood formica desks, imitation-leather vinyl sofas, and real metal square wastebaskets.

The building was narrow, and not very deep, so there was minimal floor-space. One entered from the street into a vestibule with a staircase leading up; the staircase too was covered with cheap carpeting. A sign hanging over the stairs was neatly hand-printed AUTHORIZED PERSONNEL ONLY. Another sign, waist-height, standing on its own chrome leg in front of the stairs, said INFORMATION, with an arrow pointing to the right.

An interior wall had apparently been removed here, so that the vestibule and the former living room had become one oddly shaped receptionist's office. It was appropriately furnished, including paintings that might have been views of the forests and lakes of Visaria but that looked to me like the forests and lakes of northern Michigan. A small rack of tourist literature near the entrance had an indefinably scraggy and hopeless air about it, as though even the Visarians could think of no sensible reason for anyone to visit their country.

Several people were now in this room. Two of them were Staples and Bray, several others appeared also to have some sort of official connection with today's event, and the last two were a weepy-eyed heavyset girl sitting at the receptionist's desk and a truculent-looking bruiser hulking on one of the vinyl sofas. He reminded me for some reason of this morning's funeral, probably because he seemed ethnic in much the same way. If Laura's husband had grown up big enough to play professional football he might have looked a lot like this fellow.

Staples, seeing me arrive, came over and said, quietly, "I won't introduce you. We'll just take a little walk through and I'll describe the situation."

"Right."

"You see the girl sitting at the desk?"

"The receptionist?"

"Right. She came back from lunch at one o'clock this afternoon. So did the guard."

"The blocking back on the sofa?"

"That's the one. Visaria has its own political problems, just like everybody else. His job is to sit out here and make sure there aren't any incidents."

"No wonder he doesn't look happy."

"The point is," Staples said, "both of those characters were in this room from one o'clock until after the body was found. Neither of them left for a second, not to go to the john, not for anything. They both swear to it."

"Could they be in cahoots with one another?"

"Look at them," Staples suggested.

I looked at them. Judging from appearances—generally a good way to judge, by the way—between them they might just be able to figure out how to open a box of corn flakes. "Okay," I said.

"Now let's go to the scene of the crime."

Staples led the way. We had to walk through the little cluster of people near the inner door, and it turned out that at least two of them were Visarian. Or anyway foreign, since they were speaking together in some language that seemed to consist principally of the letter "k," spoken with varying degrees of emphasis. One of these two intercepted Staples on his way by, saying, "You are making progress?"

"We are making progress," Staples told him. They smiled at one another, and Staples moved on, me following. I too smiled at the Visarian, and he smiled back.

Staples paused at the door. "As you see, it had to be broken in."

"Locked from the inside, eh?"

"Locked and bolted. The door fit snugly. There's no way to throw that bolt except from this side."

I studied the door, the wrenched wood, the hardware. I said, "And I assume the only fingerprints on the bolt belonged to the dead man."

"Of course."

"This is a pretty elaborate setup," I said. "What's it all about?"

"There'd been threats on this fellow's life," Staples said. "Some political thing at home. So he spent his working hours in this room with the door locked on the inside. If anyone wanted to see him, the receptionist would buzz, tell him who was waiting, and he'd come over and unlock the door."

"All right." I looked hesitantly into this inner room. "The body still here?"

"No, it was taken away. He'd been strangled with wire, sitting there at his desk."

My adam's apple gave a little twinge. "Charming," I said, and roved around the room a bit.

It was almost identical with the room outside; same ceiling, same paneled walls, same spongy carpeted floor. A little money had been spent on the desk, but the other furnishings were still bottom-of-the-line from some office furniture discount house. There was, however, a paper shredder in one corner, to show that this was a serious diplomatic operation.

A pair of tall windows at the back had a clear close view of a brick wall. Heavy iron bars masked both windows on the outside. I said, "I assume those bars have been checked."

"Just as solid as they look," Staples assured me.

A door behind the desk led to a small bathroom done in the same minimal style as everything else. This would be the corner of the house directly behind the staircase. The one window in the bathroom was also guarded by iron bars, and was in any event too small to crawl through. I noticed two dirt smudges on the vinyl tile floor, but nothing else in here of interest.

When I returned to the office, Bray had come in looking glum and harassed. "I hope you feel brilliant," he told me.

"Not yet," I admitted.

Staples said to Bray, "Give the man time."

"All he wants," Bray said. To me he said, "By the way, in that Templeton case, the woman that went off the terrace, it looks as though you and Fred were right."

"Oh, really?"

Bray shrugged. "We never came up with anything," he said. "I resisted the idea, but I guess it really was suicide after all."

So George had gotten away with it. Good for him. I said, "They can't all be murders, can they?"

"I suppose not," Bray said.

Staples said, "But this one definitely is. Let me tell you the situation, Carey. The chief of mission, Ivor Kaklov, lived here in the building, up on the top floor. The receptionist and the guard also live here. They spent an ordinary morning, Kaklov in this office and the other two outside, and at twelve Kaklov came out and they went upstairs for lunch."

I said, "Locking the office behind them?"

"No," Staples said. "It was only kept locked when Kaklov was in it."

"How about the front door?"

Bray said, "That was locked, but it doesn't matter. It's the kind you can open by slipping a credit card down between the door and the jamb."

I said, "So the killer came into the building while everybody was at lunch, and hid in here. In the bathroom, in fact."

Staples said, "Ah, good man. You saw those smudges on the bathroom floor."

"Of course," I said. "We have sloppy weather outside. Even if the killer took a cab he wouldn't get out right at this address, so he did some walking and he tracked dirty snow in with him. It melted while he waited for Kaklov to finish lunch."

Bray said, "That part we can work out for ourselves. We know how the killer got in, and what he did after he got here. The question is, how in hell did he get out again?"

I nodded. "That's the question, all right. I wonder what the answer is."

Nobody told me. So I turned away again, wandering around the room, looking at this and that. There was a certain atmosphere of disarrangement in the area of the desk, which was only to be expected, but otherwise the place retained its neat anonymity.

Well, not quite. The paper shredder was out about three feet from the wall, standing alone and awkward into the room like a volunteer robot. It didn't look as though it belonged there, so I went over to check, and from the indentations in the carpet I could see that the machine usually stood against the wall. It had been moved out here, by some person for some reason.

It was a heavy machine, about waist height, but it moved readily enough on its casters. There was nothing underneath it. There was no shredded paper in the white plastic bag in the bottom half. A dirt smudge on the beige metal top suggested nothing in particular. When I pushed the *On* button the machine gnashed its many teeth but nothing came out.

Staples and Bray had been watching me, and now Staples came over to say, "Something?"

"I'm not sure." I frowned at him, frowned at the room, at all its lumber yard banality.

"You're onto something." Staples was staring at me as though I were an egg and he'd just heard cracking sounds.

I said, "Kaklov and the receptionist and the guard all went upstairs at twelve. They all came down together at one?"

"Right."

"Kaklov came in here, and the other two stayed outside. That was at one o'clock. When was the body found?"

"Three-thirty. A phone call from outside came through for Kaklov, the receptionist buzzed, there wasn't any answer, she knocked on the door, she and the guard talked it over, and finally the guard broke the door in."

"Between one and three-thirty, did Kaklov have any visitors?"

"No."

"Any other phone calls?"

"No."

Bray had also come over, and now he said, "The preliminary medical report says he'd been dead at least a couple of hours when he was examined. Meaning probably before two."

I said, "Or as close to one o'clock as the assassin could make it."

"Looks that way."

I frowned at the room. The answer was in here somewhere. I felt I could almost reach out and touch it. I said, "The assassin came in during lunch and hid in the bathroom. Kaklov came in at one o'clock, locked the door, and the assassin killed him. The guard broke the door down at three-thirty, and Kaklov was in here alone." Looking back at Bray, I said, "What about *after* they found the body? Any time when there wasn't anyone around?"

But Bray shook his head. "There's a special police detachment a block from here," he said. "For the UN. There were officers on the scene within five minutes, and both the receptionist and the guard swear they stayed right in that office the whole time."

"I was afraid that was the answer." I leaned against the paneled wall, folding my arms and looking around this damn bland enigmatic room. I said, "I find myself thinking of the Sherlock Holmes dictum: 'When you have eliminated the impossible, whatever remains, however improbable, must be the truth.' So what are the impossibilities here?"

Bray said, "The whole thing is impossible. This isn't the kind of case I like."

"No, let's think about it." I looked over at the desk again, where the killing had taken place. "The assassin getting in was possible. The assassin committing the crime was possible."

"The assassin getting out again," Bray said. "*That's* impossible."

"So we eliminate that." Smiling as though I knew what I was doing, I said, "In approved Sherlock Holmes style, we eliminate the impossible. The assassin did get out. So where does that leave us?"

"Up a tree," suggested Staples.

"Up a—" Then it hit me. "Of course!"

They both stared at me. Half-whispering, Staples said, "You've got it?"

"Of course I've got it. If the assassin didn't get out of this room, Fred, then he's *still here*."

Bray said, "If you mean suicide, Kaklov did it himself, it won't work. A man can't strangle himself, not that way."

"No, there was a killer," I agreed. "But the point is, he's still in this room. That's what the dirt on the paper shredder is all about."

"Dirt on the paper shredder?" Staples went over to frown at it. "Yeah, you're right. So what?"

"Think, Fred. Think about the dirt on the bathroom floor."

"Smudged footprints." He transferred his bewildered frown from the paper shredder to me. "He stood on the paper shredder?"

"Certainly. Don't you know where he is?" I pointed up. "He's in the ceiling."

I was right, of course. Dropped ceilings are constructed of a metal gridwork hung by wires from the beams of the original ceiling. The two-foot by four-foot fiberboard rectangles simply lie in this grid, and can be pushed up and out of the way. A space of a foot or more is left below the old ceiling, to leave room for the fluorescent light fixtures and for the fiberboard pieces to be slipped up over the grid.

The gridwork isn't very strong, and wouldn't normally support the weight of a man, but this was a special case. First, the killer had brought in two six-foot lengths of thin lumber and placed them diagonally across the grid, spreading the weight. Second, the killer wasn't a man but a woman, a slender twentyish girl who couldn't have weighed over a hundred pounds.

A hundred very nasty pounds, I might say. When Fred Staples, following my suggestion, climbed up on the paper shredder, lifted the nearest section of fiberboard and stuck his head in between the ceilings to look, she kicked him in the face. He gave a yelp and came catapulting off the shredder and into my arms, the fiberboard rectangle bouncing and careening around us, while at the same time the girl came *through* another ceiling section and landed feet first on Al Bray's head.

Both cops were yelling, I was falling down from the weight of Fred Staples, and Al Bray was being beaten to the ground by the furious knees, heels, elbows, fists and forehead of the woman wrapped around his neck. She was dressed all in black—shoes, slacks, sweater—and she'd descended more like a demon than a human being.

"Stop her!" Bray yelled from the floor, and I wriggled out from under Staples just in time to snap my fingers around her near ankle as she scurried for the door.

I learned to regret that. She turned back the way a cat does when its hind leg is grabbed. The first thing she did was leave three long fingernail gashes on my right wrist, and the second thing she did was leave four long fingernail gashes on my left cheek. Then Bray arrived, and hit her very very hard with his fist on the side of her head, just above the ear. (He later explained that in all head-punching the target should be an area covered by hair, to minimize visible bruises later. Every trade has its expertise.)

The girl fell down when Bray hit her, and he immediately stepped on her long hair, so she couldn't get up again. When she snapped her head around to bite his ankle he rested his other foot on her throat and said, "Think it over."

She thought it over, glaring up at everybody, and while she was thinking Fred Staples put her wrists in handcuffs behind her back. They stood her up then, and frisked her in a thorough blunt irritable way that had nothing of sex in it at all.

Meantime, my wrist and face were both beginning to sting. I licked my wrist, but couldn't do much about my face. I also went to the nearest vinyl divan and sat down, feeling a bit shaky.

The girl had suddenly become very vocal. She shouted a lot of fierce things, undoubtedly of a political nature, burning with passion and historical ignorance, but since this Nathan Halizing was being done in that k-k-k language I took to be Visarian I remained ignorant of her specific quarrel with the late Mr. Kaklov. Al Bray rapped her with a knuckle in the hair a couple of times and she subsided, but continued muttering and glaring at everybody.

Bray and a uniformed cop then took the girl away, and Fred Staples came over to me with a handkerchief extended in his right hand. "What's that for?" I said. "I'm not crying."

"No, you're bleeding."

"I'm *what*?" Grabbing the handkerchief, I pressed it to the stinging side of my face, and it came away with diagonal red lines on it. "That's *my* blood!"

"Better come with me," he said.

NINE
The Death of the Party

After the hospital, where they gave me a shot and a scrub and some gauze bandage on my cheek, I went with Staples back to my apartment and we discussed the Laura Penney murder some more. He assured me they were investigating possibilities other than the guilt of Kit Markowitz, meaning they were still checking into the five original male suspects. I asked him the questions Kit had assigned me, and he said no, they hadn't established solid alibis for Jay English or Dave Poumon, mostly because the initial interview with that pair had seemed conclusive enough. As for Claire and Ellen, Kit's two alternate female suspects. Staples acknowledged they'd studied Claire a bit without establishing much of anything, but Ellen came as a surprise to him. He made himself a note, and I said, "Our investigations overlap."

"The more the merrier," he told me. "I really want to solve this Laura Penney murder, Carey."

"Good," I said.

Next I asked him about the anonymous letter, and he turned out to have a Xerox copy of it on his person. He let me make my own copy, in longhand, and then a phone call from his office summoned him away.

I hadn't wanted to check my messages while he was there, not being absolutely certain Patricia wouldn't be cute in spite of my warning, but it turned out to be just the usual dull band of voices, including Shirley, calling from Boston again about those damned papers she wanted signed: "I know you have them by now, and this time I'm serious. If I don't receive them by tomorrow, my Boston attorney is going to hire a New York attorney. At *your* expense."

Papers, papers. Yes, I remembered receiving them, but had I ever signed and returned them? With all this other stuff going on, I was pretty sure I hadn't, but when I went through the crap on my desk they weren't there.

Damn. Who needed this annoyance? I spent ten minutes searching the apartment, in every likely and unlikely corner, and finally had to give up and call Shirley, a thing I hate to do. One of the brats answered—until John's voice changes, which I presume it will some day, there's no way to tell them apart, even if I wanted to—but then Shirley came on the line and I said, "Look, I'm not trying to make trouble, but I lost those damn papers."

"You're such a bullshitter, Carey."

"Well, that's all right, you do what you want to do, only if you send me another set I'll sign them right away and send them straight back."

Some snarling followed, until it was agreed I'd be sent another set of papers, and then we both hung up and off I went for the Valium. That, plus the medication I'd been given at the hospital, plus the hectic life I'd been leading recently, combined to knock me out all of a sudden, and I staggered to the bed and slept until seven-thirty, when the phone woke me, being Kit, wondering where I was.

"Sorry," I said. "I'll be right there." And I was, extending the anonymous letter out in front of me as a peace offering.

"Wonderful!" she said, clutching at it. "How did you do it?"

"I have my methods, Watson."

So then dinner, which was already late, had to be delayed further while Kit immersed herself in the anonymous letter, reading aloud its cryptic algebra: "If A got too close to B, what would C do?" With paper and pencil, she proceeded to put columns of names under the letters A and C, reserving B for Laura. Gradually she demonstrated to her own satisfaction that everybody she knew could go in one column or the other, and that most names could go in both. "Oh, *really!*" she said, at last. "Being anonymous is one thing, but being a smartass is something else. Why didn't she *say* what she meant?"

"She?"

"This was obviously written by a woman."

"Ah."

"Look at this sentence about the husband. '*He* doesn't know anything about it.' That's a woman saying that. A man wouldn't even mention the husband at all."

"I see. Very clever."

Having announced this deduction, Kit went back to studying the columns of names again, and it began to look as though we'd never get to dinner, until I pointed out that Laura need not necessarily be character B, but could also be character C. Kit frowned at the sheets of paper in front of her and said, "How could that be?"

"Well, for instance, what if Laura had a secret yen for Jack Freelander, but—"

"That's ridiculous. Jack?"

"Wait a minute. What if she thought Claire Wallace was the competition? Then that sentence could read, 'If Claire Wallace got too close to Jack Freelander, what would Laura Penney do?' "

Kit mouthed the words, vertical frown lines in her forehead. "Meaning what?"

"Meaning Laura might have Claire over to her place to talk it out. There's an argument, Claire hits her, and that's it."

"Claire? Is that possible?"

"It could be a lot of people. Let's see." I ran a finger down column A. "Now, what if—?"

"Oh, I've had enough! Let's have dinner." Kit flung down her pencil, got up from her desk, and gave me a puzzled frown. "What happened to your face?"

"You noticed," I said, touching the bandage. "A girl fell out of a ceiling and scratched me."

"What?"

So at last I had her attention away from the anonymous letter, and over dinner I told her my latest exr ploit, and she was properly impressed. Of course, after dinner we had to play with the names and the columns again for another hour or so, but I didn't mind, now that I'd been fed. This detective business could be rather restful at times.

The whole week was very restful, in fact, much more so than the preceding seven days. By Tuesday afternoon Kit had finished inviting all her suspects to the Friday night party, and all had agreed to come. (No reason for the get-together was given, the guests being allowed to believe it was simply an ordinary Thank-God-It's-Friday & Isn't-Winter-Awful party.) After I'd delivered to Kit the copy of the anonymous letter, plus Staples' answers to her other questions, she had no further active role for me to play other than as the sounding board who listened every evening to that day's sleuthing and conclusions. At different times between Tuesday morning and Friday afternoon she conclusively demonstrated the guilt of four different people, and subsequently just as conclusively exonerated all four of them again. It was a pleasure to observe all of this deducing and detecting, particularly since I had already peeked at the last chapter.

When I wasn't being Dr. Watson with Kit, I was playing a very different kind of doctor with Patricia Staples. Fascinating woman! My initial impression could not have been more wrong. I had thought of her as the ultimate mousy housewife, totally absorbed in husband and casseroles, when in fact her absorption was totally with Patricia Staples. She was incredible to watch, a woman with no more concept of the world outside herself than a canary. She agreed with everything Fred said—and now with everything I said—not because she was lost in her man but because she was lost in herself. Fred admired her and kept her comfortable, so she responded by being agreeable. If he said a particular movie was wonderful or a particular politician was no good, why not agree with him? Neither the movie nor the politician mattered at all, even *existed* at all, insofar as she was concerned, so what difference did it make what anybody said about them?

This self-absorption might have been annoying if it had taken some other form—selfishness, for instance, or arrogance. As it was, her pleasure in her own existence kept her sunny in temperament, and left her with no great requirement for anything more. Should someone—Fred, me, whoever it might be—do something to make her happy (give her a compliment, say, or take her out to dinner, or screw her inventively), she accepted it as her due, and with gratitude returned the favor fourfold. Make *her* happy, she'll make *you* happy. *Gaslight*, it turned out, made us both very happy indeed, several times that week.

At the same time, the riskiness of our game—my game—kept me from ever fully concentrating on its rewards. *I am the quarry*, I kept reminding myself, *in a murder investigation which is still very much alive. It is insane for me to be cuckolding the primary investigating officer.* And yet I could never bring myself to kick Patricia Staples out of bed.

As for her husband and Bray, they came up with no more "interesting" homicides, though Staples did call from time to time with some piece of news about one or another of our recent cases. Jack St. Pierre, for instance, the fellow I'd pegged as the murderer of the copywriter, Bart Ailburg (misplaced island), had run away but had been found staying with a cousin

in San Diego, and when apprehended had immediately con-
fessed. As to the Visaria murder, the assassin had now been
identified as one Kora Haaket, and two of her co-conspirators
had been found lurking in a Volkswagen up the block from the
mission. Their guilt had been established by their Visarian
nationality, their history of anti-government politics, the presence in their Beetle of a woman's coat with Kora Haaket's name
sewn in it, and their mistake of not only carrying guns but actually shooting these guns at the police who approached their car
to question them. A double mistake, that; one of the guns, a
defective American product bought locally, had blown up in its
operator's hand. Both co-conspirators were now in the hospital
and doing well, though their future was in doubt. Since legally
the Visarian mission was considered Visarian territory rather
than American, the Visarians were asking for extradition of
Kora Haaket and the other two for trial in their native land.
Since trial in Visaria would inevitably lead to execution, and
since execution in Visaria was by flaying, the Legal Aid defense
attorney assigned to the trio was trying to obfuscate due pro-
cess in every way he could. It was likely the three Visarians
would remain in jail for the rest of their natural lives, awaiting a
final decision on the extradition order.

On the Laura Penney murder, Staples continued to have no
further news, except that he'd followed Kit's idea about Ellen
Richter, and had found her to have an unimpeachable alibi for
the time of the killing.

Oh, and the matter of Edgarson. He was found, in a TWA
storage room at the Seattle airport, sometime Wednesday night,
as Staples informed me over the phone on Thursday afternoon.
"His office isn't sure what he was going out to Seattle for," he
said, "but apparently one of his cases had got him involved with
some mob types. He bought the ticket himself, at the airport,
three hours before takeoff, but then apparently he got lured to

some quiet place and was murdered. Hit on the head. He had one of those big folding suitcase things, and they stuffed his body in it and checked it through to Seattle on Edgarson's own ticket."

"Mob types, you say?"

"It has all the earmarks. We're putting the question out to some of our informants now."

"This is bad news for Kit," I said. "I know for sure he would have exonerated her."

"Well, it keeps the situation pretty much the way it was," he said. "We'll keep working on it."

That day also I got the substitute set of papers from Shirley— I never had found the first set—and I immediately signed them and sent them back to Boston.

I also got some work done at last. The first several days after Laura's death I'd been so busy with these other things that almost none of my real work got done, but during the course of this week I finished the Cassavetes piece and made major headway in carving a rational interview out of the block of wood left me by Big John Brant.

Then came Friday, and Kit's party.

I don't much like parties. Too many people in too small a space, drinking too much and talking too loudly and usually creating at least one new set of permanent enemies. No matter how carefully the guest list is assembled, there's usually one social gaffe to start the ball rolling—or roiling—and the discontent breeds like maggots in a dead horse.

This time, the guest list had been compiled with no reference at all to the usual social niceties. Jack Meacher and Perry Stokes were both invited, for instance, even though Perry would naturally bring his wife Grace, who had run away briefly to East St. Louis with that same Jack Meacher three summers ago. But

Jack and Perry were among the male suspects, so here they were, willy-nilly, glowering at one another across Kit's living room while Grace sat unobtrusively near the bar, putting away the cheap Scotch with a funnel.

Jack Meacher provided an added fillip by showing up with Audrey Feebleman; the first hint to anybody that there was trouble between Audrey and her husband Mort. Irv and Karen Leonard, who had managed to keep their marriage green—if not to say gangrenous—for nine wonderful years by combining moral disapproval of others with very tight security on their own peccadilloes, spent most of the party standing in a corner together backbiting everyone else present, until Karen suddenly went off to dance the hustle with Mark Banbury, who had arrived with Honey Hamilton, an absolutely luscious blonde I had always coveted.

Let's see; and who else? Ellen Richter, who had been invited as a suspect but who had since been cleared by Staples, arrived with Jack Freelander, who was still a suspect and who was still determined to pick my brains for that asinine magazine piece of his. He hummed and stuttered at me all evening, like a defective hearing aid.

The other female suspect, Claire Wallace, a tall cool girl of the sort who models long skirts in the women's magazines, showed up with a lurking shifty-eyed fellow introduced as Lou, who had long graying hair and heavy bags under his eyes, who wore dungarees and a flannel shirt and a leather vest, and who looked generally like an unsuccessful train robber. And the representatives of the sexual Third World, Jay English and Dave Poumon, brought along some messy fag hag named Madge Stockton; one of those plump girls who wears forty shawls and combs her hair with barbed wire.

So there we were, seventeen oddly assorted people in one smallish living room, with February taking place outside. Kit had a stack of easy rock music on the turntable, to fill in the sound until conversation should commence, and I served as bartender for the first hour, until the guests were properly lubricated. The secret of a successful party, if there is any such thing, is to get *some* alcohol into each guest right away, but then slow the liquor and provide some food, to keep them from becoming dysfunctional. Also hide the chairs; if everybody sits down, the party dies. Also have the food and liquor tables as far from one another as possible; that way, the drinkers will cluster in one place, the eaters will cluster in another, and the well-rounded types will circulate. Keep them standing and walking and drinking and eating, and pretty soon they'll act as though they're at a party.

Which they did. The usual conversations took place, I traveled around trying unsuccessfully to avoid Jack Freelander, and Kit prowled among her suspects like a choirmaster through a chorus in which one voice is singing flat. Her method was fairly direct; she just kept talking with people about Laura Penney's murder, which was now an event ten days in the past, so it could be discussed as unsolved history, like the John F. Kennedy assassination. Fairly early on, I passed her in conversation with Jack Meacher and heard her say, "One of the people in this room is a murderer."

"Oh, I think it was a burglar did it," Jack said. "Do these little sandwiches come from Smiler's?"

I didn't listen to Kit's response, since Jack Freelander was gliding toward me again, but several times later that evening I heard her deliver the same old-movie line to several other guests, and the responses ranged from Karen Leonard's jaded, "Well, *I'm* never surprised by anything *anybody* does," to Jay English's avid, "Who?"

"One of them. One of the people in this room is a murderer."

Well, it was true, wasn't it? I danced with Honey Hamilton

while her date, Mark Banbury, was busy dancing with Karen Leonard, and Kit just kept hacking through the underbrush. And the party, despite its origins, became a party.

My flight from Jack Freelander made me unwary in other directions, and I abruptly found myself in conversation with Madge Stockton, the pudgy girl brought by Jay English and Dave Poumon. "I understand a friend of yours was murdered recently," she said.

"Most of us knew her," I admitted, nodding my head to include the other partygoers.

"It's so hard to keep track of an individual death, isn't it?" she said. "There are so many deaths, so many injustices, they all blend together."

"Well, that depends how closely they affect you."

She smiled; she had bad teeth. "That's right," she said. "It isn't morality at all, it's personal convenience, personal emotions. None of us really care how many strangers get killed."

Well, if you're going to a cocktail party you have to expect cocktail party conversation. I said, "Naturally, it affects you more if it happens to somebody you know." And even as I was saying it, I knew I was giving this girl an irresistible opportunity to quote John Donne.

Which she took. I received the tolling of the bell with my best glazed smile, and she said, "But the point really is morality, isn't it? People are liberal or conservative these days, they believe in women's rights or property rights or whatever, some of them are even still ethical, but nobody's actually moral any more. Nobody hates sin." Then she nodded, looking amused at herself, and said, "See? People smile if you even *use* the word sin."

Was I smiling? Yes, I was. Wiping it off, I tried another catchphrase: "The only sin is getting caught."

But I wasn't to get off so lightly. "Not even that," she said. "That was twenty years ago, when people were much more naive. Now we know what happens if you get caught. A lecture tour and a best-seller."

"And Laura Penney's killer?"

"He probably regrets it," she said. "Because of the inconvenience. But I don't suppose he's ashamed of himself, do you?"

"Ashamed?" What an odd word.

She gave me another flash of her bad teeth. "Nobody's ashamed of anything any more, are they?"

"Well, there's a lot in what you say," I said. "Woops, looks like I need a new drink. Excuse me." And I fled.

While I was making that new drink, which in fact I did need, Grace Stokes, extremely drunk, got into a sudden unintelligible loud argument with her husband Perry and then stormed out, thumping her right shoulder against the doorpost on the way by. Jack Meacher, the Don Juan of East St. Louis, kept his attentions firmly fixed on his current date, Audrey Feebleman, until Perry Stokes also left, following his wife's trail but not repeating the shoulder–doorpost thump.

Time passed. I made a date with Honey Hamilton for lunch and an afternoon screening next Tuesday. Jay English and Dave Poumon shook everybody's hand and left, taking their moral fruit fly with them. Lou, the apparent train robber, shot up in the john, an action of which we all disapproved; Claire Wallace apologized for him and took him away. Feeling mellow after my successful gambit with Honey Hamilton, I gave Jack Freelander fifteen minutes of my valuable time and the son of a bitch actually took *notes*. He and Ellen Richter left shortly afterward, and I heard Kit trying to talk about Laura's murder with Mark Banbury, whose reaction was to tell her how he was coming along with his analysis: "Doctor Glund says I'm very nearly ready to start dealing with my repressed hostilities."

Repressed hostilities; the world could use more of those.

✿

"We'll clean up in the morning," Kit said.

"Good," I said, and yawned. Mark Banbury and Honey Hamilton, the last of our guests, had just departed, and the old clock on the wall read two-fifteen.

"What we'll do now," she went on, "is put down on paper everything we got."

"Everything we got?" Then I remembered; we were investigating a murder. "Have mercy, Kit," I said. "We'll do that in the morning, too."

"No, we might forget things." She was already opening her secretary-desk, sitting down, gathering pencils and sheets of blank paper. "One thing I know for sure," she said. "It isn't Irv Leonard."

Intrigued despite myself, I drew up a chair and said, "Why not?"

"If the killer was a man," she explained, "then it follows that he was the secret lover, and Irv wasn't the secret lover."

"How can you be so sure? He and Karen both play around on the side, you know that as well as I do. They're the biggest marital hypocrites in New York."

"Yes," Kit agreed, "and each of them always knows *exactly* what the other one's doing. Neither of them ever admits it, but they always know who the other one is hanging around with. So I had a little chat with Karen, and I just kept mentioning names until she froze up, and she froze up when I mentioned Susan Rasmussen. Remember the New Year's party at Hal's place? Irv was hanging around with Susan then, so if he's still hanging around with her he definitely wasn't involved with Laura."

"Why not? Why couldn't he have two girls?"

"Not Irv Leonard," she said. "Some men might do that. You could do it, for instance. But not Irv Leonard."

I didn't much care for that crack. "If you say so, Sherlock."

"Oh, and it isn't Jack Meacher either." She made another note.

"How do you figure that?"

"I talked with Audrey," she told me. "Jack was with her that evening, but she hadn't split with Mort yet, so Jack lied to the police. But if the police ever come back and ask again, he'll tell the truth this time."

"Not Sherlock," I said. "I was wrong. You're Inspector Maigret."

"I knew I'd get somewhere, if I could only bring all the suspects together in one place."

"And now you've cut the list to six, out of an original nine. Fast work."

"Oh, we can cut more than that." She was scribbling furiously on her sheets of paper now. "Like, it isn't Jay English or Dave, so that's two more gone."

"And what made them go?"

"They got married last month," she said. "To each other, in San Francisco. Dave showed me their newspaper clipping. The only way either of them could have been a suspect was if Jay was trying to go straight by having an affair with Laura, and he obviously wasn't."

"Out of the closet and off the hook."

But Kit was in no mood for jokes. "That leaves four," she said. "No, three; it wasn't Claire Wallace."

"Not Maigret either," I said. "Maybe Miss Marple. Why isn't it Claire Wallace?"

"Because the only reason she would have had for fighting with Laura was over Jerry Fishback, assuming Jerry was the secret lover. But I found out tonight she broke up with Jerry just after New Year's, and started going with that whatever-his-name-was…"

"Lou. The shooting gallery king."

"Dreadful man."

"The last survivor of the sixties," I agreed.

"They've been going together for two weeks. So Claire didn't have any motive."

"I stand in awe of you," I said.

"So that leaves Jack Freelander and Mark Banbury and Perry Stokes." She gave me a quick look, saying, "You were talking with Jack Freelander. Did you get anything?"

I was in a quandary. I hadn't actually been engaged in sleuthing tonight, since I knew damn well there was nothing to sleuth about, but wouldn't it look strange if I had nothing at all to report? So I took the plunge and said, "Well, you can cross him off your list."

She pounced on that. "I can? How do you know for sure?"

How *did* I know for sure? "Well," I said, "you know he's doing that piece on pornographic movies for *Esquire*."

"I think everybody on earth knows that," she said, "except the people at *Esquire*."

"Well, um— He borrowed that Farber book from me, *Negative Space*. I hadn't thought of it before, but he borrowed it that afternoon and he called me that night to ask—"

"What night? You mean the night Laura was killed?"

"Right. He borrowed the book from me that afternoon, I gave it to him at the screening I took Laura to." Which was perfectly true. Everything I'd said so far was true, but the conversation I was about to report as having taken place the night of the killing had actually taken place two hours ago in this room. "So he called that same night," I said, "and he—"

"But you had your machine on. Remember? You were running a film."

Damn. Suddenly things were getting complicated, it was hard to remember the safe places to put my feet. "That would have been later," I said. "Around, uhh, eleven-thirty. Anyway, he called and he'd read most of the book by then, and he had a million questions to ask. You can imagine, reading the collected reviews of Manny Farber. But the thing is, he couldn't possibly have done that much reading in the Farber book and at the same time have gone off and gotten into a quarrel with a girl-friend and killed her and all the rest of it."

Kit continued to peer closely at me. She said, "What movie was that you were running?"

"Why? What difference does it make?"

"You told me what it was, and I'm trying to remember."

So was I. The titles of the twenty-four prints I own blurred together in my mind. "*Gaslight*," I guessed. "I think that was it."

"Ah," she said.

"Anyway," I pointed out, "that eliminates Jack Freelander. So all we have left is Mark Banbury and Perry Stokes."

"No, we don't," she said. With a strange little smile on her lips, she drew a big pencil X through the notes she'd just made.

I said, "What's that for?"

"It was *Top Hat*," she said.

I looked at her. I knew what she was talking about, but I couldn't bring myself to acknowledge it. I said, "What was *Top Hat*?"

She looked at me, studying me as though trying to guess my weight. "I knew you were the secret lover," she said. "I knew it all along. But I thought there had to be somebody else besides you."

"Kit," I said. "Hold on a minute. Are you accusing *me*?"

"You were seeing an awful lot of Laura Penney," Kit said. "And the only reason the police think *I'm* guilty is because even they know you're the likeliest one to have been the secret lover."

"But I've been exonerated, remember? I'm the one with the cast-iron alibi."

"Are you really? Let's look at that alibi again, why don't we?"

"Kit," I said, "this isn't doing either one of us any good. It's late, we're both tired, we've both been drinking, we're both likely to say foolish things."

"I want to talk about your alibi, Carey."

"Well, I don't." And then I was on my feet, irritated beyond endurance. "What the hell does Laura Penney's death mean to you anyway?" I remembered the fat girl and her talk of morality and sin, and I said, "You aren't involved in this out of any moral anguish or anything like that. The cops got down on *you*, that's all, that's the only reason you're even thinking about the subject or asking the question."

Kit, very quiet, was watching me pace back and forth. She said, "Meaning what?"

"Meaning you know you're innocent, and you know they can't prove you guilty, so leave it alone. Don't play detective, leave that to the pros."

"Meaning I might get hurt?"

"Meaning we're already into B-movie dialogue," I pointed out. "Don't complicate things, all right?"

"You killed her, Carey."

It was said, stated out loud, hanging there in the air between us. I closed my eyes, and when I opened them again she was watching me. I said, "The private detective saw me leave."

"You bribed him," she said. "And he's disappeared. But the police are looking for him, and when they find him maybe he'll tell a different story."

So she didn't yet know that Edgarson was dead. But when she found out—and the way she was poking around, she was bound to find out—she would not make Staples' mistake. She would draw the lines correctly, and they would lead straight to me.

"Oh, Kit," I said. "Why did you have to get into all this?" And I took a step toward her.

"I'll scream," she said.

"Only once," I told her.

What a mess. I hadn't wanted any of this, and one thing had led to the next, and now I had the death of Kit Markowitz to deal with. And she was the best girlfriend I ever had.

All the way uptown in the cab, dabbing at the new scratches on my face and wrists, I tried to figure out what to do, and by the time I got home I had a plan. It was desperate and dramatic, but under the circumstances I didn't see what else there was to do.

I left my overcoat on when I entered the apartment, went directly to the kitchen, blew out the two pilot lights on the top of the stove, and switched on all four burners. With gas hissing into the room, I went back to the living room, picked up my heaviest glass ashtray, and prepared to hit myself on the back of the head with it. Which turned out to be very difficult to do. In the first place, I had this automatic tendency to duck, combined with this other automatic tendency to pull my punches. Also, I didn't want to hit myself hard enough to knock myself out. All I wanted was a bump, a bruise, some indication that violence had taken place, and finally, after three painful glancing blows, I gave myself a good one that hurt like *fury*. "Ow ow ow ow ow," I said, dancing around the room, dropping the ashtray and clutching at my head, getting so angry from the pain that I actually went back and kicked the ashtray, and then I hurt at both ends.

Well, anyway, the job was done, and when I touched the sore spot on the back of my head a minute later my fingertips came away a little damp with blood. Fine. Now we give the seeping gas five minutes or so to make some headway in the apartment, and then we throw that rotten ashtray through a window and we stagger out into the hall yelling *help help help*, and the obvious conclusion is that the murderer of Laura Penney, believing that Kit and I were getting too close to him, had attempted to murder us both, succeeding with Kit and nearly succeeding with me.

If there had only been some point at which everything could have been reversed. Sitting in the black leather director's chair with my overcoat still on and my head still aching, I kept going over and over the events of the last ten days, trying to find something that could have been done differently, some decision that would have ended with Kit still alive now, and the more I thought about it the more inevitable it all became. From the moment I'd lost my temper and punched Laura and she'd slipped on that shiny floor, every step had followed with the regularity and inevitability of a heartbeat.

Funny smell the gas company adds to their product, so you'll know when it's in the air. I'll wait till it gets a bit stronger, then get up from here and find the ashtray...kicked it under the sofa...throw it out the window...run out to the hall...stagger out to the hall...sleepy...very heavy body in this chair...stagger out to hall soon...be able to relax after this...danger all gone... relax...relax...head doesn't hurt so much any more...

TEN
Memoirs of a Master Detective

"You were lucky," Staples said.

"I sure was."

I sure was. The explosion had saved my life. I'd gone to sleep in that damn chair, overcome by the gas, and if I hadn't forgotten about the pilot light in the oven Staples would have had two unsolved murders that night. As it was, the explosion knocked out windows and summoned help just as efficiently and much more dramatically than I could have done, and when I woke up I was in a private room in a city hospital with a policeman on the door, and I was swathed in enough bandages to make me qualify as snow sculpture.

The policeman at the door, seeing me awake, summoned a nurse and a doctor and Staples, in that order. The nurse refused to answer my questions; she was there only to take my temperature, pulse and half a dozen other things. The doctor joked away all my questions; he was there only to read the nurse's report. But Staples was perfectly willing to answer questions: "It's Saturday," he said. "Twenty minutes to three in the afternoon."

"But what happened?"

"Somebody tried to kill you," he said.

"Tried to *kill* me!"

"Tell me about last night."

So I told him about last night, the party, the assembled suspects, the post-mortem that Kit and I had done in which we'd eliminated three names from the list but had come to no other firm conclusions, then my departure, the cab ride home, "and then I don't know. I can't remember anything after I went into the apartment."

"You were hit on the head," Staples told me. "The killer set your oven to explode, hoping it would look like an accident. You're lucky to be alive."

"The oven?" Suddenly I realized what I'd done. Good God! "I might have been killed!"

Staples nodded soberly. "I think that was the general idea."

I wiggled my various parts under the covers, trying to figure out if they were all still there. "How bad— What hap— How *am* I?"

"Concussion. Some scratches and bruises, a few minor burns. Nothing serious. You were lucky."

"I sure was." Then I realized my distraction was keeping me from getting on with the original scenario. I could brood about exploding ovens later; for the moment, I had a role to play: "But why?" was my first prepared line. "Why would anybody do such a thing?"

Staples looked grim. "It seems," he said, "you and Miss Markowitz did better than you knew last night. You must have gotten close to the killer without realizing it."

"You mean, he thought we were onto him? And that's why he tried— Good God, *Kit!*" I struggled up off the pillow. "Call her, Fred, she's in danger!"

His grimness increased, as he rested a hand on my shoulder. "I already thought of that, Carey. I'm sorry, we were too late."

"Too late? What do you mean? You don't mean—"

He nodded. "I'm sorry. He must have gone down to her place as soon as he left your apartment last night."

"Kit," I said.

He patted my arm. "Don't worry, Carey. We'll get him."

"Kit," I said.

*

I spent nine days in the hospital, and all in all it was very pleasant. I had visitors as often as I wanted, I had as much rest as I wanted, and by the fourth day I had my typewriter and manuscripts and could even get some work done.

Staples visited at least twice a day, sometimes with Al Bray and sometimes alone. On his second visit I gave him Kit's conclusions about the innocence of Jay English and Dave Poumon, plus the unrevealed alibi of Jack Meacher, and we agreed it was ironic that Kit had proved her own innocence by becoming another victim. He kept assuring me he was making progress, and indicated he was leaning more now in the direction of Irv Leonard. (I hadn't mentioned Kit's conclusions in re Irv, feeling the list of suspects was shrinking rather alarmingly as it was.) Staples also had me go over and over and over the events of the party searching for that one small item that had scared the killer, but we never seemed to find it.

Patricia visited several times, with her husband's knowledge, and once we managed to perform an unnatural sex act together. Honey Hamilton also visited, twice, seeming very warm and sympathetic and eager to console me for my tragic loss. Other friends visited, some smuggling in bottles of bourbon, but most of the time I remembered to keep a long face.

There were only two bad moments. One was when Jack Freelander arrived with a rough draft of his porno article; trapped in bed, I had no choice but to read the damn thing and make comments. The other incident, more serious, was one of the times Staples brought my mail. He was stopping at my apartment every day to see how the reconstruction was coming along—they were putting in a new kitchen and fixing the walls— and was also picking up my mail. On Wednesday when he arrived, the bundle included a large white envelope with a familiar-looking blue logo on the return address. What was it?

Tobin–Global!

The detective agency, Edgarson's private detective agency!

(I had by now been living a Valium-free existence for nearly a week, and it was astonishing what a difference it made in moments of stress. What did Mankind *do* before these wonderful pills? Reality is drabber and slower and grayer without them, but the scary moments are suddenly faster and far more terrifying. My three murders had been serious, of course, but they had happened at a pace where I could retain control over myself and events. Now, with only the hospital's grudgingly dispensed pain killers inside me, a simple matter like this envelope nearly killed me with fright. Consequences seemed more real, dangers more possible. Valium had made it possible for me to walk my tightrope *as though there were a net.* Now, the chasm yawned plainly beneath me.)

Had Staples seen this return address? Had he made the connection? Should I explain it somehow, make up some story? Should I look in the envelope?

No. No to everything. In a panic situation, the best thing to do is nothing. If Staples had made the connection he'd mention it himself. (But officially I'd never met Edgarson! How could I explain this discrepancy?)

Closing my eyes to that drop, forcing myself to an appearance of calm without the assistance of pills, I casually put the mail on the bed, the Tobin–Global envelope face down, and Staples and I spent ten minutes discussing the latest developments in the case. Karen Leonard had an alibi for her husband for the night of the party, but Staples had taken a dislike to her—an easy thing to do—and therefore thought she might be lying. *I can't stand it*, I kept screaming inside my head, but I did stand it, and at last he left, and I clawed my way into that white envelope, and found—

What? Shirley's papers, the original set that I hadn't been

able to find. Utterly bewildered, I read the accompanying letter:

Dear Mr. Thorpe:

Having been unable to reach you by phone, I have decided to return these documents to you, though of course Tobin-Global stands prepared to assist you in your marital situation in any way we can. Unfortunately, we have no record of your ever having engaged our services.

These documents were found in the desk file of Mr. John Edgarson, a former employee no longer with the firm. If Mr. Edgarson was working for you privately, I must point out that by the terms of Mr. Edgarson's employment he was required to relay all potential client arrangements to Tobin-Global. The resources of a large organization like Tobin-Global are, of course, much more useful in delicate marital situations than the services, no matter how well-intentioned, of any one individual.

If you were under the impression that Mr. Edgarson was taking some action on your behalf, would you get in touch with me?

Sincerely,
Walter Carter, V.P.

I liked the straightforward way in which Walter Carter maligned the dead; apparently his opinion of Edgarson was just as high as mine. And I also appreciated his decision to send these papers back. What an unsuspected little time bomb Edgarson had left in his wake! Undoubtedly he'd stolen those papers during that period when he was occupying my apartment, and I couldn't begin to guess what smarmy use he'd intended to make of them.

Well. All's well that ends well. I took from under my mattress a bottle of smuggled bourbon and made do as best I could for the absence of Valium. Shirley's papers, covering letter and envelope and all, went out with that day's trash, and on the following Monday I left the hospital and went home.

The new stove and sink and refrigerator were in, but the wall between the kitchenette and the living room had so far been only partially sheetrocked, leaving some of the raw new studs exposed. The living room windows had been replaced. There'd been some damage in the living room, primarily breakage of small objects like lamps, with the principal casualty being my answering machine. The carpet had also suffered both fire and water damage, and would have to be replaced. But most of these things were insured, and in any event the apartment was certainly livable.

I felt rested and refreshed. In the hospital, I'd finished the Cassavetes piece and now I had "Big John Brant: The Acorn And The Oak" just about ready for its final draft. Patricia was coming over tomorrow afternoon to permit me to worship once more at her shrine, and I had a date with Honey Hamilton for Thursday night. Life, which had been full of turmoil for a while, was at last settling down again.

I also felt utterly safe. Staples had begun to look guilty in my presence the last few days, meaning the investigation was stymied once more; this time, I should think, permanently. He'd suggested as I was leaving the hospital that they keep me under police protection for a while, since the killer might have it in mind to try for me again, but I pointed out the needlessness of that: "Since he hasn't been arrested by now, he knows he must be safe from me, that I don't know or didn't notice whatever it was. It would be much more dangerous for him to try to kill me again than to leave things alone." Staples agreed at last, reluctantly, and so I was finally again a private citizen. There'd been many a twist and turn in the trail since I'd stupidly lost my temper with Laura Penney that night, but it was all over now. I was home and dry.

When the doorbell rang at two o'clock Friday afternoon I was on the phone with Honey, the two of us murmuring at one another the way people will on the day after their first night together. "It's the doorbell, sweetheart," I said. "I'll call you back later." We made kissing noises at one another, and I hung up.

And who was this at the door? Patricia? But she'd said she wouldn't be able to come around any more this week; not till next Tuesday at the earliest. But I could find out who my guest was before seeing her, or him; as a part of the general renewal and repair around this place, the intercom had been fixed, and it was now possible for me to lean close to the grid in the wall, push the button to the left, and say, "Who is it?"

"Fred Staples, Carey."

"Come on up."

I hadn't seen Staples all week. He'd been avoiding me, I'd assumed, because he had nothing new to report on the Laura Penney–Kit Markowitz murder case. Since I was reasonably sure he still had nothing to report on that case, maybe this meant he had another of his unusual homicides to show me. That would be nice; it had been quite a while since I'd had the chance to flex that muscle.

Nevertheless, the thought of facing Fred Staples still made me sufficiently nervous that I went to the bathroom and popped a Valium before opening my front door. He came thumping up the stairs in his hat and raincoat—an early March rain was drizzling outside—and he had Al Bray with him. "Welcome," I said. "Come on in. Coffee?"

"No, thanks, Carey." Staples seemed a little awkward with me, and Al Bray merely nodded his hello.

Was something wrong? They came in, I shut the door, and we all stood in the living room together. I said, "Something wrong, Fred?"

"We got a new development," he said.

I made myself look eager. "In the Laura Penney case?"

"Another anonymous letter," Staples told me. "Apparently from the same source."

"Anonymous letter?" But Edgarson was the source of that first letter, how could he have sent another one now? Post-marked Seattle? Or maybe he'd made some sort of arrangement that the letter should be sent automatically if he didn't stop it.

Staples had reached down inside his raincoat and his jacket and was now extending the letter toward me. "Same kind of paper, same kind of typing," he said.

God *damn* that Edgarson, would he never leave me alone? I took the letter and opened it and read,

> *He can blow himself up all he wants,*
> *but he should have thrown away the key*
> *to the basement door at Penney's.*

That wasn't Edgarson. I'd blown myself up long after Edgarson had been removed from the scene. And what was this non-sense about a key? Looking at Staples and Bray, seeing their serious faces, I said, "This thing accuses me of being the killer."

Nodding, Staples said, "It does read that way, Carey."

"But you *know* I'm not the killer. Never mind all this business about blowing myself up, you know I didn't kill Laura Penney."

Staples was doing all the talking, while Bray just watched, and now Staples said, "The basement door to that building is around on the side street. The detective wouldn't have been able to see it, so you could have gone in that way. And I must say, Carey, that if you *did* go in that way, it suggests premeditation."

I said, "But I don't have any such key. I never did have. Why would I have a key to the basement of some building I don't even live in?"

Staples smiled a little, as though pleased with me. "I'm glad to hear that, Carey," he said. "If you'd said you *did* have a key, I would have been a little troubled."

"Well, I don't."

Staples and Bray looked at one another, both still solemn-faced, and then Staples sighed and shrugged and looked at me again and said, "We've gotten to be pretty good friends, Carey. I hope this won't spoil that."

"No, of course not, why should it?" Handing the anonymous letter back to him, I said, "I guess that must be the same nut that left the message on my answering machine that time. Probably the other anonymous letter was about me, too."

"Probably was," Staples agreed. And that should have been the end of it, except that he stood there holding the anonymous letter in one hand, rapping the folded edge of it against his other thumbnail and frowning as though unhappy about something.

I said, "Is there more?"

"I'm afraid there is, Carey. You know we're pretty much at a dead end in this case, so we have to follow any lead we get. I'm sorry."

"Well, sure. I understand that."

Into his jacket he went again, and came out with a folded document that looked vaguely like a lease. "So we went to court," he said, "and got a search warrant. I'm sorry, Carey, but we have to look for that key."

I was surprised, and more than a little annoyed. "For God's sake, Fred, I told you I never had such a key."

"We're going to have to search the premises. I'm sorry," he

added, saying that for the fourth or fifth time. He kept being sorry, but on the other hand he was obviously determined to search the apartment.

Patricia. Had she left any little something-or-other that her husband shouldn't see? No, I didn't think so, but what a hell of a complication *that* would make.

Al Bray now finally spoke. "Do you have a key ring, Carey?"

"Yes, of course." I took it from my pocket and handed it to him. From his own trouser pocket he took an ordinary Yale-type brass key, and compared it with all of mine.

What if one matched? But it couldn't, I didn't *have* any goddam basement key. This whole thing was absurd.

Nevertheless, I felt a surprising rush of relief when at last he shook his head, handed me back my keys, and said, "Not there."

"Of course not," I said.

"We'll want to search now, Carey," Staples said.

"Go right ahead. Do you want me to help?"

Staples grinned, but not with much humor. "I don't think so," he said.

Al Bray said to me, "Why not just sit down on the sofa there? We won't take very long."

So that's what I did. I sat on the sofa, and Al Bray went into the bedroom to conduct the search there while Fred Staples searched in the living room, and I tried to figure out just what the hell was going on around here.

In the first place, who had sent that anonymous letter, and why? And what was all this about a key? What was happening? For the first time, I didn't feel in control of the situation, and that was frightening.

I understand the police slang word for a search is "toss," though Staples and Bray hadn't used that word with me. In any event, they tossed my place for about five minutes before Staples looked up from my bottom desk drawer to call, "Hey, Al? I think I got it."

I stared at him across the room, and as Bray came hurrying out of the bedroom I got to my feet. But Staples pointed a severe finger at me, saying, "You wait there for just a minute, Carey."

So I waited. Whatever key Staples had just found in my desk drawer was matched against the key from Bray's pocket, and I could see by the looks they gave one another that it was a match. I said, "Fred, what have you got there? Let me see it, will you?"

So they brought it over to me, and both of their faces were much harder now. Al Bray had the two keys in the palm of one hand, and he held it out so I could see them.

Two keys. Both Yale-type, both brass. The hills and valleys looked identical. The only difference was that one of them— the one Staples had just found—was shiny and new.

I said, "I never saw that key before in my life." And even as I was saying it, I could hear what a weak cliché line it was. How many movies had contained that line, and how many times had it been believed?

Also my next remark: "Somebody planted it there!"

"I'm sorry, Carey," Staples said. But this time he didn't sound sorry at all.

I said, "Wait a minute. Look at it, it's brand new."

Bray said, "Only used once, maybe."

"But it's not *mine*!"

Bray put the two keys away in his pocket. Staples said, "Better get your coat on, Carey."

In the car, heading downtown through the pelting rain, I figured it out. Al Bray drove, up front with the police radio intermittently squawking, and Staples rode in back with me. I spent the first dozen blocks trying to get my bearings, trying to understand what had happened and why—had *Edgarson* planted that key there?—and then I turned my head and saw Staples' stony profile, saw him looking straight ahead with no expression at all on his face, and all at once I got it.

"Oh, damn it to hell," I said. I didn't speak loudly enough for Bray to hear, not over the radio and the windshield wipers and the rain, but Staples heard me all right. A muscle moved in his jaw.

I said, "You were afraid the killer might try for me again anyway, regardless of what I'd said. So you were keeping an eye on me, without letting me know. Being a pal."

Staples neither moved nor spoke. The hard gray glass of the window beyond him streamed with rainwater.

I could see it, I could see exactly how it had happened. Tuesday afternoon he'd been watching, and Patricia had come into my building, and two hours later Patricia had come out again, and when he'd questioned her casually that evening she'd undoubtedly said she'd been home all day.

In fact… In fact, now that I thought about it, there was that annoying phone call about ten minutes after Patricia'd arrived. Without my answering machine, we'd had to put up with the ringing until the caller had quit. Eighteen rings, I remember counting them.

Staples in a phone booth, counting the eighteen rings.

But what a hell of a revenge. All right, all right, he used to carry on so much about how perfect Patricia was, what a perfect couple they were, so this thing had to leave him with a certain amount of egg on his face, but wasn't he overreacting just a little? I mean, he was framing me for *murder*.

He was *framing* me. For *murder*.

He had written that anonymous letter himself. He had carried that incriminating key into my apartment in his own pocket.

All right. What man does, man can undo. I had to persuade him, that's all, I had to convince him that he didn't want to do this thing. And I only had a few minutes, because once we got downtown and the official business started, there wouldn't be any way for him to change his mind.

But how? What should I say to him? Tell him that Patricia loves him, that we'd had one brief crazy mistake and—?

No. That expressionless rockbound face told me one thing for sure; I should not mention Patricia's name. Somehow I had to get him to stop doing this thing without ever saying out loud his reason for doing it.

What, then? Friendship? No; it wasn't long enough or deep enough. Danger to himself? There wasn't any, to begin with, and in any event I was sure he didn't care.

Professionalism. Pride of accomplishment, that was my only chance. Leaning closer to him, speaking softly enough so Bray wouldn't be able to hear, I said, "You don't want to do this, Fred. If you do this, the real killer will get away."

Nothing. No response.

"You don't want that to happen, Fred. Think of poor Laura Penney, think of Kit. If you do this, their deaths will go unpunished."

Nothing.

"Fred," I said, becoming more desperate, "don't you *care* who killed Laura and Kit? Don't you *care*?"

He looked at me, at last. He studied me for five seconds with his very cold eyes, and then he said, "No." And faced front.

I couldn't believe it. "But that's your job," I said. "That's your vocation. Doesn't it matter to you?"

Apparently he was finished expressing himself. He sat silent, facing front.

I kept trying for another twenty blocks, talking at him every time the radio blare cut Al Bray out of earshot, appealing to Staples' moral sense, his ethics, his pride in a job well done, and I might as well have been talking to an Easter Island statue. The only time he spoke or moved or did anything at all was when I skirted the subject of Patricia, just hinting slightly at the reason for all this, and when I did that he said, while still facing front, "Better be careful. You could get yourself shot trying to escape."

He meant it, too.

After that I subsided, casting about in my mind for some other way off this hook, and gradually I became very annoyed. I had done everything right, everything. I had committed three murders and covered myself brilliantly and gotten away with all three of them clean, and now this overly possessive husband, this damned jealous—

Framed for a murder I committed! It isn't fair, it just isn't fair.

"Well, I'll tell you one thing," I said at last, driven by exasperation. "The wrong one of us is a detective, that's for sure. The only way you can make an arrest is to frame somebody. Who's going to solve your crimes for you after I'm gone?"

He didn't respond to that either, so I gave him some more: "You can't do anything right, do you know that? No wonder—" But, no; I did not want to be shot trying to escape. So I started again: "You couldn't even get George Templeton."

He frowned at that, and turned finally to give me a puzzled look. "Templeton?"

"The fellow whose wife went off the terrace in the snow."

"I remember him. What about him?"

"I only took your side because I thought you were my friend," I told him. "But Al Bray was right, Templeton killed his wife."

Staples squinted, apparently trying to read on my face whether I was lying or not. "You're just saying that," he decided. "Because you're sore."

"Am I? I'll tell you the two things that prove it. The frost-bitten plants in the window, and the fact that the only disturbances in the snow on the terrace were the footprints."

"Explain," he said.

"Templeton hit her and she died," I explained. "Hours before he threw her out. He kept the terrace doors open and the body nearby to delay rigor mortis, so she'd look as though she died later than she did. He put on her shoes and walked out to the end of the terrace, being very careful not to touch anything, and then walked backwards off the terrace in the same footprints. And then put the shoes back on the body."

"That's just a theory," Staples said. "There isn't any proof."

"Not now, not any more. The only way you'll get Templeton is to frame him. But that morning there was proof, only you were too dumb to see it."

He was stung, but controlling himself. "What proof?"

"Drunk *or* sober," I told him, "there was no way for Mrs. Templeton to leave that terrace without disturbing the snow on top of the railing. And it was untouched."

"Well, I'll be damned," he said.

"She never went off that terrace," I told him. "Templeton carried her downstairs and threw her out the living room window."

"You're right." He shook his head and looked at me in obvious admiration, and actually *smiled* at me. "I'm going to miss you, Carey," he said.

Which was when it finally became real for me. The chill air of prison touched the nape of my neck, and I crouched more miserably inside my coat. Staples meant what he said; he *would* miss me. He liked me, he was pleased to think of himself as my friend, despite everything. But he would also frame me for Laura Penney's murder, frame me solid and convincing, and nothing on earth would stop him.

I couldn't talk any more. I turned away, staring out the side window at the rain, looking at my future. How different it would be from my past. All my cleverness, buried inside a stone.

Staples was still marveling over my final deduction. "You really are something, Carey," he told the back of my head. "In a lot of ways I don't care for you very much, but you sure are one hell of a detective."

ORDO

ONE

My name is Ordo Tupikos, and I was born in North Flat, Wyoming on November 9th, 1936. My father was part Greek and part Swede and part American Indian, while my mother was half Irish and half Italian. Both had been born in this country, so I am one hundred percent American.

My father, whose first name was Samos, joined the United States Navy on February 17th, 1942, and he was drowned in the Coral Sea on May 15th, 1943. At that time we were living in West Bowl, Oklahoma, my mother and my two sisters and my brother and I, and on October 12th of that year my mother married a man named Eustace St. Claude, who claimed to be half Spanish and half French but who later turned out to be half Negro and half Mexican and passing for white. After the divorce, my mother moved the family to San Itari, California. She never remarried, but she did maintain a long-term relationship with an air conditioner repairman named Smith, whose background I don't know.

On July 12th, 1955, I followed my father's footsteps by joining the United States Navy. I was married for the first time in San Diego, California on March 11th, 1958, when I was twenty-one, to a girl named Estelle Anlic, whose background was German and Welsh and Polish. She put on the wedding license that she was nineteen, having told me the same, but when her mother found us in September of the same year it turned out she was only sixteen. Her mother arranged the annulment, and it looked as though I might be in some trouble, but the Navy transferred me to a ship and that was the end of that.

By the time I left the Navy, on June 17, 1959, my mother and my half brother, Jacques St. Claude, had moved from California to Deep Mine, Pennsylvania, following the air conditioner repairman named Smith, who had moved back east at his father's death in order to take over the family hardware store. Neither Smith nor Jacques was happy to have me around, and I'd by then lost touch with my two sisters and my brother, so in September of that year I moved to Old Coral, Florida, where I worked as a carpenter (non-union) and where, on January 7th, 1960, I married my second wife, Sally Fowler, who was older than me and employed as a waitress in a diner on the highway toward Fort Lauderdale.

Sally, however, was not happy tied to one man, and so we were divorced on April 12th, 1960, just three months after the marriage. I did some drinking and trouble-making around that time, and lost my job, and a Night Court judge suggested I might be better off if I rejoined the Navy, which I did on November 4th, 1960, five days before my twenty-fourth birthday.

From then on, my life settled down. I became a career man in the Navy, got into no more marriages, and except for my annual Christmas letter from my mother in Pennsylvania I had no more dealings with the past. Until October 7th, 1974, when an event occurred that knocked me right over.

I was assigned at that time to a Naval Repair Station near New London, Connecticut, and my rank was Seaman First Class. It was good weather for October in that latitude, sunny, clean air, not very cold, and some of us took our afternoon break out on the main dock. Norm and Stan and Pat and I were sitting in one group, on some stacks of two by fours, Norm and Stan talking football and Pat reading one of his magazines and me looking out over Long Island Sound. Then Pat looked up from his magazine and said, "Hey, Orry."

I turned my head and looked at him. My eyes were half-blinded from looking at the sun reflected off the water. I said, "What?"

"You never said you were married to Dawn Devayne."

Dawn Devayne was a movie star. I'd seen a couple of her movies, and once or twice I saw her talking on television. I said, "Sure."

He gave me a dirty grin and said, "You shouldn't of let that go, boy."

With Pat, you play along with the joke and then go do something else, because otherwise he won't give you any peace. So I grinned back at him and said, "I guess I shouldn't," and then I turned to look some more at the water.

But this time he didn't quit. Instead, he raised his voice and he said, "Goddamit, Orry, it's right here in this goddam magazine."

I faced him again. I said, "Come on, Pat."

By now, Norm and Stan were listening too, and Norm said, "What's in the magazine, Pat?"

Pat said, "That Orry was married to Dawn Devayne." Norm and Stan both grinned, and Stan said, "Oh, *that*."

"Goddamit!" Pat jumped to his feet and stormed over and shoved the magazine in Stan's face. "You look at that!" he shouted. "You just look at that!"

I saw Stan look, and start to frown, and I couldn't figure out what was going on. Had they set this up ahead of time? But not Stan; Norm sometimes went along with Pat's gags, but Stan always brushed them away like mosquitoes. And now Stan frowned at the magazine, and he said, "Son of a bitch."

"Now, look," I said, "a joke's a joke."

But nobody was acting like it was a joke. Norm was looking over Stan's shoulder, and he too was frowning. And Stan, shaking his head, looked at me and said, "Why try to hide it, for Christ's sake? Brother, if *I'd* been married to Dawn Devayne, I'd tell the world about it."

"But I wasn't," I said. "I swear to God, I never was."

Norm said, "How many guys you know named Ordo Tupikos?"

"It's a mistake," I said. "It's got to be a mistake."

Norm seemed to be reading aloud from the magazine. He said, "Married in San Diego, California, in 1958, to a sailor named Ordo Tu—"

"Wait a minute," I said. "I was married then to, uh, Estelle—"

"Anlic," Pat said, and nodded his head at me. "Estelle Anlic, right?"

I stared at him. I said, "How'd you know that name?"

"Because that's Dawn Devayne, dummy! That's her real name!" Pat grabbed the magazine out of Norm's hands and rushed over to jab it at me. "Is that you, or isn't it?"

There was a small black-and-white photo on the page, surrounded by printing. I hadn't seen that picture in years.

It was Estelle and me, on our wedding day, a picture taken outside City Hall by a street photographer. There I was in my whites—you don't wear winter blues in San Diego—and there was Estelle. She was wearing her big shapeless black sweater and that tight tight gray skirt down to below her knees that I liked in those days. We were both squinting in the sunlight, and Estelle's short dark hair was in little curls all around her head.

"That's not Dawn Devayne," I said. "Dawn Devayne has blonde hair."

Pat said something scornful about people dyeing their hair, but I didn't listen. I'd seen the words under the picture and I was reading them. They said: "Dawn and her first husband, Navy man Ordo Tupikos. Mama had the marriage annulled six months later."

Norm and Stan had both come over with Pat, and now Stan looked at me and said, "You didn't even know it."

"I never saw her again." I made a kind of movement with the

magazine, and I said, "When her mother took her away. The Navy put me on a ship, I never saw her after that."

Norm said, "Well, I'll be a son of a bitch."

Pat laughed, slapping himself on the hip. He said: "You're married to a movie star!"

I got to my feet and went between them and walked away along the dock toward the repair sheds. The guys shouted after me, wanting to know where I was going, and Pat yelled, "That's my magazine!"

"I'll bring it back," I said. "I want to borrow it." I don't know if they heard.

I went to the Admin Building and into the head and closed myself in a stall and sat on the toilet and started in to read about Dawn Devayne.

The magazine was called *True Man*, and the picture on the cover was a foreign sports car with a girl lying on the hood. Down the left side of the cover was lettering that read:

> WILL THE
> ENERGY CRISIS
> KILL LE MANS?
> * * * * * * * * *
>
> DAWN DEVAYNE:
> THE WORLD'S NEXT
> SEX GODDESS
> * * * * * * * * *
>
> *WHAT* SLOPE?
> CONFESSIONS OF A
> GIRL SKI BUM

Inside the magazine, the article was titled, *Is Dawn Devayne The World's New Sex Queen?* by Abbie Lancaster. And under the title in smaller letters was another question, with an answer:

"Where did all the bombshells go? Dawn Devayne is ready to burst on the scene."

Then the article didn't start out to be about Dawn Devayne at all, but about all the movie stars that had ever been considered big sex symbols, like Jean Harlow and Marilyn Monroe and Rita Hayworth and Jayne Mansfield. Then it said there hadn't been any major sex star for a long time, which was probably because of Women's Lib and television and X-rated movies and looser sexual codes. "You don't need a fantasy bedwarmer," the article said, "if you've got a real-life bedwarmer of your own." Then the article said there were a bunch of movie stars who were all set to take the crown as the next sex queen if the job ever opened up again. It mentioned Raquel Welch and Ann-Margret and Goldie Hawn and Julie Christie. But then it said Dawn Devayne was the likeliest of them all to make it, because she had that wonderful indescribable quality of being all things to all men.

Then there was a biography. It said Dawn Devayne was born Estelle Anlic in Big Meadow, Nebraska on May 19th, 1942, and her father died in the Korean conflict in 1955, and she and her mother moved to Los Angeles in 1956 because her mother had joined a religious cult that was based in Los Angeles. It said her mother was a bus driver in that period, and Dawn Devayne grew up without supervision and hung around with boys a lot. It didn't exactly say she was the neighborhood lay, but it almost said it.

Then it came to me. It said Dawn Devayne ran away from home a lot of times in her teens, and one time when she was sixteen she ran away to San Diego and married me until her mother took her home again and turned her over to the juvenile authorities, who put her in a kind of reformatory for wayward girls. It called me a "stock figure." What it said was:

"…a sailor named Ordo Tupikos, a stock figure, the San Diego sailor in every sex star's childhood."

I didn't much care for that, but what I was mostly interested in was where Estelle Anlic became Dawn Devayne, so I kept reading. The article said that after the reformatory Estelle got a job as a carhop in a drive-in restaurant in Los Angeles, and it was there she got her first crack at movie stardom, when an associate producer with Farber International Pictures met her and got her a small role in a B-movie called *Tramp Killer*. She played a prostitute who was murdered. That was in 1960, when she was eighteen. There was a black-and-white still photo from that movie, showing her cowering back from a man with a meat cleaver, and she still looked like Estelle Anlic then, except her hair was dyed platinum blonde. Her stage name for that movie was Honey White.

Then nothing more happened in the movies for a while, and Estelle went to San Francisco and was a cashier in a movie theater. The article quoted her as saying, "When 'Tramp Killer' came through, I sold tickets to myself." She had other jobs too for the next three years, and then when she was twenty-one, in 1963, a man named Les Moore, who was the director of *Tramp Killer*, met her at a party in San Francisco and remembered her and told her to come back to Los Angeles and he would give her a big part in the movie he was just starting to work on.

(The article then had a paragraph in parentheses that said Les Moore had become a very important new director in the three years since *Tramp Killer*, which had only been his second feature, and that the movie he wanted Dawn Devayne to come back to Los Angeles for was *Bubbletop*, the first of the zany comedies that had made Les Moore the Preston Sturges of the sixties.)

So Dawn Devayne—or Estelle, because her name wasn't Dawn Devayne yet and she'd quit calling herself Honey White—

went back to Los Angeles and Les Moore introduced her to a
star-making agent named Byron Cartwright, who signed her to
exclusive representation and who changed her name to Dawn
Devayne. And *Bubbletop* went on to become a smash hit and
Dawn Devayne got rave notices, and she'd been a movie star
ever since, with fifteen movies in the last eleven years, and her
price for one movie now was seven hundred fifty thousand dollars. The article said she was one of the very few stars who had
never had a box-office flop.

About her private life, the article said she was "between
marriages." I thought that would mean she was engaged to
somebody, but so far as I could see from the rest of the article
she wasn't. So I guess that's just a phrase they use for people
like movie stars when they aren't married.

Anyway, the marriages she was between were numbers four
and five. After me in 1958, her next marriage was in 1963, to a
movie star named Rick Tandem. Then in 1964 there was a fight
in a nightclub where a producer named Josh Weinstein knocked
Rick Tandem down and Rick Tandem later sued for divorce
and said John Weinstein had come between him and Dawn
Devayne. The article didn't quite say that Rick Tandem was in
reality queer, but it got the point across.

Then marriage number three, in 1966, was to another movie
actor, Ken Forrest, who was an older man, a contemporary of
Gable and Tracy who was still making movies but wasn't quite
the power he used to be. That marriage ended in 1968 when
Forrest shot himself on a yacht off the coast of Spain; Dawn
Devayne was in London making a picture when it happened.

And the fourth marriage, in 1970, was to a Dallas businessman with interests in computers and airlines and oil. His name
was Ralph Chucklin, and that marriage had ended with a quiet
divorce in 1973. "Dawn is dating now," the article said, "but no

one in particular tops her list. 'I'm still looking for the right guy,' she says."

Then the article got to talking about her age, and the person who wrote the article raised the question as to whether a thirty-two-year-old woman was young enough to still make it as the next Sex Goddess of the World. "Dawn is more beautiful every year," the article said, and then it went back to all the business about Women's Lib and television and X-rated movies and looser sexual codes, and it said the next Superstar Sex Symbol wasn't likely to be another girl-child type like the ones before, but would be more of an adult woman, who could bring brains and experience to sex. "Far from the dumb blondes of yester-year," the article said, "Dawn Devayne is a bright blonde, who combines with good old-fashioned lust the more modern femi-nine virtues of intelligence and independence. A Jane Fonda who doesn't nag." And the article finished by saying maybe the changed social conditions meant there wouldn't be any more Blonde Bombshells or Sexpot Movie Queens, which would make the world a colder and a drabber place, but the writer sure hoped there would be more, and the best bet right now to bring sex back to the world was Dawn Devayne.

There were photographs with the article, full-page color pic-tures of Dawn Devayne with her clothes off, and when I fin-ished reading I sat there on the toilet a while longer looking at the pictures and trying to remember Estelle. Nothing. The face, the eyes, the smile, all different. The stomach and legs were different. Even the nipples didn't remind me of Estelle Anlic's nipples.

There's something wrong, I thought. I wondered if maybe this Dawn Devayne woman had a criminal record or was wanted for murder somewhere or something like that, and she'd just paid Estelle money to borrow her life story. Was that possible?

It sure didn't seem possible that *this* sexy woman was Estelle. I know it was sixteen years, but how much can one person change? I sat studying the pictures until I noticed I was beginning to get an erection, so I left the head and went back to work.

All I could think about, the next three days, was Dawn Devayne. I was once married to her, married to a sexy movie star. Me. I just couldn't get used to the idea.

And the other guys didn't help. Norm and Stan and Pat spread the word, and pretty soon all the guys were coming around, even some of the younger officers, talking and grinning and winking and all that. Nobody came right out with the direct question, but what they really wanted to know was what it was like to be in bed with Dawn Devayne.

And what could I tell them? I didn't *know* what it was like to be in bed with Dawn Devayne. I knew what it was like to be in bed with Estelle Anlic—or anyway I had a kind of vague memory, after sixteen years—but that wasn't what they wanted to know, and anyway I didn't feel like telling them. She was a teenage girl, sixteen (though she told me nineteen), and I was twenty-one, and neither of us was exactly a genius about sex, but we had fun. I remember she had very very soft arms and she liked to have her arms around my neck, and she laughed with her mouth wide open, and she always drowned her french fries in so much ketchup I used to tell her I had to eat them with ice tongs and one time in bed she finally admitted she didn't know what ice tongs were and she cried because she was sure she was stupid, and we had sex that time in order for me to tell her (a) she wasn't stupid, and (b) I loved her anyway even though she was stupid, and that's the one time in particular I have any memory of at all, which is mostly because that was the time I learned I could control myself and hold back ejaculation almost as long as I wanted, almost forever. We were both learning about things then, we were both just puppies rolling in a basket of wool, but the guys didn't want to hear anything like that, it would just depress them. And I didn't want to tell them about it either. Their favorite sex story was one that Pat used to tell about being in bed with a girl with a candle in her ass. That's what they really wanted me to tell them, that Dawn Devayne had a candle in her ass.

But even though I couldn't tell them any stories that would satisfy them, they kept coming around, they kept on and on with the same subject, they couldn't seem to let it go. It fascinated them, and every time they saw me they got reminded and fascinated all over again. In fact, a couple of the guys started calling me "Devayne," as though that was going to be my new nickname, until one time I picked up a wrench and patted it into my other palm and went over to the guy and said:

"My name is Orry."

He looked surprised, and a little scared. He said:

"Sure. Sure, I know that."

I said:

"Let me hear you say it."

He said:

"Jeez, Orry, it was just a—"

"Okay, then," I said, and went back over to where I was working, and that was the last I heard of that.

But it wasn't the last I heard of Dawn Devayne. For instance, I was more or less going then with a woman in New London named Fran Skiburg, who was divorced from an Army career man and had custody of the three children. She was part Norwegian and part Belgian and her husband had been almost all German. Fran and I would go to the movies sometimes, or she'd cook me a meal, but it wasn't serious. Mostly, we didn't even go to bed together.

But then somebody told her about Dawn Devayne, and the next time I saw Fran she was a different person. She kept grinning and winking all through dinner, and she hustled the kids to bed earlier than usual, and then sort of crowded me into the living room. She liked me to rub her feet sometimes, because she was standing all day at the bank, so I sat on the sofa and she kicked off her slippers and while I rubbed her feet she kept opening and closing her knees and giggling at me.

Well, I was looking up her skirt anyway, so I slid my hand up from her feet, and the next thing we were rolling around on the wall-to-wall carpet together. She was absolutely all over me, nervous and jumpy and full of loud laughter, all the time wanting to change position or do this and that. Up till then, my one complaint about Fran was that she'd just lie there; now all of a sudden she was acting like the star of an X-movie.

I couldn't figure it out, until after it was all finished and I was lying there on the carpet on my back, breathing like a diver with the bends. Then Fran, with this big wild-eyed smile, came looming over me, scratching my chest with her fingernails and saying, "What would you like to do to me? What do you *really* want to do to me?"

This was *after*. I panted at her for a second, and then I said, "What?"

And she said, "What would you do to me if I was Dawn Devayne?"

Then I understood. I sat up and said, "Who told you that?"

"What would you do? Come on, Orry, let's do something!"

"Do what? We just did everything!"

"There's *lots* more! There's *lots* more!" Then she leaned down close to my ear, where I couldn't see her face, and whispered, "You don't want me to have to *say* it."

I don't know if she had anything special in mind, but I don't think so. I think she was just excited in general, and wanted something different to happen. Anyway, I pushed her off and got to my feet and said, "I don't know anything about any Dawn Devayne or any kind of crazy sex stuff. That's no way to act."

She sat there on the green carpet with her legs curled to the side, looking something like the nude pictures in Pat's magazines except whiter and a little heavier, and she stared up at me without saying anything at all. Her mouth was open because she was looking upward so her expression seemed to be mainly surprised. I felt grumpy. I sat down on the sofa and put on my underpants.

And all at once Fran jumped up and grabbed half her clothes and ran out of the room. I finished getting dressed, and sat on the sofa a little longer, and then went out to the kitchen and ate a bowl of raisin bran. When Fran still didn't come back, I went to her bedroom and looked in through the open door, and she wasn't there. I said, "Fran?"

No answer.

The bathroom door was closed, so I knocked on it, but nothing happened. I turned the knob and the door was locked. I said, "Fran?"

A mumble sounded from in there.

"Fran? You all right?"

"Go away."

"What?"

"Go away!"

That was the last she said. I tried talking to her through the door, and I tried to get her to come out, and I tried to find out what the problem was, but she wouldn't say anything else. There wasn't any sound of crying or anything, she was just sitting in there by herself. After a while I said, "I have to get back to the base, Fran."

She didn't say anything to that, either. I said it once or twice more, and said some other things, and then I left and went back to the base.

I was shaving the next morning when I suddenly remembered that picture, the one in the magazine of Estelle and me on our wedding day. We were squinting there in the sunlight, the both of us, and now I was squinting again because the light bulb over the mirror was too bright. Shaving, I looked at myself, looked at my nose and my eyes and my ears, and here I was. I was still here. The same guy. Same short haircut, same eyebrows, same chin.

The same guy.

What did Fran want from me, anyway? Just because it turns out I used to be married to somebody famous, all of a sudden I'm supposed to be different? I'm not any different, I'm the same guy I always was. People don't just change, they have ways that they are, and that's what they are. That's who they are, that's what you mean by personality. The way a person is.

Then I thought: Estelle changed.

That's right. Estelle Anlic is Dawn Devayne now. She's changed, she's somebody else. There isn't any—she isn't—there isn't any Estelle Anlic any more, nowhere on the face of the earth.

But it isn't the same as if she died, because her *memories* are still there inside Dawn Devayne, she'd remember being the girl with the mother that drove the bus, and she'd remember marrying the sailor in San Diego in 1958, and even in that article I'd read there'd been a part where she was remembering being Estelle Anlic and working as a movie cashier in San Francisco. But still she was changed, she was somebody else now, she was different. Like a wooden house turning itself into a brick house. How could she…how could anybody do that? How could *anybody* do that?

Then I thought: Estelle Anlic is Dawn Devayne now, but I'm still me. Ordo Tupikos, the same guy. But if she was—If I'm—

It was hard even to figure out the question. If she was that back then, and if she's this now, and if I was *that*...

I kept on shaving. More and more of my face came out from behind the white cream, and it was the same face. Getting older, a little older every minute, but not—

Not different.

I finished shaving. I looked at that face, and then I scrubbed it with hot water and dried it on a towel. And after mess I went to Headquarters office and put in for leave. Twenty-two days, all I had saved up.

TWO

The first place I went was New York, on the bus, where I looked in a magazine they have there called *Cue* that tells you what movies are playing all over the city. A Dawn Devayne movie called *The Captain's Pearls* was showing in a theater on West 86th Street, which was forty-six blocks uptown from the bus terminal, so I walked up there and sat through the second half of a western with Charles Bronson and then *The Captain's Pearls* came on.

The story was about an airline captain with two girlfriends both named Pearl, one of them in Paris and one in New York. Dawn Devayne played the one in New York, and the advertising agency she works for opens an office in Paris and she goes there to head it, and the Paris girlfriend is a model who gets hired by Dawn Devayne for a commercial for the captain's airline, and then the captain has to keep the two girls from finding out he's going out with both of them. It was a comedy.

This movie was made in 1967, which was only nine years after I was married to Estelle, so I should have been able to recognize her, but she just wasn't there. I stared and stared and stared at that woman on the screen, and the only person she reminded me of was Dawn Devayne. I mean, from before I knew who she was. But there wasn't anything of Estelle there. Not the voice, not the walk, not the smile, not anything.

But sexy. I saw what that article writer meant, because if you looked at Dawn Devayne your first thought was she'd be terrific in bed. And then you'd decide she'd also be terrific otherwise, to talk with or take a trip together or whatever it was. And then you'd realize since she was so all-around terrific she wouldn't have to settle for anybody but an all-around terrific guy, which would leave you out, so you'd naturally idolize her. I mean, you'd want it without any idea in your head that you could ever get it.

I was thinking all that, and then I thought, *But I've had it!* And then I tried to put together arms-around-neck ice-tongs-stupid Estelle Anlic with this terrific female creature on the screen here, and I just couldn't do it. I mean, not even with a fantasy. If I had a fantasy about going to bed with Dawn Devayne, not even in my fantasy did I see myself in bed with Estelle.

After the movie I walked back downtown toward the bus terminal, because I'd left my duffel bag in a locker there. It was only around four-thirty in the afternoon, but down around 42nd Street the whores were already out, strolling on the sidewalks and standing in the doorways of shoe stores. The sight of a Navy uniform really agitates a whore, and half a dozen of them called out to me as I walked along, but I didn't answer.

Then one of them stepped out from a doorway and stood right in my path and said, "Hello, sailor. You off a ship?"

I started to walk around her, but then I stopped dead and stared, and I said, "You look like Dawn Devayne!"

She grinned and ducked her head, looking pleased with herself. "You really think so, sailor?"

She did. She was wearing a blonde wig like Dawn Devayne's hair style, and her eyes and mouth were made up like Dawn Devayne, and she'd even fixed her eyebrows to look like Dawn Devayne's eyebrows.

Only at a second look none of it worked. The wig didn't look like real hair, and the make-up was too heavy, and the eyebrows looked like little false moustaches. And down inside all that phony stuff she was Puerto Rican or Cuban or something like that. It was all like a Halloween costume.

She was poking a finger at my arm, looking up at me sort of slantwise in imitation of a Dawn Devayne movement I'd just seen in *The Captain's Pearls*. "Come on, sailor," she said. "Wanna fuck a movie star?"

"No," I said. It was all too creepy. "No no," I said, and went around her and hurried on down the street.

And she shouted after me, "You been on that ship too long! What you want is Robert Redford!"

This was my first time in Los Angeles since 1963, when the Gulf of Tonkin incident got me transferred from a ship in the Mediterranean to a ship in the Pacific. They'd flown me with a bunch of other guys from Naples to Washington, then by surface transportation to Chicago and by air to Los Angeles and Honolulu, where I met my ship. I'd had a two-day layover in Los Angeles, and now I remembered thinking then about looking up Estelle. But I didn't do it, mostly because five years had already gone by since I'd last seen her, and also because her mother might start making trouble again if she caught me there.

The funny thing is, that was the year Estelle first became Dawn Devayne, in the movie called *Bubbletop*. Now I wondered what might have happened if I'd actually found her back then, got in touch somehow. I'd never seen *Bubbletop*, so I didn't know if by 1963 she was already this new person, this Dawn Devayne, if she'd already changed so completely that Estelle Anlic couldn't be found in there any more. If I'd met her that time, would something new have started? Would my whole life have been shifted, would I now be somebody in the movie business instead of being a sailor? I tried to see myself as that movie person; who would I be, what would I be like? Would I be *different*?

But there weren't any answers for questions like that. A person is who he is, and he can't guess who he would be if he was somebody else. The question doesn't even make sense. But I guess it's just impossible to think at all about movie stars without some fantasy or other creeping in.

My plane for Los Angeles left New York a little after seven P.M. and took five hours to get across the country, but because of the time zone differences it was only a little after nine at night when I landed, and still not ten o'clock when the taxi let me off at a motel on Cahuenga Boulevard, pretty much on the line separating Hollywood from Burbank. The taxi cost almost twenty dollars from the airport, which was kind of frightening. I'd taken two thousand dollars out of my savings, leaving just over three thousand in the account, and I was spending the money pretty fast.

The cabdriver was a leathery old guy who buzzed along the freeways like it was a stock car race, all the time telling me how much better the city had been before the freeways were built. Most people pronounce Los Angeles as though the middle is "angel," but he was one of those who pronounce it as though the middle is "angle." "Los Ang-gleez," he kept saying, and one time he said, "I'm a sight you won't see all that much. I'm your native son."

"Born here?"

"Nope. Come out in forty-eight."

The motel had a large neon sign out front and very small rooms in a low stucco building in back. It was impossible to tell what color the stucco was because green and yellow and orange and blue floodlights were aimed at it from fixtures stuck into the ivy border, but in the morning the color turned out to be a sort of dirty cream shade.

My room had pale blue walls and a heavy maroon bedspread and a paper ribbon around the toilet seat saying it had been sanitized. I unpacked my duffel and turned on the television set, but I was too restless to stay cooped up in that room forever. Also, I decided I was hungry. So I changed into civvies and went out and walked down Highland to Hollywood Boulevard, where I ate something in a fast-food place. It was like New York in that neighborhood, only skimpier. For some reason Los Angeles looks older than New York. It looks like an old old Pueblo Indian village with neon added to it by real estate people. New York doesn't look any older than Europe, but Los Angeles looks as old as sand. It looks like a place that almost had a Golden Age, a long long time ago, but nothing happened and now it's too late.

After I ate I walked around for half an hour, and then I went back to the motel and all of a sudden I was very sleepy. I had the television on, and the light, and I still wore all my clothes except my shoes, but I fell asleep anyway, lying on top of the bedspread, and when I woke up the TV was hissing and it was nearly four in the morning. I was very thirsty, and nervous for some reason. Lonely, I felt lonely. I drank water, and went out to the street again, and after a while I found an all-night supermarket called Hughes. I took a cart and went up and down the aisles.

There were some people in there, not many. I noticed something about them. They were all dressed up in suede and fancy denim, like people at a terrific party in some movie, but they were buying the cheapest of everything. Their baskets were filled as though by gnarled men and women wearing shabby pants or faded kerchiefs, but the men were all young and tanned and wearing platform shoes, and the women were all made up with false eyelashes and different-colored fingernails. Also, some of them had food stamps in their hands.

Another thing. When these people pushed their carts down the aisles they stood very straight and were sure of themselves and on top of the world, but when they lowered their heads to take something off a shelf they looked very worried.

Another thing. Every one of them was alone. They went up and down the aisles, pushing their carts past one another— from up above, they must have looked like pieces in a labyrinth game—and they never looked at one another, never smiled at one another. They were just alone in there, and from up front came the clatter of the cash register.

After a while I didn't want to be in that place any more. I bought shaving cream and a can of soda and an orange, and walked back to the motel and went to bed.

There wasn't anybody in the phone book named Byron Cart-wright, who was the famous agent who had changed Estelle's name to Dawn Devayne and then guided her to stardom. In the motel office they had the five different Los Angeles phone books, and he wasn't in any of them. He also wasn't in the yellow pages under "Theatrical Agencies." Finally I found a listing for something called the Screen Actors' Guild, and I called, and spoke to a girl who said, "Byron Cartwright? He's with GLA."

"I'm sorry?"

"GLA," she repeated, and hung up.

So I went back to the phone books, hoping to find something called GLA. The day clerk, a sunken-cheeked faded-eyed man of about forty with thinning yellow hair and very tanned arms, said, "You seem to be having a lot of trouble."

"I'm looking for an actor's agent," I told him.

His expression lit up a bit. "Oh, yeah? Which one?"

"Byron Cartwright."

He was impressed. "Pretty good," he said. "He's with GLA now, right?"

"That's right. Do you know him?"

"Don't I wish I did." This time he was rueful. His face seemed to jump from expression to expression with nothing in between, as though I were seeing a series of photographs instead of a person.

"I'm trying to find the phone number," I said.

I must have seemed helpless, because his next expression

showed the easy superiority of the insider. "Look under Global-Lipkin," he told me.

Global-Lipkin. I looked, among "Theatrical Agencies," and there it was: Global-Lipkin Associates. You could tell immediately it was an important organization; the phone number ended in three zeroes. "Thank you," I said.

His face now showed slightly belligerent doubt. He said, "They send for you?"

"Send for me? No."

The face was shut; rejection and disapproval. Shaking his head he said, "Forget it."

Apparently he thought I was a struggling actor. Not wanting to go through a long explanation, I just shrugged and said, "Well, I'll try it," and went back to the phone booth.

A receptionist answered. When I asked for Byron Cartwright she put me through to a secretary, who said, "Who's calling, please?"

"Ordo Tupikos."

"And the subject, Mr. Tupikos?"

"Dawn Devayne."

"One moment, please."

I waited a while, and then she came back and said, "Mr. Tupikos, could you tell me who you're with?"

"With? I'm sorry, I…"

"Which firm."

"Oh. I'm not with any firm, I'm in the Navy."

"In the Navy."

"Yes. I used to be—" But she'd gone away again. Another wait, and then she was back. "Mr. Tupikos, is this official Navy business?"

"No," I said. "I used to be married to Dawn Devayne."

There was a little silence, and then she said, "Married?"

"Yes. In San Diego."

"One moment, please."

This was a longer wait, and when she came back she said, "Mr. Tupikos, is this a legal matter?"

"No, I just want to see Estelle again."

"I beg your pardon?"

"Dawn Devayne. She was named Estelle when I married her."

A male voice suddenly said, "All right, Donna, I'll take it."

"Yes, sir," and there was a click.

The male voice said, "You're Ordo Tupikos?"

"Yes, sir," I said. It wasn't sensible to call him "sir," but the girl had just done it, and in any event he had an authoritative officer-like sound in his voice, and it just slipped out.

He said, "I suppose you can prove your identity."

That surprised me. "Of course," I said. "I still look the same." *I* still look the same.

"And what is it you want?"

"To see Estelle. Dawn. Miss Devayne."

"You told my secretary you were with the Navy."

"I'm *in* the Navy."

"You're due to retire pretty soon, aren't you?"

"Two years," I said.

"Let me be blunt, Mr. Tupikos," he said. "Are you looking for money?"

"Money?" I couldn't think what he was talking about. (Later, going over it in my mind, I realized what he'd been afraid of, but just at that moment I was bewildered.) "Money for what?" I asked him.

He didn't answer. Instead, he said, "Then why show up like this, after all these years?"

"There was something in a magazine. A friend showed it to me."

"Yes?"

"Well, it surprised me, that's all."

"*What* surprised you?"

"About Estelle turning into Dawn Devayne."

There was a very short silence. But it wasn't an ordinary empty silence, it was a kind of slammed-shut silence, a startled silence. Then he said, "You mean you didn't know? You just found out?"

"It was some surprise," I said.

He gave out with a long laugh, turning his head away from the phone so it wouldn't hurt my ears. But I could still hear it. Then he said, "God damn, Mr. Tupikos, that's a new one."

I had nothing to say to that.

"All right," he said. "Where are you?"

I told him the name of the motel.

"I'll get back to you," he said. "Some time today."

"Thank you," I said.

The phone booth was out in front of the motel, and I had to go back through the office to get to the inner courtyard and my room. When I walked into the office the day clerk motioned to me. "Come here." His expression now portrayed pride.

I went over and he handed me a large black-and-white photograph; what they call a glossy. The blacks in it were very dark and solid, which made it a little bit hard to make out what was going on, but the picture seemed to have been taken in a parking garage. Two people were in the foreground. I couldn't swear to it, but it looked as though Ernest Borgnine was strangling the day clerk. "Whadaya think of that?"

I didn't know what I thought of it. But when people hand you a picture—their wife, their girlfriend, their children, their dog, their new house, their boat, their garden—what you say is *very nice.* I handed the picture back. "Very nice," I said.

Everybody knows about the movie stars' names being embedded in the sidewalks of Hollywood Boulevard, but it's always strange when you see it. There are the squares of pavement, and on every square is a gold outline of a five-pointed star, and in every other star there is the name of a movie star. Every year, fewer of those names mean anything. The idea of the names is immortality, but what they're really about is death.

I took a walk for a while after talking to Byron Cartwright, and I walked along two or three blocks of Hollywood Boulevard with some family group behind me that had a child with a loud piercing voice, and the child kept wanting to know who people were:

"Daddy, who's Vilma Banky?"

"Daddy, who's Charles Farrell?"

"Daddy, who's Dolores Costello?"

"Daddy, who's Conrad Nagel?"

The father's answers were never loud enough for me to hear, but what could he have said? "She was a movie star." "He used to be in silent movies, a long time ago." Or maybe, "I don't know. Emil Jannings? I don't know."

I didn't look back, so I have no idea what the family looked like, or even if the child was a boy or a girl, but pretty soon I hated listening to them, so I turned in at a fast-food place to have a hamburger and onion rings and a Coke. I sat at one of the red formica tables to eat, and at the table across the plastic partition from me was another family—father, mother, son, daughter—and the daughter was saying, "Why did they put those names there anyway?"

"Just to be nice," the mother said.

The son said, "Because they're buried there."

The daughter stared at him, not knowing if that was true or not. Then she said, "They are not!"

"Sure they are," the son said. "They bury them standing up, so they can all fit. And they all wear the clothes from their most famous movie. Like their cowboy hats and the long gowns and their Civil War Army uniforms."

The father, chuckling, said, "And their white telephones?"

The son gave his father a hesitant smile and a headshake, saying, "I don't get it."

"That's okay," the father said. He grinned and ruffled the son's hair, but I could see he was irritated. He was older, so his memory stretched back farther, so his jokes wouldn't always mean anything to his son, whose memories had started later—and would probably end later. The son had reminded his father that the father would some day die.

After I ate I didn't feel like walking on the stars' names any more. I went up to the next parallel street, which is called Yucca, and took that over to Highland Avenue and then on back to the motel.

When I walked into the office the day clerk said, "Got a message for you." His expression was tough and secretive, like a character in a spy movie. The hotel clerk in a spy movie who is really a part of the spy organization; this is the point where he tells the hero that the Gestapo is in his room.

"A message?"

"From GLA," he said. His face flipped to the next expression, like a digital clock moving on to the next number. This one showed make-believe comic envy used to hide real envy. I wondered if he really did feel envy or if he was just practicing being an actor by pretending to show envy. No; pretending to *hide* envy. Maybe he himself was actually feeling envy but was hiding it by pretending to be someone who was showing envy by trying to hide it. That was too confusing to think about; it made me dizzy, like looking too long off the fantail of a ship at the swirls of water directly beneath the stem. Layers and layers of twisting white foam with bottomless black underneath; but then it all organizes itself into swinging straight white lines of wake.

I said, "What did they want?"

"They'll send a car for you at three o'clock." Flip; friendliness, conspiracy. "You could do me a favor."

"I could?"

From under the counter he took out a tan manila envelope, then halfway withdrew from it another glossy photograph; I couldn't see the subject. "This," he said, and slid the photo back into the envelope. Twisting the red string on the two little round closure tabs of the envelope, he said, "Just leave it in the office, you know? Just leave it some place where they can see it."

"Oh," I said. "All right." And I took the envelope.

The car was a black Cadillac limousine with a uniformed chauffeur who held the door for me and called me, "sir." It didn't seem to matter to him that he was picking me up at a kind of seedy motel, or that I was wearing clothes that were somewhat shabby and out of date. (I wear civvies so seldom that I almost never pay any attention to what clothing I own or what condition it's in.)

I had never been in a limousine before, with or without a chauffeur. In fact, this was the first time in my life I'd ever ridden in a Cadillac. I spent the first few blocks just looking at the interior of the car, noticing that I had my own radio in the back, and power windows, and that there were separate air conditioner controls on both sides of the rear seat.

There were grooves for a glass partition between front and rear, but the glass was lowered out of sight, and when we'd driven down Highland and made a right turn onto Hollywood Boulevard, going past Grauman's Chinese theater, the chauffeur suddenly said, "You a writer?"

"What? Me? No."

"Oh," he said. "I always try to figure out what people are. They're fascinating, you know? People."

"I'm in the Navy," I said.

"That right? I did two in the Army myself."

"Ah," I said.

He nodded. He'd look at me in the rear-view mirror from time to time while he was talking. He said, "Then I pushed a hack around Houston for six years, but I figured the hell with it, you know? Who needs it. Come out here in sixty-seven, never went back."

"I guess it's all right out here."

"No place like it," he said.

I didn't have an answer for that, and he didn't seem to have anything else to say, so I opened the day clerk's envelope and looked at the photograph he wanted me to leave in Byron Cartwright's office.

Actually it was four photographs on one eight-by-ten sheet of glossy paper, showing the day clerk in four poses, with different clothing in each one. Four different characters, I guess. In the upper left, he was wearing a light plaid jacket and a pale turtleneck sweater and a medium-shade cloth cap, and he had a cigarette in the corner of his mouth and he was squinting, looking mean and tough. In the upper right he was wearing a tuxedo, and he had a big smile on his face. His head was turned toward the camera, but his body was half-twisted away and he was holding a top hat out to the side, as though he were singing a song and was about to march offstage at the end of the music. In the bottom left, he was wearing a cowboy hat and a bandana around his neck and a plaid shirt, and he had a kind of comical-foolish expression on his face, as though somebody had just made a joke and he wasn't sure he'd understood the point. And in the bottom right he was wearing a dark suit and white shirt and pale tie, and he was leaning forward a little and smiling in a friendly way directly at the camera. I guess that was supposed to be him in his natural state, but it actually looked less like him than any of the others.

The whole back of the photograph was filled with printing. His name was at the top (MAURY DEE) and underneath was a listing of all the movies he'd been in and all the play productions, with the character he performed in each one. Down at the bottom were three or four quotes from critics about how good he was.

The driver turned left on Fairfax and went down past Selma to Sunset Boulevard, and then turned right. Then he said, "The best thing about this job is the people."

"Is that right?" I put Maury Dee's photograph away and twisted the red string around the closure tabs.

"And I'll tell you something," said the driver. "The bigger they are, the nicer they are. You'd be amazed, some of the people been sitting right where you are right now."

"I bet."

"But you know who's the best of them all? I mean, just a nice regular person, not stuck up at all."

"Who's that?"

"Dawn Devayne," he said. "She's always got a good word for you, she'll take a joke, she's just terrific."

"That's nice," I said.

"Terrific." He shook his head. "Always remembers your name. 'Hi, Harry,' she says. 'How you doing?' Just a terrific person."

"I guess she must be all right," I said.

"Terrific," he said, and turned the car in at one of the taller buildings just before the Beverly Hills line. We drove down into the basement parking garage and the driver stopped next to a bank of elevators. He hopped out and opened my door for me, and when I got out he said, "Eleventh floor."

"Thanks, Harry," I said.

THREE

All you could see was artificial plants. I stepped out of the elevator and there were great pots all over the place on the green rug, all with plastic plants in them with huge dark-green leaves. Beyond them, quite a ways back, expanses of plate glass showed the white sky.

I moved forward, not sure what to do next, and then I saw the receptionist's desk. With the white sky behind her, she was very hard to find. I went over to her and said, "Excuse me."

She'd been writing something on a long form, and now she looked up with a friendly smile and said, "May I help you?"

"I'm supposed to see Byron Cartwright."

"Name, please?"

"Ordo Tupikos."

She used her telephone, sounding very chipper, and then she smiled at me again, saying, "He'll be out in a minute. If you'll have a seat?"

There were easy chairs in among the plastic plants. I thanked her and went off to sit down, picking up a newspaper from a white formica table beside the chair. It was called *The Hollywood Reporter*, and it was magazine size and printed on glossy paper. I read all the short items about people signing to do this or that, and I read a nightclub review of somebody whose name I didn't recognize, and then a girl came along and said, "Mr. Tupikos?"

"Yes?"

"I'm Mr. Cartwright's secretary. Would you come with me?"

I put the paper down and followed her away from the plants and down a long hall with tans walls and brown carpet. We passed offices on both sides of the hall; about half were occupied, and most of the people were on the phone.

I suddenly realized I'd forgotten the day clerk's photograph. I'd left it behind in the envelope on the table with *The Hollywood Reporter*.

Well, that actually was what he'd asked me to do; leave it in the office. Maybe on the way back I should take it out of the envelope.

The girl stopped, gesturing at a door on the left. "Through here, Mr. Tupikos."

Byron Cartwright was standing in the middle of the room. He had a big heavy chest and brown leathery skin and yellow-white hair brushed straight back over his balding head. He was dressed in different shades of pale blue, and there was a white line of smoke rising from a long cigar in an ashtray on the desk behind him. The room was large and so was everything in it; massive desk, long black sofa, huge windows showing the white sky, with the city of Los Angeles down the slope on the flat land to the south, pastel colors glittering in the haze: pink, peach, coral.

Byron Cartwright strode toward me, hand outstretched. He was laughing, as though remembering a wonderful time we'd once shared together. Laughter made erosion lines crisscrossing all over his face. "Well, hello, Orry," he said. "Glad to see you." He took my hand, and patted my arm with his other hand, saying, "That's right, isn't it? Orry?"

"That's right."

"Everybody calls me By. Come in, sit down."

I was already in. We sat together on the long sofa. He crossed one leg over the other, half-turning in my direction, his arm stretched out toward me along the sofa back. He had what looked like a class ring on one finger, with a dark red stone. He said,

"You know where I got it from? The name 'Orry'? From Dawn."
There was something almost religious about the way he said the
name. It reminded me of when Jehovah's Witnesses pass out
their literature; they always smile and say, "Here's good news!"

I said, "You told her about me?"

"Phoned her the first chance I got. She's on location now.
You could've knocked her over with a feather, Orry. I could
hear it in her voice."

"It's been a long time," I said. I wasn't sure what this conversation was about, and I was sorry to hear Dawn Devayne was
"on location." It sounded as though I might not be able to get
to see her.

"Sixteen years," Byron Cartwright said, and he had that rever-
ential sound in his voice again, with the same happiness around
his mouth and eyes. "Your little girl has come a long way, Orry."

"I guess so."

"It's just amazing that you never knew. Didn't any reporters
ever come around, any magazine writers?"

"I never knew anything," I told him. "When the fellows told
me about it, I didn't believe them. Then they showed me the
magazine."

"Well, it's just astonishing." But he didn't seem to imply that
I might be a liar. He kept smiling at me, and shaking his head
with his astonishment.

"It sure was astonishing to me," I said.

He nodded, letting me know he understood completely. "So
the first thing you thought," he said, "you had to see her again.
Just had to say hello. Am I right?"

"Not to begin with." It was hard talking when looking directly
at him, because his face was so full of smiling eagerness. I
leaned forward a little, resting my elbows on my knees, and
looked across the room. There was a huge full-color blown-up
photograph of a horse taking up most of the opposite wall. I

said, looking at the horse, "At first I just thought it was eerie. Of course, nice for Estelle. Or Dawn, I guess. Nice for her, I was glad things worked out for her. But for me it was really strange."

"In what way *strange*, Orry?" This time he sounded like a chaplain, sympathetic and understanding.

"It took me a while to figure that out." I chanced looking at him again, and he had just a small smile going now, he looked expectant and receptive. It was easier to face him with that expression. I said, "There was a picture of Estelle and me in the magazine, from our wedding day."

"Got it!" He bounded up from the sofa and hurried over to the desk. I became aware then that most of the knick-knacks and things around on the desk and the tables and everywhere had some connection with golf; small statues of golfers, a gold golf ball on a gold tee, things like that.

Byron Cartwright came back with a small photo in a frame. He handed it to me, smiling, then sat down again and said, "That's the one, right?"

"Yes," I said, looking at it. Then I turned my face toward him, not so much to see him as to let him see me. "You can recognize me from that picture."

"I know that," he said. "I was noticing that, Orry, you're remarkable. You haven't aged a bit. I'd hate to see a picture of *me* taken sixteen years ago."

"I'm not talking about getting older," I said. "I'm talking about getting *different*. I'm not different."

"I believe you're right." He moved the class-ring hand to pat my knee, then put it back on the sofa. "Dawn told me a little about you, Orry," he said. "She told me you were the gentlest man she'd ever met. She told me she's thought about you often, she's always hoped you found happiness somewhere. I believe you're still the same good man you were then."

"The same." I pointed at Estelle in the photo. "But that isn't Dawn Devayne."

"Ha ha," he said. "I'll have to go along with you there."

I looked at him again. "How did that happen? How do people change, or not change?"

"Big questions, Orry." If a smile can be serious, his smile had turned serious. But still friendly.

"I kept thinking about it," I said. I almost told him about Fran then, and the changes all around me, but at the last second I decided not to. "So I came out to talk to her about it," I said. And then, because I suddenly realized this could be a brush-off, that Byron Cartwright might have the job of smiling at me and being friendly and telling me I wasn't going to be allowed to see Estelle, I added to that, "If she wants to see me."

"She does, Orry," he said. "Of course she does." And he acted surprised. But I could see he was *acting* surprised.

I said, "You were supposed to find out if I'd changed or not, weren't you? If I was going to be a pest or something."

Grinning, he said, "She told me you weren't stupid, Orry. But you could have been an impostor, you know, maybe some maniac or something. Dawn *wants* to see you, if you're still the Orry she used to know."

"That's the problem."

He laughed hugely, as though I'd said a joke. "She's filming up in Stockton today," he said, "but she'll be flying back when they're done. She wants you to go out to the house, and she'll meet you there."

"Her house?"

"Well, naturally." Chuckling at me, he got to his feet, saying, "You'll be driven out there now, unless you have other plans."

"No, nothing." I also stood.

"I'll phone down for the car. You came in through the parking area?"

"Yes."

"Just go straight back down. The car will be by the elevators."

"Thank you."

We shook hands again, at his prompting, and this time he held my hand in both of his and gazed at me. The religious feeling was there once more, this time as though he were an evangelist and I a cripple he was determined would walk. Total sincerity filled his eyes and his smile. "She's my little girl now, too, Orry," he said.

The envelope containing the day clerk's pictures was gone from the table out front.

"Hello, Harry," I said. He was holding the door open for me.

He gave me a kind of roguish grin, and waggled a finger at me. "You didn't tell me you were pals with Dawn Devayne."

"It was a long story," I said.

"Good thing I didn't have anything bad to say, huh?" And I could see that inside his joking he was very upset.

I didn't know what to answer. I gave him an apologetic smile and got into the car and he shut the door behind me. It wasn't until we were out on Sunset driving across the line into Beverly Hills, that I decided what to say: "I don't really know Dawn Devayne," I told him. "I haven't seen her for sixteen years. I wasn't trying to be smart with you or anything."

"Sixteen years, huh?" That seemed to make things better. Lifting his head to look at me in the rear-view mirror, he said, "Old high school pals?"

I might as well tell him the truth; he'd probably find out sooner or later anyway. "I was married to her."

The eyes in the rear-view mirror got sharper, and then fuzzier, and then he looked out at Sunset Boulevard and shifted position so I could no longer see his face in the mirror. I don't suppose he disbelieved me. I guess he didn't know what attitude to take. He didn't know what to think about me, or about what I'd told him, or about anything. He didn't say another word the whole trip.

The house was in Bel Air, way up in the hills at the very end of a curving steep street with almost no houses on it. What residences I did see were very spread out and expensive-looking, though mostly only one story high, and tucked away in folds and dimples of the slope, above or below the road. Many had flat roofs with white stones sprinkled on top for decoration. Like pound cake with confectioner's sugar on it.

At the end of the street was a driveway with a No Trespassing sign. Great huge plants surrounded the entrance to the driveway; they reminded me of the plants in Byron Cartwright's outer office, except that these were real. But the leaves were so big and shiny and green that the real ones looked just as fake as the plastic ones.

The driveway curved upward to the right and then came to a closed chain-link gate. The driver stopped next to a small box mounted on a pipe beside the driveway, and pushed a button on the box. After a minute a metallic voice spoke from the box, and the driver responded, and then the gate swung open and we drove on up, still through this forest of plastic-like plants, until we suddenly came out on a flat place where there was a white stucco house with many windows. The center section was two stories high, with tall white pillars out front, but the wings angling back on both sides were only one story, with flat roofs. These side sections were bent back at acute angles, so that they really did look like wings, so that the taller middle section would be the body of the bird. Either that, or the central part could be thought of as a ship, with the side sections as the wake.

The driver stopped before the main entrance, hopped out, and opened the door for me. "Thanks, Harry," I said.

Something about me—my eyes, my stance, something—made him soften in his attitude. He nodded as I got out, and almost smiled, and said, "Good luck."

The Filipino who let me in said his name was Wang. "Miss Dawn told me you were coming," he said. "She said you should swim."

"She did?"

"This way. No luggage? This way."

The inside was supposed to look like a Spanish mission, or maybe an old ranch house. There were shiny dark wood floors, and rough plaster walls painted white, and exposed dark beams in the ceiling, and many rough chandeliers of wood or brass, some with amber glass.

Wang led me through different rooms into a corridor in the right wing, and down the corridor to a large room at the end with bluish-green drapes hanging ceiling-to-floor on two walls, making a great L of underwater cloth through which light seemed to shimmer. A king-size bed with a blue spread took up very little of the room, which had a lot of throw rugs here and there on the dark-stained random-plank floor. Wang went to one of the dressers—there were three, two with mirrors—and opened a drawer full of clothing. "Swim suit," he said. "Change of linen. Everything." Going to one of two doors in the end wall, he opened it and waved at the jackets and coats and slacks in the closet there. "Everything." He tugged the sleeve of a white terrycloth robe hanging inside the door. "Very nice robe."

"Everything's fine," I said.

"Here." He shut the closet door, opened the other one, flicked a light switch. "Bathroom," he said. "Everything here."

"Fine. Thank you."

He wasn't finished. Back by the entrance, he demonstrated the different light switches, then pointed to a lever sticking horizontally out from the wall, and raised a finger to get my complete attention. "Now this," he said. He pushed the lever down, and the drapes on the two walls silently slid open, moving from the two ends toward the right angle where the walls met.

Beyond the drapes were walls of sliding glass doors, and beyond the glass doors were two separate views. The view to the right, out the end wall, was of a neat clipped lawn sweeping out to a border of those lush green plants. The view straight ahead, of the section enclosed by the three sides of the house, was of a large oval swimming pool, with big urns and statues around it, and with a small narrow white structure on the fourth side, consisting mostly of doors; a cabana, probably, changing rooms for guests who weren't staying in rooms like this.

Wang showed me that the drapes opened when the lever was pushed down, and closed when it was pulled up. He demonstrated several times; back and forth ran the drapes, indecisively. Then he said, "You swim."

"All right."

"Miss Dawn say she be back, seven o'clock."

The digital clock on one of the dressers read three fifty-two. "All right," I said, and Wang grinned at me and left.

It was a heated pool. When I finally came out and slipped into the terrycloth robe I felt very rested and comfortable. In the room I found a small bottle of white wine, and a glass, and half a dozen different cheeses on a plate under a glass dome. I had some cheese and wine, and then I shaved, and then I looked at the clothing here.

There was a lot of it, but in all different sizes, so I really didn't have that much to choose from. Still, I found a pair of soft gray slacks, and a kind of ivory shirt with full sleeves, and a black jacket in a sort of Edwardian style, and in the mirror I almost didn't recognize myself. I looked taller, and thinner, and successful. I picked up the wine glass and stood in front of the mirror and watched myself drink. All right, I thought. Not bad at all.

I went out by the pool and walked around, wearing the clothes and carrying the wine glass. Part of the area was in late afternoon sun and part in shade. I strolled this way and that, admiring my reflections in the glass doors all around, and trying not to smile too much. I wondered if Wang was watching, and what he thought about me. I wondered if there were other servants around the place, and what kind of job it was to be a servant for a famous movie star. Like being assigned to an Admiral, I supposed. I was once on a ship with a guy who'd been an Admiral's servant for three years, and he said it was terrific duty, the best in the world. He lost his job because he started sleeping with some other officer's wife. He always claimed he'd kept strictly away from the Admiral's family and friends, but there was this Lieutenant Commander who lived in the same area near Arlington, Virginia, and whose wife kept trying to suck up to the Admiral's wife. That's how Tony met her, one time when she came over and the Admiral's wife wasn't there. According to Tony it wasn't his fault there was trouble; it was just that the Lieutenant Commander's wife kept making things so obvious, hanging around all the time, honking horns at him, calling him on the phone in the Admiral's house. "So they kicked me out," he said. (Tony wasn't very popular with the guys on the ship, which probably wasn't fair, but we couldn't help it. The rest of us had been assigned here as a normal thing, but he'd been sent to this ship as a *punishment*. If this was punishment duty, what did that say about the rest of us? Nobody particularly wanted to think about that, so Tony was generally avoided.)

Anyway, he did always claim that the job of servant to the brass was the best duty in the world, and I suppose it is. Except for *being* the brass, of course, which is probably even better duty, except who thinks that way?

After a while I went back into the room, and the digital clock said six twenty-four. I looked at myself in the mirror one more time, and all of a sudden it occurred to me I was looking at Dawn Devayne's clothes. Not my clothes. She'd come home, she wouldn't see somebody looking terrific, she'd see somebody wearing *her* clothes.

No. I changed into my own things, and went back to the living room by the main entrance. There were long low soft sofas there, in brown corduroy. I sat on one, and read more *Hollywood Reporters*, and pretty soon Wang came and asked me if I wanted a drink.

I did.

She arrived at twenty after seven, with a bunch of people. It later turned out there were only five, but at first it seemed like hundreds. To me, anyway. I didn't give them separate existences then; they were just a bunch of laughing, hand-waving, talking people surrounding a beautiful woman named Dawn Devayne.

Dawn Devayne. No question. The clear, bright, level gray eyes. The skin as smooth as a lion's coat. Those slightly sunken cheeks. (Estelle had round cheeks.) The look of intelligence, sexiness, recklessness. Of course that was Dawn Devayne; I'd seen her in the movies.

I got to my feet, looking through the wide arched doorway from the living room to the entrance hall, where they were clustered around her. That group all bunched there made me realize Dawn Devayne already had her own full life, as much as she wanted. What was I doing here? Did I think I could wedge myself into Dawn Devayne's life? How? And why?

"Wang!" she yelled. "God damn it, Wang, bring me liquor! I've been kissing a faggot all day!" Then she turned, and over someone's shoulder, past someone else's laugh, she caught a glimpse of me beyond the doorway, and she put an expression on her face that I remembered from movies; quizzical-amused. She said something, quietly, that I couldn't hear, but from the way her lips moved I thought it was just my own name: "Orry." Then she nodded at two things that were being said to her, stepped through the people as though they were grouped statues, and came through the doorway with her hand out for shaking and her mouth widely smiling. "Orry," she said. "God damn, Orry, if you don't bring it back."

Her hand was strong when I took it; I could feel the bones, as though I were holding a small wild bird in my palm. "Hello…" I said, stumbling because I didn't know what name to use. I couldn't call her Estelle, and I couldn't call her Dawn, and I wouldn't call her Miss Devayne.

"We'll talk later on," she said, squeezing my hand, then turned to the others, who had followed her. "This is Orry," she said. "An old friend of mine." And said the names of everybody else.

Wang arrived then, and while he took drink orders Dawn Devayne looked at me, frowning slightly at my clothing, saying, "Didn't Wang give you a room?"

"Yes. Down at the end there."

Her glance at my clothes was a bit puzzled, but then her expression cleared and she grinned at me, saying, "Yes, Orry. I'm beginning to remember you now."

"I don't remember you at all," I told her. Which was true. So far, Estelle Anlic had made no appearance in this room.

She still didn't. Dawn Devayne laughed, patting my arm, saying, "We'll talk later, after this crowd goes." She turned half away: "Wang! Get over here." Back to me: "What are you drinking?"

❖

I tried not to drink too much, not wanting to make a fool of myself. Though Dawn Devayne had spoken about the others as though they would leave at any instant, in fact they stayed on for an hour or more, mostly gossiping about absent people involved in the movie they were currently making. Then we all got into two cars and drove down to Beverly Hills for dinner at a Chinese restaurant. I rode in the same car with Dawn Devayne, a tan-colored Mercedes Benz with the license plate WIPPER, but I didn't sit beside her. I rode in back with a grim-faced moustached man named Frank, whose job I didn't yet know, while Dawn Devayne sat beside the driver, a tall and skinny, leathery-faced, sly-smiling man named Rod, who I remembered as having played the airline pilot in the *The Captain's Pearls*, and who was apparently Dawn Devayne's co-star again this time. The other three people, an actor named Wally and an unidentified man called Bobo and a heavyset girl named June, followed us in Wally's black Porsche, which also had a special license plate; BIG JR.

Phone-calling had been done before we'd left the house, and four more people joined us at the restaurant; Frank's plump wife, a tough-looking blonde girl for Wally, a grinning hippie-type guy in blue denim for June, and a willowy young man in a black jumpsuit for Rod. I realized Rod must be the faggot Dawn Devayne had been kissing all day, and the fact of his homosexuality startled me a lot less than what she had shouted in his presence.

The eleven of us filled an alcove at the rear of the restaurant. Eleven people can't possibly be quiet; we made our presence felt. There was a party atmosphere, and I saw other patrons glancing our way with envy. We were, after all, quite obviously having a wonderful time. Not only that, but at least two of us were famous. But perhaps in Beverly Hills there's more sophistication about movie fame than in most other places; no one came by the table in search of autographs.

As for the party atmosphere, that was more apparent than real. Dawn Devayne and Rod and Wally and June's hippie-type friend did a lot of loud talking, mostly anecdotes about the movie world or the record business, to which June's friend belonged, but the rest of us were no more than audience. We laughed at the right moments, and otherwise sat silent, eating one platter of Chinese food after another. Rounds of drinks kept being ordered, but I let them pile up in front of me—four glasses, eventually— while I drank tea.

Rod drove us back home. Again Dawn Devayne sat up front with him, while I shared the back seat with Rod's friend, who was called Dennis. In the dark, wearing his black jumpsuit and with his pale-skinned hands and face and wispy yellow hair, Dennis was startling to look at, almost unearthly. And when he touched the back of my hand with a fingertip, his skin was so cold that I automatically flinched away.

He ignored that; maybe people always flinched when he touched them. "I know who you are," he said, and his small head floating there had a smile on it that was very sweet and innocent, as though he were on his way to his First Communion. *My God*, I thought, *you'd last six hours on a ship. They'd shove what was left in a canvas bag.*

I said, "You do?"

"Orry," he said. "That's not a common name."

"No, I guess it isn't."

"You were in the Navy."

"I still am."

"You were married to Dawn."

"That's right," I said.

He turned his sweet smile and his wide eyes toward the two heads up front. They were talking seriously together now, Dawn Devayne and Rod, about some disagreement they were having with the director, and what they should do about it tomorrow.

Dennis, staring and smiling so hard that it was as though he wanted to burrow into their ears and live inside their brains, said, "It must have been wonderful. To know her at the very beginning of her career. If only I'd met Rod, all those years ago." When he looked at me again, his eyes were luminous. Maybe he was crying. "I keep everything that's ever written about him," he said. "I have dozens of scrapbooks, dozens. That's how I know about *you*."

"Ah."

"Do you keep scrapbooks?"

"About what?" Then I understood. "Oh, you mean Dawn Devayne."

"You don't? I'll *never* be blasé about Rod. Never."

In the house Dawn Devayne held my forearm and said, "Orry, I'm bushed. I'm sorry, baby, I can't talk tonight. Come along with me tomorrow, all right? We'll have some time together."

"All right." I was disappointed, but she did look tired. Also, my own body was still more on East Coast time, three hours later; I wouldn't mind sleeping, after such a long day. I don't know why it is, but emotions are exhausting.

"I'm going to swim for five minutes," she said, "and then hit the sack. We get up at seven around here. You ready for that?"

"I will be." And I smiled at her. God knows she wasn't Estelle, but I felt just the same as though I knew her. We were old friends in some other way, entirely different and apart from reality. I suspected that was a form of human contact she had learned to develop, as a means of dealing with all the faces a movie star has to meet. It wasn't the real thing, but that didn't matter. It was a friendly falseness, a fakery that made life smoother.

I watched her swim. She was naked, and she spent as much time diving as she did swimming, and it was the same nude body that had excited me so much in the magazine pictures, and yet my sexual feelings were thwarted, imprisoned. Maybe it was because I was being a peeping tom and felt ashamed of myself. Or maybe it was because, in accepting the counterfeit friendship of Dawn Devayne, I had lessened the existence of Estelle Anlic just that much more, and I felt guilty about *that*. Whatever it was, for as long as I looked at her I kept feeling the lust rise, and then become strangled, and then rise, and then become strangled.

I should have stopped looking, of course, but I couldn't. The most I could do was close my eyes from time to time and argue with myself. But I couldn't leave, I had to stay kneeling at a corner of the darkened room, with one edge of the drapes pulled back just far enough to peek out during the ten minutes that Dawn Devayne spent moving, diving, swimming, the green-white underwater lights and yellow surrounding lanterns glinting and flashing off the wet sheen slickness of her flesh. Drops of water caught in her hair made tiny flashing round rainbows. Her legs were long, her body strong and sleek, a tanned thorough-bred, graceful and self-contained.

When at last she put on a white robe and walked away, I awkwardly stood, padded across the room by the dim light filtering through the drapes, and slid into the cool bed. A few seconds later, as though waiting for me to settle, the pool lights went off.

FOUR

I must have gone to sleep almost at once, though I'd been sure I would stay awake for hours. But the pool lights ceased to shine on the blue-green drapes, darkness and silence drifted down like a collapsing tent—four white numerals floating in the black said 11:42, then 11:43—and I closed my eyes and slept.

To awake in the same darkness, with the white numbers reading 12:12 and some fuss taking place at the edge of my consciousness. I didn't know where I was, I didn't know what that pair of twelves meant, and I couldn't understand the rustling and whooshing going on. In my bewilderment I thought I was assigned to a ship again, and we were in a storm; but the double twelve made no sense.

Then one of the twelves became thirteen, and I remembered where I was, and I understood that someone was at the glass doors leading to the pool, making a racket. Then Dawn Devayne's voice, loud and rather exasperated, said, "Orry?"

"Yes?"

"Open these damn drapes, will you?"

At the Chinese restaurant there had been a red-jacketed young man who parked the cars. He leaped into every car that came along, and whipped it away with practiced skill, as though he'd been driving *that* car all his life. At some point he must have had a first car, of course, the car in which he'd learned to drive and with which he'd gotten his first license, but if some customer of the restaurant were to drive up in that car today would the young man recognize it? Would it feel *different* to him? Since his driving technique was already perfect with any car, what special familiarity would he be able to display? It could not be by skill that he would show his particular relationship with this car; possibly it would be with a breakdown of skill, a tiny reminiscent awkwardness.

Dawn Devayne was wonderful in bed. It's true, she was what men thought she would be, she was agile and quick and lustful and friendly and funny and demanding and responsive and exhausting and exhilarating and plunging and utterly skillful. Her skill produced in me responses of invention I hadn't known I possessed. Fran Skiburg was right; there *are* other things to do. I did things with Dawn Devayne that I'd never done before, that it had never occurred to me to do but that now came spontaneously into my mind. For instance, I followed with the tip of my tongue all the creases of her body; the curving borders of her rump, the line at the inside of each elbow, the arcs below her breasts. She laughed and hugged me and gave me a great deal of pleasure, and not once did I think of Estelle Anlic, who was not there.

We'd turned the lights on for our meeting, and when she kissed my shoulder and leaned away to turn them off again the digital clock read 2:02. In the dark she kissed my mouth, bending over me, and whispered, "Welcome back, Orry."

"Mmm." I said nothing more, partly because I was tired and partly because I still hadn't fixed on a name to call her.

She rolled away, adjusting her head on the pillow next to me, settling down with a pleasant sigh, and when next I opened my eyes vague daylight pressed grayly at the drapes and the clock read 6:03, and Dawn Devayne was asleep on her back beside me, tousled but beautiful, one hand, palm up, with curled fingers, on the pillow by her ear.

How did Estelle look asleep? She was becoming harder to remember. We had lived together in off-base quarters, a two-room apartment with a used bed. Sunlight never entered the bedroom, where the sheets and clothing and the very air itself were always just slightly damp. Estelle would curl against me in her sleep, and at times I would awake to find her arm across my chest. A memory returned; Estelle once told me she'd slept with a toy panda in her childhood, and at times she would call me Panda. I hadn't thought of that in years. Panda.

Dawn Devayne's eyes opened. They focused on me at once, and she smiled, saying, "Don't frown, Orry, Dawn is here." Then she looked startled, stared toward the drapes, and cried, "My God, dawn *is* here! What time is it?"

"Six oh six," I read.

"Oh." She relaxed a little, but said, "I have to get back to my room." Then she looked at me with another of her private smiles and said, "Orry, do you know you're terrific in bed?"

"No," I said. "But you are."

"A workman is as good as his tools," she said, grinning, and reached under the covers for me. "And you've been practicing."

"So have you."

She laughed, pulling me closer, with easy ownership. "Time for a quickie," she said.

We swam together naked in the pool while the sun came up. ("If Wang *does* look," she'd answered me, "I'll blind him.") Then at last she climbed out of the pool, wet, glistening gold and orange in the fresh sunlight, saying, "Time to face the new day, baby."

"All right." I followed her up to the blue tiles.

"Orry."

"Yes?"

"Take a look in the closet," she said. "See if there's something that fits you. Wang can have your other stuff cleaned."

I knew she was laughing at me, but in a friendly way.

And the problem of what to call her was solved. "Thanks, Dawn," I said. "I will."

"See you at breakfast."

I wore the gray slacks, but neither the full-sleeved shirt nor the Edwardian jacket seemed right for me, so I found instead a green shirt and a gray pullover sweater. "That's fine," Dawn said, with neutral disinterest.

A limousine took us to Burbank Airport, over the hills and across the stucco floor of the San Fernando Valley, a place that looks like an over-exposed photograph. Dawn asked me questions as we rode together, and I told her about my marriage to Sally Fowler and my years in the Navy, and even a little about Fran Skiburg, though not the part where Fran got so excited about me having once been married to Dawn Devayne. There were spaces of silence as we rode, and I could have asked her my question several times, but there didn't seem to be any way to phrase it. I tried different practice sentences in my head, but none of them were right:

"Why aren't you Estelle Anlic any more, when I'm still Orry Tupikos?" No. That sounded as though I was blaming her for something.

"Who would I be, if I wasn't me?" No. That wasn't even the right question.

"How do you stop being the person you are and become somebody entirely different? What's it like?" No. That was like a panel-show question on television, and anyway not exactly what I was trying for.

Dawn herself gave me a chance to open the subject, when

she asked me what I figured to do after I retired from the Navy two years from now, but all I said was, "I haven't thought about it very much. Maybe I'll just travel around a while, and find some place, and settle down."

"Will you marry Fran?"

"That might be an idea."

At Burbank Airport we got on a private plane with the two actors, Rod and Wally, and the grim-faced man named Frank and the heavyset quiet man called Bobo, all of whom I'd met last night. Listening to conversations during the flight, I finally worked it out that Frank was a photographer whose job it was to take pictures while the movie was being made; the "stills man," he was called. Bobo's job was harder to describe; he seemed to be somewhere between servant and bodyguard, and mostly he just sat and smiled at everybody and looked alert but not very bright.

We flew from Burbank to Stockton, where another limousine took us to the movie location, which was an imitation Louisiana bayou in the San Joaquin River delta. The rest of the movie people, who were staying in nearby motels and not commuting home every night, were already there, and most of the morning was spent with the crew endlessly preparing things—setting up reflectors to catch sunlight, laying a track for the camera to roll along, moving potted plants this way and that along the water's edge—while Dawn and Rod argued for hours with the director, a fat man with pasty jowls and an amused-angry expression and a habit of constantly taking off and putting back on his old black cardigan sweater. His name was Harvey, and when I was introduced to him he nodded without looking at me and said, "Ted, they really *are* putting that fucking dock the wrong place," and a short man with a moustache went away to do something about it.

The argument, with Dawn and Rod on one side and Harvey on the other, wasn't like anything I'd ever seen in my life. When the people I've known get into an argument, they either settle it pretty soon or they get violent; the men hit and the women throw things. Dawn and Rod and Harvey almost immediately got to the point where hitting and throwing would start, except it never happened. Dawn Devayne stood with her feet apart and her hands on her hips, as though leaning into a strong wind, and made firm logical statements of her point of view, salted with insults; for instance, "The motivation throughout the whole story, you cocksucker, is for my character to feel protective toward Jenny." Rod's style, on the other hand, was heavy sarcasm: "Since it's a *given* that you have the sensitivity of a storm drain, Harvey, why not simply accept the fact that Dawn and I have thought this over very carefully." Harvey, with his angry-amused smile, always looked as though he was either just about to say something horribly insulting or would suddenly start pounding the other two with a piece of wood, and his *manner* was very insulting-patronizing-hostile, but in fact he merely kept saying things like, "Well, I think we'll simply all be much happier if we do it my way."

Unless there's a fist fight, the person who remains the calmest usually wins most arguments, so I knew from the beginning Harvey would win this one, but it went on for hours anyway, and when it ended (Harvey won, and Dawn and Rod both sulked) they only had time before lunch to shoot one small scene with Dawn and Wally on the riverbank. It was just a scene where Dawn said, "I don't think they'll ever come back, Billy." They shot it eight times, with the camera in three different positions, and then we all had a buffet lunch brought out from Stockton by a catering service.

Dawn's dressing room was a small motor home, where she

took a nap by herself after lunch, while I walked around looking at everything. Another part of the Dawn–Wally scene was shot, with just Wally visible in the picture, talking to an empty spot in space where Dawn was supposed to be, and then they set up a more complicated scene involving Dawn and Rod and some other people getting into a boat and rowing away. Dawn woke up while the crew was still preparing that one, and she and Rod groused together about Harvey, but when they went out to shoot the scene everybody was polite to everybody else, and then the day was over, and we flew back to Los Angeles.

There was a huge gift-wrapped package in the front hall at Dawn's house. It was about the size and shape of a door, all wrapped up in colorful paper and miles of ribbon and a big red bow, and a card hung from the bow reading, "Love to Dawn and Orry, from By."

Dawn frowned and said, "What's that asshole up to now?"

Rod and Wally and Frank and Bobo had come in with us, and Wally said, "It's an aircraft carrier. By gave you an aircraft carrier."

"For God's sake, open it," Rod said.

"I'm afraid to," Dawn told him. She tried to make that sound like a joke, but I could see she really was afraid to open it. I later learned that Byron Cartwright's sentimentalism was famous for causing embarrassment, but I don't think even Dawn suspected what he had chosen to send us. I know I didn't.

Finally it was Wally and Rod who pulled off the bow and the ribbon and the paper, and inside was the wedding day picture, Estelle and me in San Diego, squinting in the sunlight. The picture had been blown up to be slightly bigger than life, and it was in a wooden frame with a piece of glass in front of it, and here were these two stiff uncomfortable figures in grainy gray, staring out of some horrible painful prison of the past. Usually this picture was perfectly ordinary, neither wonderful nor awful, but blown up to life size—larger than life—it became a kind of cruelty.

Everybody stared at it. Wally said, "What the hell is *that*?"

They hadn't recognized that earlier me. Dawn wouldn't have been recognizable anyway, of course, but expanding the original photo had strained the rough quality of the negative beyond its capacity, so that I myself might not have guessed at first the white blob face was mine.

After the first shock of staring at the picture, I turned to look at Dawn, to see her with a face of stone, glaring—with hatred? rage? revulsion? bitterness? resentment?—at her own image in the photograph. She turned her head, flashed me a look of irritation that I'd been watching her, and without a word strode out of the room.

Rod, with the eager look of the born gossip, said, "I don't know what's going on here, but it looks to *me* like By's done it again."

Wally was still frowning at the picture. "What *is* that?" he said. "Who *are* those people?"

"Orry? Isn't that you?"

It was the voice of Frank, the stills man, the professional photographer, who had backed away from the giant picture, across the hall and through the doorway into the next room, until he was distant enough to see it clear. Head cocked to one side, eyes half closed, he was standing against the back of a sofa in there, studying the picture.

At first I didn't say anything. Wally turned to frown at Frank, then at me, then at the picture, then at me again. "You? That's you?"

Rod and Bobo were moving toward Frank, squinting over

their shoulders at the picture as they went. I said to Wally, "Yes. It's me."

"That girl is familiar," Frank said.

I felt obscurely that Dawn would want to be protected, though I didn't see how it was going to be possible. "That's my wife," I said. "Or, she *was* my wife. That was our wedding day."

Rod and Bobo were now standing next to Frank, gazing at the picture, and Wally was moving back to join them. I was like a stage performer, and they were my audience, and the picture was used in my act. Frank said, "I know that girl. What's her name?"

Rod suddenly said, "Wait a minute, *I* know that picture! That's Dawn!"

"Yes," I said, but before I could say anything else—explain, apologize, defend—Wang came in to say, "Miss Dawn say, everybody out."

Rod, nodding at the picture and ignoring Wang, said thoughtfully, "Byron Cartwright, the avalanche that walks like a man."

Wang said to me, "You, too. Miss Dawn say, go away, eat dinner, come back."

"All right," I said.

We were joined by Frank's wife and Wally's girl and Rod's friend Dennis in an Italian restaurant that looked like something from a silent movie about Biblical times. Bronze-colored plaster statues, lots of columns, heavily framed paintings of Roman emperors on the walls. The food was covered with too much tomato sauce.

My story was amazing but short, and when I was done Rod and Wally told stories for the rest of dinner about other disastrous gestures made by Byron Cartwright in the past. He was everyone's warmhearted uncle, except that his instincts were constantly betrayed by his inability to think through the effect of his activities. As a businessman he was considered one of the best (toughest, coldest, coolest) in his very tough business, but away from the office his affection toward his clients and other acquaintances led him to one horrible misjudgment after another.

(These acts of Byron Cartwright's were not simple goofs like sending flowers to a hay-fever victim. As with the picture to Dawn and me, each story took about five minutes to explain the characters and relationships involved, the nuances that turned Byron Cartwright's offerings into Molotov cocktails, and while some of the errors were funny, most of them produced only groans among the listeners at the table. It was Wally who finally summed it up, saying, "Most mutations don't work, and By is simply one more proof of it. You can't have an agent with a heart of gold, it isn't a viable combination.") After dinner, Rod drove me back to Dawn's house, with Dennis a silent worshipper vibrating behind us on the back seat. As we neared the house, Rod said, "May I give you a piece of advice, Orry?"

"Sure."

"You haven't known Dawn for a long time, and she's probably changed a lot."

"Yes, she has."

"I don't think she'll ever mention that picture again," Rod told me, "and I don't think you ought to bring it up either."

"You may be right."

"If it's still there, have Wang get rid of it. If you want it yourself, tell Wang to ship it off to your home. But don't show it to Dawn, don't ask her about it. Just deal with Wang."

"Thank you," I said. "I agree with you."

We reached the house, and Rod stopped in front of the door. "Good luck," he said.

I didn't immediately leave the car. I said, "Do you mind if I ask you a question?"

"Go ahead."

"You saw how different Dawn used to be, when she was Estelle Anlic. And if you remember the picture, I haven't changed very much."

"Hardly at all. The Navy must agree with you."

"The reason I came out here," I said, "was because I had a question in my mind about that. I wanted to know how a person could change so completely into somebody different. Somebody with different looks, a different personality, a whole different kind of life. I mean, when I married Estelle, she wasn't anybody who could even *hope* to be a movie star."

Rod seemed both amused and in some hidden way upset by the question. He said, "You want to know how she did it?"

"I suppose. Not exactly. Something like that."

"She decided to," he said. He had a crinkly, masculine, self-confident smile, but at the same time he had another expression going behind the smile, an expression that told me the smile was a fake, a mask. The inner expression was also smiling, but it was more intelligent, and more truly friendly. He said, using that inner expression, "Why did you ask *me* that question, Orry?"

It was, of course, because I believed he'd somehow done the same sort of thing as Dawn, that somewhere there existed photos of him in some unimaginable other person. But it would sound like an insult to say that, and I said nothing, floundering around for an alternate answer.

He nodded. "You're right," he said.

"Then how?" I asked him. "She decided to be somebody else. How is it possible to *do* that?"

He shrugged and grinned, friendly and amiable but not really able to describe colors to a blind man. "You find somebody you'd rather be," he said. "It really is as simple as that, Orry."

I knew he was wrong. There was truth in the idea that people like Dawn and himself had found somebody else they'd rather be, but it surely couldn't be as simple as that. Everybody has fantasies, but not everybody throws away the real self and lives in the fantasy.

Still, it would have been both rude and useless to press him, so I said, "Thank you," and got out of the car.

"Hold the door," he said. Then he patted the front seat, as though calling a dog, and said, "Dennis, come on up." And Dennis, a nervous high-bred afghan hound in his fawn-colored jumpsuit, clambered gratefully into the front seat.

I was about to shut the door when Rod leaned over Dennis and said, "One more little piece of advice, Orry."

"Yes?"

"Don't ask Dawn that question."

"Oh," I said.

The picture was gone from the front hallway. My luggage from the motel was in my room, and Dawn was naked in the pool, her slender long intricate body golden-green in the underwater lights. I opened the drapes and stepped out to the tepid California air and said, "Shall I join you in there?"

"Hey, baby," she called, treading water, grinning at me, sunny and untroubled. "Come on in, the water's fine."

FIVE

The rest of the days that week were all the same, except that no more unfortunate presents came from Byron Cartwright. Dawn and I got up early every morning, flew to Stockton, she worked in the movie and napped—alone—after lunch, we flew back to Los Angeles, and then there'd be dinner in a restaurant with several other people, a shifting cast that usually included Rod and Wally and Dennis, plus others, sometimes strangers and sometimes known to me. Then Dawn and I would go back to the house and swim and go to bed and play with one another's bodies until we slept. The sex was wonderful, and endlessly various, but afterwards it never seemed real. I would look at Dawn during the daytime, and I would remember this or that specific thing we had done together the night before, and it wasn't as though I'd actually done it with *her*. It was more as though I'd dreamed it, or fantasized it.

Maybe that was partly because we always slept in the guest room, in what had become my bed. Dawn never took me to her own bed, or even brought me into her private bedroom. Until the second week I was there, I was never actually in that wing of the house.

On the Thursday evening we stayed longer in Stockton, to see the film shot the day before. Movie companies when they're filming generally show the previous day's work every evening, which some people call the *dailies* and some call the *rushes*. Its purpose is to give the director and performers and other people involved a chance to see how they're doing, and also so the film editor and director can begin discussing the way the pieces of film will be organized together to make the movie. Dawn normally stayed away from the rushes, but on Thursday evening they would be viewing the sequence that she and Rod had argued about with Harvey, so the whole group of us stayed and watched.

I suppose movie people get so they can tell from the rushes whether things are working right or not, but when I look at half a dozen strips of film each recording the same action sequence or lines of dialogue, over and over and over, all I get is bored. Nevertheless, I could sense when the lights came up in the screening room that almost everybody now believed Harvey to have been right all along. Rod wouldn't come right out and admit it, but it was clear his objections were no longer important to him. Dawn, on the other hand, had some sort of emotional commitment to her position, and all she had to say afterwards was, grumpily, "Well, I suppose the picture will survive, despite that." And off she stomped, me in her wake.

Still, by the time we reached the plane to go back to Los Angeles, she was in a cheerful mood again. Bad temper never lasted long with her.

Friday afternoon there were technical problems of some sort, delaying the shooting, so after Dawn's nap she and I sat in the parlor of her dressing room and talked together about the past. It was one of those conversations full of sentences beginning, "Do you remember when—?" We talked about troubles we'd had with the landlord, about the time we snuck into a movie theater when we didn't have any money, things like that. She didn't seem to have any particular attitude about these memories, neither nostalgia nor revulsion; they were simply interesting anecdotes out of our shared history.

But they led me finally, despite Rod's advice, to ask her the question that had brought me out here. "You've changed an awful lot since then," I said. "How did you do that?"

She frowned at me, apparently not understanding. "What do you mean, changed?"

"Changed. Different. Somebody else."

"I'm not somebody else," she said. Now she looked and sounded annoyed, as though somebody were pestering her with stupidities. "I dyed my hair, that's all. I learned about makeup, I learned how to dress."

"Personality," I said. "Emotions. Everything about you is different"

"It is not." Her annoyance was making her almost petulant. "People change when they grow older, that's all. It's been sixteen years, Orry."

"I'm still the same."

"Yes, you are," she said. "You still plod along with those flat feet of yours."

"I suppose I do," I said.

Abruptly she shifted, shaking her head and softening her expression and saying, "I'm sorry, Orry, you didn't deserve that. You're right, you are the same man. You were wonderful then, and you're wonderful now."

"I think the flat feet was more like the truth," I said, because that is what I think.

But she shook her head, saying, "No. I loved living with you, Orry, I loved being your wife. That was the first time in my life I ever relaxed. You know what you taught me?"

"Taught you?"

"That I didn't have to just run all the time, in a panic. That I could slow down, and look around."

I wanted to ask her if that was when she realized she could become somebody else, but I understood by now that Rod had been right, it wasn't something I could ask her directly, so I changed the subject. But I remembered what the magazine article had said about me being a "stock figure, the San Diego sailor in every sex star's childhood," and I wondered if what Dawn had just said was really true, if being with me had in some way started the change that turned Estelle Anlic into Dawn Devayne. Plodding with my flat feet? Most of the Estelle Anlics in the world marry flat-footed Orry Tupikoses; what had been different with us?

Saturday we drove to Palm Springs, to the home of a famous comedian named Lennie Hacker, for a party. There were about two hundred people there, many of them famous, and maybe thirty of them staying on as house guests for the rest of the weekend. Lennie Hacker had his own movie theater on his land, and we all watched one of his movies plus some silent comedies. That was in the afternoon. In the evening, different guests who were professional entertainers performed, singing, dancing, playing the piano, telling jokes. It was too big a party for anybody to notice one face more or less, so I didn't have to explain myself to anybody. (There was only one bad moment, at the beginning, when I was introduced to the host. Lennie Hacker was a short round man with sparkly black eyes and a built-in grin on his face, and when he shook my hand he said, "Hiya, sailor." I thought that was meant to be some kind of insult joke, but later on I heard him say the same thing to different other people, so it was just a way he had of saying hello.)

I'd never been to a party like this—a famous composer sat at the piano, singing his own songs and interrupting himself to make put-down gags about the lyrics—and I just walked around with a drink in my hand, looking at everything, enjoying being a spectator. (I was wearing the Edwardian jacket and the full-sleeved shirt, no longer self-conscious about my appearance.) Dawn and I crossed one another's paths from time to time, but we didn't stay together; she had lots of friends she wanted to spend time with.

As for me, I had very few conversations. Rod and Dennis were there, and I had a few words with Rod about the silent comedies we'd seen, and I also made small talk with a few other people I'd met at different restaurant dinners over the last week. At one point, when I was standing in a corner watching two television comedians trade insult jokes in front of an audience of twenty or thirty other guests, Lennie Hacker came over to me and said, "Listen."

"Yes?"

"You look like an intelligent fella," he said. He looked out at the crowd of his guests, and made a sweeping gesture to include them all. "Tell me," he said, "who the fuck *are* all these people?"

"Movie stars," I said.

"Yeah?" He studied them, skeptical but interested. "They look like a bunch a bums," he said. "See ya." And he drifted away.

A little later I ran into Byron Cartwright, who beamed at me and took my hand in both of his and said, "How *are* you, Orry?"

"Fine," I said.

"Listen, Orry," he said. He kept my hand in one of his, and put his other arm around my shoulders, turning me a bit away from the room and the party, making ours a private conversation. "I've wanted to have a *good* talk with you," he said.

"You have?"

"I'm sorry about that picture." He looked at me with a pained smile. "The way Dawn talked about you, I thought she'd *like* that reminder."

I didn't know what to say. "I guess so," I told him.

"But things are good between *you* two, aren't they? No trouble there."

"No, we're fine."

"That's good, that's good." He thumped my back, and finally released my hand. "You two look good together, Orry," he said. "You did way back then, and you do now."

"Well, *she* looks good."

"The two of you," he insisted. "Together. When's your leave up, Orry? When do you have to go back to the Navy?"

"In two weeks."

"Do you want me to fix it?"

"Fix it?"

"We could get you an early release," he said. "Get you out of the Navy."

"I've only got two years before I collect my pension."

"We could probably work something out," he told me. "Make some arrangement with the Navy. Believe me, Orry, I know people who know people."

I said, "But I couldn't go on living at Dawn's house."

"Orry," he said, chuckling at me and patting my arm. "You were her first love, Orry. You're her man. Look how she took you right in again, the minute you showed up. Look how well you're getting along. In some little corner of that girl, Orry, you've always been her husband. She left the others, but she was taken away from you."

I stared at him. "*Marry* her? Dawn Devayne? Mr. Cartwright, I don't—"

"By. Call me By. And think about it, Orry. Will you do that? Just think about it."

There was no question in the Hacker household about our belonging together. Dawn and me. We'd been initially shown by a uniformed maid to a bedroom we were to share on the second floor, overlooking Hacker's private three-hole golf course, and by one o'clock in the morning I was ready to return to it and go to sleep, although the party was still going strong. I found Dawn with a group of people singing show tunes around the piano, and I told her, "I'm going to sleep now."

"Stick around five minutes, we'll go up together."

I did—it's surprising how many old lyrics we all remember, the words to songs we no longer know we know—and then we found our way to the right bedroom, used the private bath next door, and went to bed. When I reached for Dawn, though, she laughed and said, "You must be kidding."

I was. I realized I was too sleepy to have any true interest in sex, that I'd started only out of a sense of obligation, that I'd felt it was my duty to perform at this point. "You're right," I said. "See you in the morning."

"You're a good old boy, Orry," she said, and kissed my chin, and rolled away, and I guess we both went right to sleep.

When I woke up it was still dark, but light of some sort was glittering faintly outside the window, and there were distant voices. I'd lived with Dawn Devayne less than a week, but already I was used to the rounded shapes of her asleep beside me, and already I missed the numerals of the digital clock shimmering white in the darkness. I didn't know what time it was, but it had to be very late.

I got up from bed and looked out the window, and the illumination came from floodlights over the golf course. Lennie Hacker and some of his male guests were playing golf out there. I recognized Byron Cartwright among them. Lennie Hacker's distinctive nasal voice said something, and the others laughed, and somebody drove a white ball high up out of the light, briefly out of existence before it suddenly bounced, small and white and clear, on the clipped grass of the green.

The men moved as a group, accompanied by a servant driving a golf cart filled with bags and clubs. A portable bar was mounted on the back of the cart, and they were all having drinks from it, but no one appeared drunk, or sloppy, or tired. None of them were particularly young, but none of them were in any way old.

The golf course made a wobbly triangle around an artificial pond, with the first tee and the third green forming the angle nearest the house. As the players moved away toward the first green, I looked beyond the lit triangle, seeing only black darkness, but sensing the other Palm Springs estates around us, and then the great circle of desert around that. Desert. These men—*some* men—had come out to this desert and by force of will had converted it into a royal domain. "To live like kings." That's a cliché, but here it was the truth. In high school I read that the ancient Roman emperors had ordered snow carted down from the mountain peaks to cool their palaces in summer. It has always been the prerogative of kings to make a comfortable toy of their environment. Here, where a hundred years ago they would have broiled and starved and died grindingly of thirst, these men strolled on clipped green grass under floodlights, laughing together and reaching for their drinks from the back of a golf cart.

If I married Dawn Devayne—

I shook my head, and closed my eyes, and then turned away from the window to look at the mound of her asleep in the bed. It was a good thing I'd been warned about Byron Cartwright's sentimental errors, or I might actually have started dreaming about such impossibilities, and wound up a character in another Byron Cartwright horror story: "And the poor fellow actually proposed to her!" If an Indian who had grubbed his lean and careful existence from this desert a hundred years ago were to return here now, how could he set up his tent? How could he take up his life again? He's never been *here*. I was married to Estelle Anlic once, a long time ago. I was never married to Dawn Devayne.

SIX

After the weekend, we went back to the old routine until Wednesday evening, when, on the plane back to Los Angeles, Dawn said, "We won't be going out to dinner tonight."

"No?"

"My mother's coming over, with her husband."

I felt a sudden nervousness. "Oh," I said.

She laughed at my expression. "Don't worry, she won't even remember you."

"She won't?"

"And if she does, she won't care. I'm not sixteen any more."

Nevertheless, it seemed to me that Dawn was also nervous, and when we got to the house she immediately started finding fault with Wang and the other servants. These servants, a staff of four or five, I almost never saw—except for the cook at breakfast—but now they were abruptly visible, cleaning, carrying things, being yelled at for no particular reason. Dawn had said her mother would arrive at eight, so I went off to my own room with today's *Hollywood Reporter*—I was getting so I recognized some of the names in the stories there—until the digital clock read 7:55. Then I went out to the living room, got a drink from Wang, and sat there waiting. Dawn was out of both sight and hearing now, probably changing her clothes.

They came in about ten after eight, two short leathery-skinned people in pastel clothing that looked all wrong. Dawn's mother had on a fuzzy pink sweater of the kind worn by young women twenty years ago, with a stiff-looking skirt and jacket in checks of pale green and white. Her shoes were white and she carried a white patent leather purse with a brass clasp. None of the parts went together, though it was understandable that they would all belong in the same wardrobe. She looked like a blind person who'd been dressed by an indifferent volunteer.

Her husband, as short as she was but considerably thinner, was dressed more consistently, in white casual shoes, pale blue slacks, white plastic belt, and white and blue short-sleeved shirt. He had a seamed and bony face, the tendons stood out on his neck, and his elbows looked like the kind of bone sooth-sayers once used to tell the future. With his thin black hair slicked to the side over his browned scalp, and his habit of leaning slightly forward from the waist at all times, and his sur-prisingly bright pale blue eyes, he looked like a finalist in some Senior Citizens' golf tournament.

I stood up when the doorbell rang, and moved tentatively forward as Wang let them both in, but I was saved from intro-ducing (explaining) myself by Dawn's sudden arrival from the opposite direction. Striding forward in a swirl of floor-length white skirt, she held both arms straight out from the shoulder and cried, "Mother! Leo! Delighted!"

All I could do was stare. She had redone herself from top to bottom, had changed her hair, covered herself with necklaces and bracelets and rings, made up her face differently, dressed herself in a white ballgown I'd never seen before, and she was coming forward with such patently false joy that I could hardly believe I'd ever watched her do a *good* job of acting. I was sud-denly reminded of that whore back in New York, and I realized that now Dawn herself was pretending to be Dawn Devayne. Some imitation Dawn Devayne, utterly impregnable and larger than life, had been wrapped around the original, and the aston-ishing thing was, the real Dawn Devayne was just as bad at imi-tating Dawn Devayne as that whore had been.

I don't mean to say that finally I saw Estelle again, tucked away inside those layers of Dawn, as I had seen the Hispanic hidden inside the whore. It was Dawn Devayne, the one I had come to know over the last week, who was inside this masquerade.

But now Dawn was introducing me, saying, "Mother, this is a friend of mine called Orry. Orry, this is my mother, Mrs. Hettick, and her husband Leo."

Leo gave me a firm if bony handclasp, and a nod of his pointed jaw. "Good to know you," he said.

Dawn's mother gave me a sharp look. Inside her mismatched vacation clothing and her plump body and her expensive beauty shop hair treatment she was some kind of scrawny bird. She said, "You in pictures?"

"No, I'm not."

"Seen you someplace."

"Come along, everybody," Dawn said, swirling and swinging her arms so all her jewelry jangled, "we'll sit out by the pool for a while."

I didn't think there was anything wrong with the evening except that Dawn was so tense all the time. Her mother, whom I'd never met before except when she was yelling at me, did a lot of talking about arguments she'd had with different people in stores—"So then *I* said, so then *she* said…"—but she wasn't terrible about it, and she did have an amusing way of phrasing herself sometimes. Leo Hettick, who sat to my right in the formal dining room where we had our formal dinner, was an old Navy man as it turned out, who'd done a full thirty years and got out in 1972, so he and I talked about different tours we'd spent, ships we'd been on, what we thought of different ports and things like that. Meantime, Dawn mostly listened to her mother, pretending the things she said were funnier than they were.

What started the fight was when Mrs. Hettick turned to me, over the parfait and coffee, and said, "You gonna be number five?"

I had to pretend I didn't know what she was talking about. "I beg pardon?"

"You're living here, aren't you?"

"I'm a houseguest," I said. "For a couple of weeks."

"I know that kind of houseguest," she said. "I've seen a lot of them."

Dawn said, "Mother, eat your parfait." Her tension had suddenly closed down in from all that sprightliness, had become very tightly knotted and quiet.

Her mother ignored her. Watching me with her quick bird eyes she said, "You can't be worse than any of the others. The first one was a child molester, you know, and the second was a faggot."

"Stop, Mother," Dawn said.

"The third was impotent," her mother said. "He couldn't get it up if the flag went by. What do you think *of that*?"

"I don't think people should talk about other people's marriages," I said.

Leo Hettick said, "Edna, let it go now."

"You stay out of this, Leo," she told him, and turned back to say to me, "The whole world talks about my daughter's marriages, why shouldn't I? If you *are* number five, you'll find your picture in newspapers you wouldn't use to wrap fish."

"I don't think I read those papers," I said.

"No, but my mother does," Dawn said. Some deep bitterness had twisted her face into someone I'd never seen before. "My mother has the instincts of a pig," she said. "Show her some mud and she can't wait to start rooting in it."

"Being *your* mother, I get plenty of mud to root in."

I said, "I was the first husband, Mrs. Hettick, and I always thought *you* were the child molester."

"Oh, Orry," Dawn said; not angry but sad, as though I'd just made some terrible mistake that we both would suffer for.

Slowly, delightedly, as though receiving an unexpected extra dessert, Mrs. Hettick turned to stare at me, considering me, observing me. Slowly she nodded, slowly she said, "By God, you are, aren't you? That filthy sailor."

"You treated your daughter badly, Mrs. Hettick. If you'd ever—"

But she didn't care what I had to say. Turning back to her daughter, crowing, she said, "You running through the whole lot again? A triumphant return tour! Let me know when you dig up Ken Forrest, will you? At least he'll be stiff this time."

Leo Hettick said, "That's just about enough, Edna."

His wife glared at him. "What do *you* know about it?"

"I know when you're being impolite, Edna," he said. "If you remember, you made me a promise, some little time ago."

She sat there, glaring at him with a sullen stare, her body looking more than ever at odds with her clothing; the fuzzy pink sweater, most of all, seeming like some unfunny joke. While the Hetticks looked at one another, deciding who was in charge, I found myself remembering that magazine's description of me as "a stock figure," and of course here was another stock figure, the quarrelsome mother of the movie star. I thought of myself as something other than, or more than, a stock figure; was Mrs. Hettick also more than she seemed? What did it mean that she had broken up her daughter's first marriage, to a sailor, and later had married a sailor herself, and wore clothing dating from the time of her daughter's marriage? What promise had she made her husband, "some little time ago"? Was *he* a stock figure? The feisty old man telling stories on the porch of the old folks' home; all the rest of us were simply characters in one of his reminiscences.

Maybe that was the truth, and he was the hero of the story

after all. He was certainly the one who decided how this evening would end; he won the battle of wills with his wife, while Dawn and I both sat out of the picture, having no influence, having no part to play until Edna Hettick's face finally softened, she gave a quick awkward nod, and she said, "You're right, Leo. I get carried away." She even apologized to her daughter, to some extent, turning to Dawn and saying, "I guess I live in the past too much."

"Well, it's over and forgotten," Dawn said, and invented a smile.

After they left—not late—the smile at last fell like a dead thing from Dawn's mouth. "I have a headache," she said, not looking at me. "I don't feel like swimming tonight, I'm going to bed."

Her own bed, she meant. I went off to my room, and left the drapes partway open, and didn't go to sleep till very late, but she never came by.

It was ten forty-three by the digital clock when I awoke. I put on the white robe and wandered through the house, and found Wang in the kitchen. Nodding at me with his usual polite smile, he said, "Breakfast?"

"Is Dawn up yet?"

"Gone to work."

I couldn't understand that. Last night she'd been upset, and of course she'd wanted to be alone for a while. But why ignore me this morning? I had breakfast, and then I settled down with magazines and the television set, and waited for the evening.

By nine o'clock I understood she wasn't coming home. It had been a long long day, an empty day, but at least I'd been able to tell myself it would eventually end. Dawn would come home around seven and everything would be the same again. Now it was nine o'clock, she wasn't here, I knew she wouldn't be here tonight at all, and I didn't know what to do.

I thought of all the people I'd met in the last week and a half, Dawn's friends, and the only ones I might talk to at all were Byron Cartwright or Rod, but even if I did talk to one of them what would I say? "Dawn and her mother had a little argument, and Dawn didn't sleep with me, and she left alone this morning and hasn't come back." Rod, I was certain, would simply advise me to sit tight, wait, do nothing. As for Byron Cartwright, this was a situation tailor-made for him to do the wrong thing. So I talked to no one, I stayed where I was, I watched more television, read more magazines, and I waited for Dawn.

The next day, driven more by boredom than anything else, I finally explored that other wing of the house. Dawn's bedroom, directly across the pool from mine, was all done in pinks and golds, with a thick white rug on the floor. Several awkward paintings of white clapboard houses in rural settings were on the walls. They weren't signed, and I never found out who'd done them.

But a more interesting room was also over there, down a short side corridor. A small cluttered attic-like place, it was filled with luggage and old pieces of furniture and mounds of clothing. Leaning with its face to the wall was the blown-up photograph, unharmed, and atop a ratty bureau in the farthest corner slumped a small brown stuffed animal; a panda? The room had a damp smell— it reminded me of our old apartment in San Diego—and I didn't like being in there, so I went back once more to the television set.

People on game shows are very emotional.

✿

Saturday morning I finally admitted to myself that Dawn was staying away only because I was still there. I'd been alone now for three days, except for Wang and the silent anonymous other servants—from time to time the phone would ring, but it was Wang's right to answer it, and he always assured me afterward it was nothing, nothing, unimportant—and all I'd done was sit around and think, and try to ignore the truth, and by Saturday morning I couldn't hide it from myself any more.

Dawn would not come back until I had given up and left. She couldn't throw me out of her house, but she couldn't face me either, not now or ever again. I belonged in the room with the photograph and the panda and the old clothing, the furniture, the bits and pieces of Estelle Anlic.

I knew the answer now to the question I'd brought out here. In order to create a new person to be, you have to hate the old person enough to kill it. Estelle *was* Dawn, and Dawn was happy.

She had dealt with my sudden reappearance out of the past by forcing me also to accept Dawn Devayne, to put this new person in Estelle's place in my memory, so that once more Estelle would cease to exist.

But the mother remained outside control, with her dirty knowledge; in front of her, Estelle was only pretending to be Dawn Devayne. After Wednesday night, Dawn must believe her mother had recreated Estelle also in my mind, turned Dawn back into Estelle in my eyes. No wonder she couldn't be in my presence any longer.

I put the borrowed clothes away and packed my bag and asked Wang to call a taxi. There wasn't anybody to say goodbye to.

Back on the base a week early, I explained part of the situation to the Commander and applied for a transfer, and got it. I told Fran everything—almost everything—and she moved to Norfolk to be near me at my new post (where my history with Dawn Devayne never came to light), and when I retired this year we were married.

I don't go to Dawn Devayne movies. I also don't do those things with Fran that I'd first done with Dawn. I don't have any reason not to, it's just I don't feel that way any more. And Fran's vehemence for new sexual activity was only a temporary thing anyway; she very quickly cooled back down to what she had been before. We get along very well.

Sometimes I have a dream. In the dream, I'm walking on Hollywood Boulevard, on the stars' names, and I stop at one point, and look down, and the name in the pavement is ESTELLE ANLIC. I just stand there. That's the dream. Later, when I wake up, I understand there isn't any Estelle Anlic any more; she's buried out there, on Hollywood Boulevard, underneath her name, standing up, squinting in the San Diego sun.